Living with the Dead

(Walking with the Dead, Book 3)

Living with the Dead

(Walking with the Dead, Book 3)

PJ Dziekan

ISBN-13: 9798676346423

For the others who raised me and watched over me

My siblings
Cougy, Sandi, Al, Milo, Carl

BOOK ONE

CHAPTER ONE

Gunfire peppered the air around them. Sarah Louis ran, one hand wrapped around her abdomen, the other gripping the 9mm tight. Mick Cooke followed close behind, his shotgun empty, hanging from a cord around his neck. The weapon bounced against his hip with every step, but he couldn't leave it. If they got back to the apartment or the market, they would find more shells. For now, they needed to find a place to hole up, to wait for the trouble to pass, for help to arrive.

The pain ripped through her again and she couldn't hold back the scream. "What is it?" Mick asked, his head swiveling to check their surroundings.

"It's your kid," Sarah panted as the pain subsided.

"What?!?" He exclaimed, his hand moving to her distended belly. "Now?"

"For a while now," she admitted. She felt an odd sensation, then her pants dampened. "And my water just broke."

"Are you fucking serious? Jesus, Sarah!! You shouldn't be out here!"

"No shit." She swiped a hand across her brow. "Neither of us should be here. How the hell did they get in?" She spotted one just about 20 feet away, probably drawn by her scream. She took aim and shot it in the head. The body dropped with a barely heard thump.

"That doesn't matter! What are we going to do?" Mick held his free hand on her belly, the other clutching a prybar, his only defense against what raged around them.

"We're going to have a baby." Another pain, she bit her lip to stop another scream. "Pretty damn soon."

"Come on, we have to find somewhere out of the open." He took her hand and started down the street.

"Where?" She gasped. "We took down most of the buildings around here to build the greenhouses."

"I don't know, babe, but we have to get out of the middle of the street." He pulled her along, wincing when she tightened her hand on his. The pains were coming fast.

"Mick, I – I don't think I can go much further." He hated to hear the pain in her voice.

"OK." He steered her towards the sidewalk, where there was a tiny patch of green where a tree once stood. The grass would be softer than the hard ground. He dropped the pry bar and pulled off his jacket, laying it face down on the grass. It wasn't very clean, but it was better than nothing. He helped her to lay down on the jacket, watching her face as the pain washed over her. "What do I do?" He asked as he dropped to his knees beside her.

"Help me get my pants off."

"Not now, you're having a baby." He had to joke. If not, he'd scream.

"Ass," she laughed weakly. Another pain struck and she moaned.

"Sarah, I don't know what to do," Mick said. He shifted to kneel between her legs, wishing he could do something, anything.

"I don't either." Her voice was thick with pain and yes, tears. "I've never done this before." She looked up at his blood splattered face as a contraction ripped thru her. She gritted her teeth against the pain, swallowing the scream that threatened to break through. "I'm never doing it again."

Mick smiled. "Will you know when it's time?"

She could hear the sounds of gunfire in the distance. Another contraction hit and she dropped her gun from her right hand and clutched her belly. They were coming right on top of each other. Her left held Mick's, squeezing tight. "I think—I think soon."

He waited until her pain eased, then dragged her wet jeans and panties down her legs. "Sarah, I see something. Is it time to push?"

"With the next contraction," she panted. "Be ready."

"I am." His eyes met hers and he smiled. Biting her lip, she smiled back.

Less than fifteen seconds later, the next contraction began. "Mick, it's coming!" She cried out as she pushed, the pain unbelievable.

"The head's out! I'm holding his head!" Mick exclaimed. He couldn't believe he held his child's head in his hands, that soon, they would be a family.

Sarah fell back, her chest heaving. "Her head," she said weakly. She heard Mick's chuckle. "This is the hardest part," she said.

"I'm here for you, Sarah."

"I know." She felt the next one coming. "Get ready…" She bit her lip, keeping the scream inside as she pushed, hard, wanting this done, wanting it over. She tasted blood in her mouth, but she couldn't let them hear her, even though she felt like she was being ripped apart. Then, all of a sudden, it was over. She heard a small cry.

"Sarah…" Mick breathed. He placed their child on her belly, still connected to her. Her hand came up to rest on the baby's stomach. Blinking away tears, he looked up at her. "Oh, Sarah, I love you."

He shifted back on his heels, bringing a bloodied hand up to wipe his eyes. Sarah opened her mouth to reply when Mick pitched over on his side, the sound of the gunshot reaching her after he had fallen. She saw the hole in the side of his head, just a drop of blood visible. Her eyes wide, she screamed, her voice merging with that of her fatherless child.

♦

Sarah's eyes flew open and she bit off her scream. She looked to her right, seeing Mick curled up beside her, his hand resting on her hip. She looked to her left, seeing the silhouette of their baby, sleeping peacefully in the bassinet. She sighed, bringing her hand up to scrub at her eyes. The damn dream was coming more often.

She knew she wouldn't get back to sleep. She eased out from under Mick's hand and sat on the edge of the bed. Her jeans were hanging over the chair. She slipped those on, fastening her belt, then slid her feet into her boots, not bothering to tie them, just tucking the laces inside, then stood. On her way out of the bedroom, she stopped to look down at their sleeping daughter. Josephine Ryan Cooke was a handful when awake, an absolute angel when she slept. But at least she slept. Unlike Missy's son, Louis, who at 18 months of age barely slept 3 hours in a row.

With a smile, Sarah tiptoed past the bassinet into the living room. She grabbed the battery powered lantern from the side table by the door and turned it on low. She carried it into the kitchen and set it on the counter. She quickly brewed herself a cup of tea, still lamenting the loss of cream after all these years. She got used to drinking it without, but damn, she still missed it. The milk from the few cows they had was too precious to waste on cream. She carried the lantern and the tea back into the living room and set them on the coffee table before settling on the sofa. She picked up her well-worn notebook and started to work.

Nearly three years after the end of the world, pre-ZA food supplies were hard to find. Every so often, someone would find a hidden cache and they'd have a few cans of peaches or her favorite, pineapple. Mostly, they grew what they could, bartered for what they couldn't. They managed to connect with a few other communities and trade between them was brisk. According to the list from Troy, they were getting low on fruit, which the community at Kittington grew and stored in abundance. They could trade some fish, maybe even some of their precious batteries. She made a note to send a scout.

She looked over the work schedule created by Troy and Annie, surprised to see a few unfamiliar names. She was supposed to meet all new arrivals. She'd have to find out how she missed the newcomers. She made another note for herself in her ever-present notepad.

"Hey," a voice softly said. She lifted her head to see Mick standing in the doorway.

"Hey yourself." She smiled.

"Why are you up?"

She shrugged. "Couldn't sleep, figured I'd get a start on the day. Did you know we had a few new people here?"

"Is it the dream again?" Mick walked over to sit next to her on the sofa.

"I just couldn't sleep." She didn't look at him as she lied. He didn't need to worry about her. He worried enough in the past couple years.

"Sarah…" She looked up at him, at the beautiful blue eyes their daughter had inherited. "You don't have to keep it to yourself. Tell me about the dream."

She shook her head. "Just a nightmare. I barely remember it." Liar. You remember every single detail. Her eyes searched out the spot in the dream where the bullet entered his skull.

Mick sighed. She never shared. She held it and held it until she broke under the weight. And he was always there to pick up the pieces. "What are you doing?" He asked, nodding at the notebook.

"We need to set up a trade with Kittington. And like I said, there's some new folks in town that I didn't meet. I'll have to search them out tomorrow."

"Who are you sending to Kittington?"

"I'll send Alan and Mark with a request for trade. We don't need to send a four-man crew since it's basically a scouting mission. If they're agreeable, do you want to go make the trade?" She asked with a smile. "I wouldn't mind getting out of town for a bit."

"Are we walking or riding?" With the diesel supply reserved for the generators, they rarely drove anywhere. The vehicles were restricted to large supply runs.

"If we start early in the day, I think we can walk it. If the booty is too much, maybe we can have someone there ride us back and we'll replenish their diesel. Should be in and out in twelve hours."

Mick leaned back on the sofa and stifled a yawn. "Who else is going?"

"I don't know yet. Why don't you go back to sleep? Josey is going to be wide awake in a few hours and it's your turn to wrangle her." Sarah smiled. Her favorite thing to see in this world was Josey and Mick together. Their daughter had her father wrapped around her finger.

"Nah, I'll be OK." He lifted his long legs and put his feet on the coffee table. Sarah arched an eyebrow. With a sheepish smile, he put his feet down.

"Stretch out on the sofa," she said, moving forward. Mick laid on the sofa, his 6'2" frame barely fitting.

"Lay with me," he said.

"I have to take care of this." She indicated the notebook on the table.

"No, you don't. You can do it in the morning."

"It is the morning." She laughed.

"It's two o'clock in the morning. The time normal people sleep." The expression on her face was painful. "At least rest with me."

With a loud sigh, she toed off her boots and laid next to him on the couch. He turned, spooning her, his arm around her belly. "Happy?" She asked.

He breathed deep, her scent a part of him. He placed a kiss on the top of her head. "Yes."

Sarah smiled. So was she.

CHAPTER TWO

Sarah awoke to the sound of her daughter laughing. She opened her eyes, surprised to see that Mick had somehow got up from the sofa without disturbing her. She swung her feet to the floor and looked for the source of the laughter. Mick was sitting at the kitchen table, bouncing Josey on his knee. She giggled, clapping her chubby hands together.

Sarah stood up, stretching as she walked across the room. "Hey, bug!" She said, holding out her hands. Josey made the sound they assumed meant "Mama" and lifted her arms. Sarah scooped her up.

"How's my girl?" Sarah balanced Josey on her hip and Josey laid her head on Sarah's shoulder. "How did you get up without waking me?" Sarah asked Mick.

"My secret," he said with a wink. He got up from the table and headed to the counter. "I'll make you a cup of tea while you feed her."

"You hungry, bug?" Sarah sat in the seat Mick had vacated and lifted her tee. Josey began to nurse. Sarah never thought she'd have a child let alone be comfortable breast feeding. But any formula was long since expired and besides, her baby would always have food. At least for a little while longer. Michelle said she should be weaned soon. Josey was already eating many solids, her chubby arms and legs a testament to her love of food.

Mick assumed he would be a father someday, but when the dead rose, he was more concerned with surviving. He didn't think he would ever have a child. It took the zombie apocalypse to meet the love of his life, the mother of his child. He watched the two of them as Josey fed. Josey had a few strands of Sarah's auburn hair, free of its customary braid, twisted in her fingers. A few more strands laid across Josey's head, highlighting the bright red of their daughter's hair. "What's happening today?" He asked as he put the cup of tea in front of Sarah.

"I need to send Alan and Mark to Kittington. I want to check with Troy and Annie about these new arrivals. I think I have a turn on gate duty." Sarah took a sip of her tea, wincing when Josey bit a little too hard.

"What's on my schedule?" He asked as the lamp on the end table flickered on. It was 7:00 a.m., the time when the generators kicked on every day.

"Your daughter," Sarah laughed. Josey was biting more than usual. "OK, bug, that's enough." Sarah pulled her from her breast and tugged her shirt back down.

"Da!" Josey reached out for Mick.

Mick took her as Sarah finished her tea. "What are we feeding her today?"

Sarah shrugged. "See what's available. We can eat what she doesn't." Since refrigeration was still only available in one building, they were unable to keep food in the apartment more than a day or two. Often, the three of them ate carrots or peas or some other food that was easy to mash up for Josey. Most days, they ate in the communal dining room, where Donna made meals for anyone who cared to eat. But at least once a week, they ate alone as a family.

Sarah finished her tea and took her cup to the sink. She poured a tiny bit of water from the jug into the cup and rinsed it, then set it in the drainer. "I'll be ready to go in a few minutes." Dropping a kiss on Josey's head, she went to the bathroom where she quickly braided her hair and brushed her teeth. In the bedroom, she strapped on her holster. Reaching under the bed, she pulled out a box locked with a combination. She spun the dials and pulled out her Glock, tucking it into the holster. She grabbed the knife and sheath, clipping them on her belt. The walkie talkie sat on the nightstand, where she put it every night, volume turned low so as not to disturb Josey. She clipped it on her belt next to the knife. By the time she was done, Mick and Josey were both dressed for the weather, Josey looking like a pink marshmallow in her winter coat. "Let's go, guys." She picked up her ever-present note pad from the table and tucked it in her back pocket. She grabbed her jacket on the way out the door.

The sun was barely up and the morning air was cold. They moved quickly from their building, Ash, to Shaun, where the refrigerators were kept. They had found some solar panels and were looking for more, hoping to get each building its own set. For now, they used the juice from the solar array to keep the power in Shaun on 24/7. They could have lived in that building, but Sarah was happy in Ash. He was, after all, one of her favorite movie characters.

There were two apartments on the first floor, which originally held four. One was their medical area, complete with exam rooms, where April and Michelle took care of everything from the flu to broken bones. Luckily, they hadn't seen anything more serious. They really weren't equipped for much else. The second apartment was their kitchen. In both, walls had been strategically removed, the work supervised by Bobby. The medical area was converted to a small waiting area, three exam rooms and two "hospital" rooms. In the kitchen, most walls were removed, except those needed for support. Refrigerators and freezers lined two of the three walls of the large room, while the fourth held a counter with propane stoves and a dumbwaiter designed by Bobby to move food from the kitchen to the communal dining room on the second floor. In the center of the room was a large island, complete with a sink that had to be manually filled and drained and cabinets for storage. It was at that counter in what used to be apartment 1A that they found Donna, sipping a cup of hot chocolate.

"'Morning," she said as they walked in. She smiled at Josey. "Hey, Josey girl!" Josey babbled happily.

"How's things today?" Sarah asked.

"Well, I don't know, since you're the first in this morning as usual and nothing has happened yet."

Sarah rolled her eyes. "You know what I mean."

"Things are fine," Donna said. "I did an inventory last night and we're still good on most everything. Susan wanted to try and make some cheese with some of the milk; I told her to check with you."

"Are we getting a lot of milk?" Mick asked.

"Three cows don't produce a hell of a lot, but it sure would be nice to have some cheese."

"I'll talk to her." Sarah pulled her notepad from her back pocket. "We're low on fruit, so I'm going to see if we can trade with Kittington. Anything else you think we need?"

Donna shook her head. "Meat's good, veggies are good. The last scavenging crew even managed to find a huge stockpile of flour on their last run. It was in a bakery and sealed up in giant metal canisters. I'll have to sift it; there were a few bugs in it, but it'll be nice to have some biscuits or the like."

"Sure would," Mick said. He missed bread. He missed a lot of things, but bread was high on the list.

"We'll need some turkey, then we're heading to the store for veggies. What do we have the most of left?" Sarah put her notepad back into her pocket as she walked back to the fridge that held the turkey. She pulled a small resealable bag from the fridge. She walked back to the island and marked her initials on the sheet next to "1/2 pound turkey."

Donna consulted a typed list. Where Troy found a manual typewriter, no one knew. "Looks like carrots."

"OK, thanks."

"Wait." Donna got up and went to a stainless-steel refrigerator. She opened it up and pulled out a sealed pint-sized mason jar. With a smile, she brought it over to Sarah. "I saved some pears for Josey."

"Donna, you don't have to do that." Sarah knew if she told her to stop saving food for Josey, she would. But Sarah was torn. She wanted the best for Josey. She wanted her to grow up strong. She would need to be.

"I want to. I know Josey loves those pears. Don't you, Josey girl?" The baby gurgled happily, clapping her chubby hands together.

"Thanks, Donna." Sarah took the pears. "We'll see you later."

The small family left the kitchen apartment. Mick shifted Josey on his hip. She squirmed and reached for Sarah. "No, baby, stay with Da." Sarah didn't carry the baby when she was armed. She looked at Mick. "Do you want to take her home and feed her the turkey and pears? I'll bring some carrots up in a bit."

"No, she should have her veggies before her dessert."

"Old world rules, Mick." Sarah smiled. "It won't hurt for her to have her pears now."

"No, we'll come along, won't we, Jojo."

"Don't call her that."

They walked down the road a bit, heading for the community market. It actually had been a supermarket before the apocalypse. All the shelving was already in place, so they decided to use it as their central point for all non-refrigerated supplies. Troy Smith, with his head for organization, was in charge, with Christa and Helen as his assistants. Annie assisted him with the scheduling. Troy smiled when they walked in. "Hi, Sarah, Mick. Josey."

"We're going to need some carrots," Sarah said, moving to the sign out sheet. Every item was catalogued both in the market and the kitchen. Whenever someone took something, they initialed the item. Troy maintained the inventory, sending a list to Sarah every other day.

"We have plenty of carrots. You know where they are." He held his arms out to Josey and she clapped her hands together before reaching for him. He took her in his arms, laughing as she pulled on his beard. Mick smiled, leaning against what was formerly the customer service counter and was now Troy's desk.

"List says we're low on fruit. What do we have to trade?" Sarah headed back to the aisle where the preserved vegetables were kept.

"We've a lot of fish. A good supply of potatoes. There's also that crate of candles that the last crew brought back. Oh, and a case of beer, probably skunky but you never know."

"Hey, leave the beer," Mick said.

"We'll see what they'll take. The candles would be best. I don't think they have full power out there yet." Sarah came back with a two-quart jar of steamed carrots. She found a reusable tote under the counter and put the pears, turkey and carrots in the bag. "Why don't you take Josey back and feed her? I need to talk to Troy, then I'll be along."

"OK." Mick took Josey from Troy. "Don't be too long or we might not leave anything for you. Right, boo?" Josey babbled.

Sarah put the bag over Mick's free shoulder. "I won't be long." She kissed Josey's pink cheek, then kissed Mick. "I'll see you in a bit."

Mick said goodbye to Troy and they left, Josey's babble making both Sarah and Troy smile. With a sigh, she turned from the door and pulled out a chair. She sank into it, grateful for a few minutes off her feet. She'd be on them most of the day. "I saw a few names I didn't recognize on the duty roster," she said. "Frank and Chris?"

Troy nodded. "They came in a few days ago. I tried to get you on the walkie, but Mick said you were in the shower. It was the day you and he found a nest of them and you came home covered in gore."

Sarah remembered. They were scavenging and found an isolated house set back in some woods. Since it was so isolated, they assumed there would still be supplies. There were, but there were also four zombies. They had been closed up in the house since close to the beginning of the apocalypse. They exploded when they took them out, both of them ending up covered in blood, brain and other disgusting fluids. They did manage to come back with some rifles, ammo, and camping supplies, along with some canned goods. They both needed showers when they returned and since Josey was with Missy and Louis, they took a little extra time for themselves.

"I want to meet with them today. You have Chris with Bobby?" Troy nodded. "What about Frank? I saw his name on the list, but no assignment."

"He was pretty banged up. I thought he could rest a few more days before we gave him something to do. Both he and Chris are staying in Ash, let me check the apartment number." Troy pulled a clipboard from a drawer and ran his finger down the typed page. "They're in 2B."

"Thanks, Troy." Sarah got up. "I better get home before there's no breakfast left for me. Then I'll go see Frank."

CHAPTER THREE

After a somewhat satisfying breakfast of turkey, carrots and pears, Mick stored the leftovers in a small cooler and they headed back out for the day. "I'm going to meet with these two new guys, Frank and Chris, then I'll head to the greenhouse for a bit," Sarah said.

Mick nodded. "I'll be at Missy's or, if I can leave Josey with her, I'll go help Bobby with the new solar panels. We'll be back for lunch."

"You don't have to work on the solar panels. You're not on the schedule."

"I want to. I hate sitting around."

Sarah smiled. "Not cut out to be a househusband, huh?"

"Shutty." He turned to Josey. "Do you want to go see Missy and Louis?" Josey giggled and turned her head away. "I think she has a crush on Louis." Sarah laughed.

♦

Sarah stood in front of the door to 2B and knocked three times. After a minute, she knocked again, louder. She was raising her hand to knock a third time when the door flew open. "Who the hell are you?" The guy at the door was tall, nearly as tall as Mick. He had a full beard of black and grey, matching his shoulder length hair. His left arm was in a sling.

"Sarah Louis. And you're Frank?"

He leaned against the door. "Yeah. What do you want?"

"I wanted to introduce myself, see how things are going for you."

His eyes roamed up and down her body. "Why do you get a gun?"

"Because I'm in charge here."

"You?" He laughed.

She fought the urge to straighten up to her full 5'2". "Yes. Me. Is there a problem?"

He shook his head. "You're serious? I thought that black guy we talked to was in charge."

"Nope, all me." She smiled, but it didn't quite reach her eyes. Her first impression of him wasn't going so well.

"Oh! I just didn't expect someone so…so…"

"Don't finish that thought," Sarah said. "Can I come in?"

"Sure, sure!" Frank stepped aside and Sarah walked in. She noticed that every light in the apartment was on, at least those she could see. The room was also very warm.

"You like the lights?" She asked.

"Yeah, missed the things. Before we came here, I hadn't seen electric light in two and a half years."

"I'd appreciate it if you didn't use so much light. Less work for the generators."

"Oh, sure, sure, sorry." He moved around the place, turning off most of the lights. "I didn't expect this when we got here." She could hear him say from the bedroom.

"What did you expect?" She sat herself on the sofa, perched on the edge. She never fully relaxed anymore, except when she was home with Mick and Josey.

"Oh, just a bunch of people trying to survive, like the last place I was." He came back into the living room. He sat in a chair opposite her.

"Where did you come from? Your last place?" She asked.

"It wasn't really a place. Me and Chris, he came in with me, we've been together since almost the beginning. We ended up with a group for a while, then zombies came, killed a few people. Everyone scattered so we moved on, too." He leaned back in the chair. "We were on our own for a while, then we found another group. There was a guy who wanted to be in charge, he was friendly with Chris. I had no dog in the fight, but when it looked like Chris' friend was going to go down and take everyone with him, we left." He sighed. "We ended up down the road at another community. We didn't have anything like this, but we had something. I had a girl there…"

He trailed off and looked down at the floor. After a moment, he collected himself. "Raiders came, took all the supplies, killed some people. Almost got me, but Chris saved my life." He lifted his left arm. "Your doc, April, said this isn't healing right. She said something about rebreaking it, but I don't think I can handle that."

"She's smart, you should listen to her." Sarah pulled out her notepad. "What did you do before?"

"Before the world went to hell? I sold cellphones." Frank laughed. "Lotta good that does me now."

She gave him a small smile. "What can you do now?" She had her pen poised over the pad.

"I don't know. Troy said he'd find me something, but I had a few days because of my arm."

Sarah nodded. "Everyone gets a few days when they first get here, so they can acclimate to the situation. But we have to find you something to do. Everyone works here, not all day or all the time, but everyone has to contribute." She closed the pad and put it back in her pocket. "Think on what you can offer the community and let Troy or Annie know. We'd rather you do something you want than assign you to something you hate." She stood up. Frank hopped to his feet.

"I just don't know what I can do."

"There's always grunt work. The gardens, gate duty, clean up. Think about your skills and let Troy know. I'm going to go over and talk to your friend Chris." She held out her hand and Frank took it. "Welcome to Thornville."

"Thank you."

Sarah nodded at him. "I'll see you later, maybe at dinner."

"OK, thanks." They walked to the door. "Can I ask you something?" Sarah cocked her head, waiting for what she knew was coming. "How'd you get to be in charge? You're younger than most of the people I've met here and you don't seem like…" He trailed off, unsure how to finish.

"Just lucky, I guess." She smiled as she took her leave.

♦

Sarah walked through town, which was about twenty blocks from gate to gate. She stopped in one of the greenhouses and saw Frannie and Chuck hard at work on their shift. Even though it was January, they still had plants growing, some producing. Feeding over 40 people regular meals took a lot of food. They did have meat, mostly deer and turkeys and the occasional wild pig, but most of it was vegetables. "We'll have some peppers in a week or so," Chuck said, pointing to the plants.

"Weren't there brussels sprouts coming in?" Sarah asked. She loved brussels sprouts.

"Next few days we should get some."

"Take them when they're small. I hate the big ones, they get bitter."

Chuck laughed. "I'll make sure we do."

Sarah left the greenhouse and wandered down the street. She had finally gotten used to the lack of background noise, other than the occasional voice or bird call. She liked it. After a heavy rain, when it was quiet, she could even hear the river running. She did miss a few things from her old life, but not the noise.

She passed by one of the outside gardens that had been a vacant a lot between buildings. The ground was covered with plastic, waiting for the spring. The wind gusted, rattling the edges of the plastic. She put her hands in her pockets and made a mental note to send someone out to make sure the plastic was secure. They didn't want the few animals that hung around to get in the garden and dig up their bulbs.

Her route took her past the war memorial and the two crosses planted in front of the stone. She stopped and stared down at the graves. One cross represented Elaine, the oldest member of their community who had died of natural causes at the end of summer. At least she died surrounded by friends. The other represented Mick's brother Ryan, the first person she had encountered when the world went to shit. He saved her from certain death that first day and many other days after. She couldn't save him. Raiders had kidnapped Mick and Ryan to force them to leave their town. One of the raiders executed Ryan right in front of her. The man didn't live long. Sarah, along with Mick, Ben and Jack, tracked him down and crippled him, letting the zombies tear him apart. Sometimes she still heard his screams.

"We're doing good, Ryan," she said softly. "Josey's getting big. She has Mick's eyes and a lot brighter shade of my hair." Sarah laughed. "She's a handful. Just like I'm sure you were." She touched his cross. "We miss you."

She heard someone call her name. She pulled her hand from the memorial and turned to face the voice. It was Paul, a former police officer who joined them last year. She started towards him. "Hi, Paul."

"I need to talk to you, Sarah." He was a short stocky guy, but still a good 5 inches taller than she was.

"Sure, what's up?" She started walking away from the graves. Paul followed.

"When I was out on yesterday's supply run, I saw a few things." He had to adjust his stride to keep up with her.

"What did you see, Paul?"

"In the basement of one of the houses we checked, we found a bunch of reloading equipment. I'd like to take the truck and bring it back. We can make our own ammo."

Sarah walked a few steps without responding. "Was there anything else there to make the trip worth the diesel? I know we could use the ammo, but we're good with other weapons."

"There wasn't in that house, no, but there were more we could check. It was a gated community and there were a lot of houses there." Paul shoved his hands deeper in his pockets. The day was warming up, but it was still chilly.

"Let me think on it. I'll let you know later today. What else was there?"

"We saw a few out there that looked fresh. I didn't see any wounds on them, either."

Sarah shrugged. "Maybe they were under their clothes. You know we're not the only people out here. Maybe someone from another camp got too close to one and got bit, then covered it up so their people didn't find out."

"Could be, but it wasn't just one." He shook his head. "It was really odd."

She stopped in front of her next destination. "Let Troy know. He'll tell everyone going out about it. Have them keep an eye out."

Paul nodded. "Who's next to go out?"

"I'm planning to send Alan and Mark out to Kittington to see if they'll trade some fruit. I'm not sure who's on the next scavenging team; Troy will have that info."

Paul nodded again. "I'll go tell him now. See you at dinner?"

"Yup."

She stood in front of Bobby's workshop, which was a former mechanic's garage. It had ample space for his work, with most of the tools he needed already in place. She walked into the office, the bell above the door ringing merrily. She stepped past the chair, five-year old magazines, and desk covered in dust to head into the garage area. "Bobby!" she called as she stepped over the threshold.

He turned to see who was calling him, an average sized man with long brown hair and a short-trimmed beard. He had gained back all the weight he had lost during his time in Sugar Creek and looked rather healthy. "Sarah!" He said with a smile. He put the wrench he was holding on the work bench and crossed the garage floor. "How are you? How's Josey?"

"All good," she answered, returning his smile. "How's things going here?" She indicated the solar panels with a nod of her head.

"Not bad. The mounting brackets on the panels have a bit of damage that I can fix. We'll get these ones installed on Ash." He grinned.

"I like the sound of that. I hear you have a new helper."

Bobby nodded. "Yeah, Chris. He did some mechanical work back in the day, so this was the best place for him."

"Is he around?" Sarah didn't see him on the floor.

"Yeah, he's out back –uh—taking care of things." Bobby blushed.

Sarah laughed. "It's natural, Bobby, no need to get weird about it."

"Yeah, well…"

He was saved from answering further when a guy walked in from the alley behind the garage, average height, blond hair and heavy beard. He was wiping his hands on a shop rag. "Bobby?" He walked up to them.

"You're Chris?" Sarah asked. He nodded, looking over at Bobby, then back at Sarah. "I'm Sarah Louis. Pleased to meet you." She held out her hand.

Gingerly, he took her hand and gave her a limp shake. "I've heard about you. You're not quite what I expected."

"I never am." She took her hand back. "How are you doing here? Feeling OK?"

"Oh, yeah, I like it. Enough food, a warm place to sleep, a job that makes sense." He looked at Bobby. "The boss isn't too bad, either."

Bobby laughed. "Yeah, he's not that bad a worker, Sarah."

She smiled. "How'd you end up here?" She listened as he told her almost exactly what Frank had, with a few minor details.

"I want to fit in here," Chris finished. "I really like this place."

"We're glad to have you," Sarah replied. "Bobby needs someone who actually knows what they're doing. His last assistant didn't know the difference between a wrench and a ratchet."

"Yes, you did," Bobby said. "It was the hammer and screwdriver that confused you." Sarah laughed. After a moment, Chris joined in.

Her walkie squawked. "Sarah, I need you at the south gate."

She stepped away from Bobby and Chris and unclipped the walkie from her belt. She brought it to her mouth. "Everything OK?" She asked.

"I don't know. Can you just get here?"

She wasn't sure who was on the south gate. She didn't recognize the voice over the static of the walkie, but she did recognize the trepidation in it. "On my way." She clipped the walkie back to her belt and turned to Bobby and Chris. "Duty calls. I'll see you two later."

As she turned to go, Bobby stepped up to her. "Is there a problem?" he asked softly.

She shook her head. "No, it's nothing. I'll see you at dinner." She walked slowly away from Bobby, trying to project an air of calm. Once she was outside, she began to jog to the south gate. Luckily, she had been heading in that direction and reached it in just a few minutes. She didn't approach immediately; she wanted to scout the area, see what had the sentry so freaked.

She saw the sentry – she still wasn't sure who it was – on top of the fast food restaurant they used for surveillance. Whoever it was had their back to Sarah, staring down at the other side of the gate. With a hand on her gun, she walked to the restaurant. She climbed the ladder at the back of the building, accessing the roof. She unsnapped the strap on her holster and quietly moved to where the sentry was standing.

"What's the problem?" She asked softly, dismayed to see the sentry jump.

The sentry was Sid, one of their more recent immigrants. He had come, with his wife Helen, just a few months prior. They were a middle-aged couple, probably in their late 50s. She would have never put him on gate duty; he tended to be nervous around people.

"Them," he said, pointing over the gate.

Sarah rested her hand on the butt of her gun as she peered over the wall. She broke into a smile and dropped her hand to her side. "Nice horses."

Two mounted men looked up at her. "How are you, Sarah?" Staff Sgt. Tony McGuire asked. With him was Sgt. John Sullivan, known as Sully.

"Good, you guys?"

"We need to talk." Sarah caught the seriousness of his voice.

"I'll let you in. You know the drill. You can leave the horses tied to those trees there." She turned to Sid. "Keep an eye on those horses. Anything gets near them, shoot."

His eyes widened. "Even people?"

Sid would not be on wall duty again. "Give them one warning, then shoot. If something happens to those horses, it's your ass." She moved quickly across the roof, scrambling down the ladder. She walked around the building to the gate, a school bus and a truck nose to nose across the street, the back ends of each butting against a building. Metal had been welded where the vehicles met and along the bottoms of both. There was a door in the middle of the bus, leading from one side of the road to the other. The door was nearly invisible, but Tony and Sully had visited before.

The first time they visited, as representatives from the United States Government, they expected a docile group. They were shocked when Sarah and Mick held them at gunpoint. However, after the rocky start, they became friendlier with each visit. Sarah was actually happy to see them now. They brought news from the outside, sometimes good, sometimes bad. Sarah had the feeling that this was going to a bad news visit.

Tony and Sully were waiting at the door when Sarah opened it. "Come on." The two men stepped past her, watching as she locked the entry door with a padlock, then slid a steel bar over the entrance. The three of them walked through the bus. Sarah repeated her actions on the town side of the bus. Once the bar was in place, she turned to her visitors. "Nice to see you guys," she said with a smile.

"You, too, ma'am." Sully smirked.

"Don't call me ma'am, Sully."

Sully laughed. "Here, got something for Josey." He rummaged in his pack and came out with a red-headed doll, nearly as big as Josey was.

"You think my daughter plays with dolls?" Sarah asked with a smile.

"No, but Mick's does." Sully laughed.

"Give it to her when you see her," Sarah said and Sully returned the doll to his pack.

"Is there somewhere we can talk?" Tony interrupted.

Sarah didn't like the look on his face. There was something serious going on. "Sure. There's an empty storefront right up here." She started walking, the guys falling in behind her. She took them to what was once a florist shop. The faint smell of roses greeted them when they pushed through the door. Sarah leaned against the cashier stand and folded her arms. "What's going on?" She asked.

"About six months ago, the virus mutated," Tony said. "It's killing nearly everyone now, not just those who were bit."

"How did it mutate? How did you figure this out?" Sarah didn't give in to her panic.

"The scientists aren't sure how it happened," Sully answered. "But it seems that anyone who has had any contact with the bodily fluids of the zeds in the past six months are infected now. They had a blood test to check before the mutation and it's showing the same thing now on people who weren't bitten. To make things even more fun, those who were infected by the bodily fluids can pass the infection themselves via their bodily fluids."

"So we're all infected." Sarah blew out a sigh.

"If you've killed them and got splattered, you're infected." Tony swiped a hand across his eyes. "If you're exchanging bodily fluids with someone who was killing them, you're infected. It's possible that if you were around them, or somewhere where they were in the last six months, you're infected. We're just not sure."

Josey. Sarah's knees nearly buckled. Her daughter was infected. She swallowed hard. "What—what do we do now?" Sarah could feel the headache forming. She thought once they all died out, things could go back to a somewhat normal world.

"Keep doing what you're doing. Isolate anyone who looks sick or dying." Sully shrugged. "Same old, same old."

"And if someone has a heart attack in the middle of the night and dies?"

"Then you have a problem." Tony shook his head. "That's how the scientists discovered it. Since they were working with them, there were always fluids around and despite their precautions, they were in contact with them. One of them died in the middle of the night. The next day, when their relief came, the whole crew were zeds."

"Shit." Sarah kicked at the ground. "I have to tell the council. Are you guys just spreading the joyful news?"

"Yes, we're headed to Kittington after this," Sully said. "Then Boyer."

"I need to get to Kittington. Can you wait about an hour or so while I tell the council? It would be nice to have a military escort. I've never had one."

Sully looked at Tony. "Yeah, we can wait about an hour."

"Let's go to the kitchen. Donna can get you fed while you wait."

They left the florist shop and started walking back towards Shaun. "Are you going to tell your people?" Tony asked.

"I don't think I have a choice."

CHAPTER FOUR

Sarah left Tony and Sully with Donna, who promised to feed them a good meal. It was no hardship to Donna. She had a little crush on Sully. Sarah headed to what they termed the daycare, which was really just Missy keeping an eye on the three kids who were under school age. She figured Mick was there with Josey. She needed to talk to him.

On her way, she saw Grant heading to his shift in one of the greenhouses. "Hey, Grant!" she called.

Grant turned and saw her, grinning when he realized it was Sarah. "Sarah!" He trotted over to her, a sixteen-year old kid in need of a haircut. His thick eyeglasses were two separate halves joined together in the middle. Not a fashionable choice, but a necessary one so he could see. He was nearly legally blind without them.

"Can you do me a favor? Find Troy, Bobby, Annie, April and Paul and send them to my place right away?"

"Sure! Annie might be with Missy, I'll start there."

Sarah shook her head. "I'm heading there now. Just find the rest and if Annie's not there, I'll find her myself."

"I'll get them now." He raced off. Sarah was tempted to tell him to slow down, but time was of the essence.

She made her way to Missy's apartment and knocked on the door. A few minutes later, Missy opened. "Sarah, you don't have to knock. Come in!"

Sarah never walked into someone's apartment without knocking. There was precious little privacy in their small settlement. Everyone needed that last little bit. She stepped in and saw Mick on the floor, Josey crawling around him. "Figured I'd find you here." Josey saw her and rapid crawled her way to her mother. She held up her arms. Sarah looked over at Mick.

But Missy was there first. "Not now, Josey-girl. Mama's all geared up for the day." She carried her into the kitchen. "Want a cracker?"

Mick got up from the floor. He didn't like the look on Sarah's face. "What's wrong?"

"Council needs to meet. We have some news."

Mick nodded. "I guess it's bad?"

"Yeah, it's bad. Get Josey and we'll head over to the house." Sarah started to pack up Josey's bag. "Grant is gathering up everyone else."

"Aunt Sarah!!!!" Two and a half feet of boy launched at her. Sarah stood quickly, angling her body so that her gun and knife were not within reach.

"Hey, Louis!!" She exclaimed as he clutched her legs in a tight hug. She tousled his light brown hair.

"Come see!!" He pulled away and tugged on her hand, intending to take her to his room to show her his latest treasure.

"Not now, sweetie. I have to go back to work. I'll see you later, OK?" She smiled down at him, gently pulling her hand from his sticky one.

"OK." He turned away and headed back into his room.

Sarah shook her head. If it wasn't for the fact that he barely slept more than 3 hours at time, he'd be the perfect kid. She'd rather have her daily firebrand so she could have a good night's sleep.

Missy came back from the kitchen with said firebrand, who was gnawing on a stale cracker. "You can leave her here with me, if you want," she said.

Sarah looked at Mick, who shrugged. "If you wouldn't mind," she said. "It won't be for long."

"Take as long as you need. Josey and I will have some fun, won't we, Josey-girl?" Josey babbled happily.

"Do you know where Annie is?" Sarah asked.

"She left about ten minutes ago. She said she was headed to the greenhouse by the north gate."

Sarah sighed. The opposite end of town. "OK, thanks. We'll be back for Josey in a bit."

Mick and Sarah walked quickly up the road. Sarah knew her time was limited. Tony and Sully wouldn't wait for long. "What's going on?" Mick asked.

She took a breath. "The virus mutated. Anyone who's been exposed to their fluids in the last six months is now infected. We'll turn when we die." She kept her voice low, just in case someone was around to hear.

"Fuck." Mick and Sarah had both been exposed multiple times in the last six months. "Is it going to kill us?"

"It won't kill us, but when we die, we'll turn." She nodded to Steven as he walked by.

"What do we do?"

"What can we do?" She asked. "Lock everyone up at night in separate apartments?" She smiled. "You think I'm sleeping without your warmth in the winter, you're crazy."

"Sarah, this isn't funny."

"No shit, Mick. I don't know what we do. We talk it over with the council and we figure it out from there." They had reached the north greenhouse.

Annie was wrist deep in soil when they walked in. "Hi Sarah, Mick. What brings you down here?" There was a smear of dirt on her cheek.

"We need to have a quick council meeting," Sarah said.

"Now?" Annie pulled her hands from the potting soil and brushed the excess back into the bucket. She saw the tension in Sarah's face. "Give me a minute to get cleaned up."

"We'll meet you back at our place, OK?" Sarah didn't give her a chance to answer. She turned and walked out, Mick following.

When they got back to their place, Troy and April were already there, waiting outside the door. "Why are we meeting?" Troy asked as they came down the hall. April knew better than to ask. Sarah didn't like to repeat herself. She would tell them when everyone was gathered.

Sarah said nothing. She opened their apartment door and ushered Troy and April inside. "Want something to drink? Coffee? Water?" she asked as she headed into the kitchen to make herself a cup of tea. Both declined as they sat in the living room. April looked at Mick, who gave nothing away. Sarah was their leader; it was her place to lead the meetings. He was just her second.

The rest of the council members arrived quickly. Once everyone was in, and had been offered refreshment, Sarah sat on the arm of an oversized chair and surveyed the room. April was their senior medical officer, as she was a former paramedic. Bobby was their chief engineer since he had the talent to make things work again. Annie was their human resources director, having the skill to work with Troy to fit workers to jobs. Troy was their accountant, keeping track of their supplies, which were much more precious than money. Paul was a former police officer. Sarah thought having someone with law enforcement experience on the council was a good idea. And Mick was her moral support, sometimes even her conscious. They were her council.

She decided to just get it over with. "Tony and Sully are here. The government has just discovered that the virus has mutated." She noticed that everyone had a reaction. Except Mick. "Anyone who's been in contact with the zombies in the last six months is now infected."

"What does that mean?" April asked.

"It means that when we die, we turn." Annie's gasp almost drowned out Sarah's next words. "It also means that anyone who's been in contact with the zombies can infect others through bodily fluids."

"That explains those zombies we saw on the last run. What are we going to do about this?" Paul asked. "What if someone dies in the middle of the night?"

"Then we're fucked," Sarah said simply. "The best we can do is make sure individual apartments are locked at night. That way, if something happens, we won't lose the whole town."

"Yeah, but we'll lose whoever is in the apartment," April said.

"Then we'll give people the option to lock themselves in separate rooms within the apartments. I don't see our couples taking that option, though." She looked at April. "Do you want to sleep separate from Mandy?"

April shook her head. "Is there nothing else we can do?"

Sarah rubbed her forehead. "If anyone has a better idea, I'm all ears." No one responded. She looked up at Bobby. "Bobby, I need you to make sure every apartment has a working lock. I know some of them, like ours, don't. Leave the keys hanging in the lock. We may need to get in if there's an issue."

"I'm on it. We'll probably need more locksets."

"I'll make sure the next salvage team looks for a hardware store." Sarah stood up. "Tony and Sully are heading to Kittington to give them the news. I'm going to tag along, since I want to arrange a trade and I'd like to hear Evan's thoughts. Since we're leaving so late in the morning, we may have to stay overnight, so you guys may have to sit on this news." They all looked uncomfortable, but she knew they'd keep her confidence. They wouldn't be on her council if they couldn't.

"I'll find someone to fill your spot on the gate," Annie said. "I think Ben has some free time today."

"Thanks," Sarah said. She was itching to go.

Bobby sensed her impatience. "I better go see what we have in the way of locks," he said, standing. Everyone else took that as their cue to leave.

"Wait, Troy, Annie. We need to talk about a personnel matter," Sarah said. The rest of the council filed out; their hearts heavy with the news.

"What is it?" Troy asked.

"I don't want Sid on gate duty anymore."

"Did he do something wrong?" Annie stood, clasping her hands in front of her.

"No, but he's not very observant up there. I snuck up on him. And when I told him to shoot anything that went near the horses, he practically wet himself. We need better people on the gate."

Troy nodded. "We'll find something else for him. You have any ideas?" He looked at Annie.

"Teaching? Gardening? Does he have any building experience?"

"I don't know. We'll pull him off the gate and talk to him. Who can we put up there now?" Troy slid his arms into his jacket.

Annie and Troy left, discussing the revised schedule. As Sarah cleaned up the remains of their meeting, Mick spoke. "I thought you were sending Alan to Kittington."

Sarah carried glasses into the kitchen. "I was going to, but I thought maybe I could talk to Evan, see if he has any ideas about how to handle this." Evan was the leader of Kittington.

"I wish you would have told me you were going." Mick grabbed the rest of the glasses.

"Why? You're coming with me." She took the glasses from him and headed to the kitchen.

"Is Missy going to watch Josey?"

"I thought she could go, too. It's not a supply run and besides, we'll have Tony and Sully with us to watch our backs." She put the rest of the glasses in the sink and used a bit of water to rinse them.

Mick knew his daughter needed to be exposed to the world outside their walls. He just didn't know if he was ready. "You really think it's a good idea?"

She smiled. "Yeah, Mick, it's a good idea. She'll be fine. You worry too much." He shrugged. "Come on, let's go get her. I need to stop at the market before we meet up with Tony and Sully."

♦

Tony and Sully didn't laugh, but it was close. It looked like Mick had sprouted a miniature conjoined twin, with arms and legs barely under control. "How you doin', Mick?" Sully asked as he shook Mick's hand. Josey laughed, reaching out to Sully from the carrier Mick wore.

"Good, you?"

Sarah pulled Tony aside while Mick and Sully talked. "I've told the council. We're going to lock the apartments from now on. Might not save everyone, but it will save most."

Tony nodded. "That's what we're doing back at the base. Someone wanted everyone to move into the stockade, but no one wants to live in a cell."

Sarah sighed. "This shit sucks," she said. "I mean, it sucked before, but I thought once they all died, it would be OK."

"We all did."

Donna moved from behind the counter. "I've packed you some lunches, nothing fancy." She handed Sarah a small soft sided insulated cooler.

Sarah slung it across her chest. It rested on her hip, just under the edge of her backpack. It would take a bit to get used to as she walked. "Thanks, Donna."

"I put some of those pickles you liked in there, Sully," Donna said.

"I appreciate it, Donna, thanks," the soldier said.

Sarah hid her smile as she walked up to Mick and Sully. "We ready to go?" Josey babbled happily. "You ready to go on an adventure, bug?" She tickled Josey under the cheek just to hear her daughter's laughter. There wasn't enough of that in the world.

CHAPTER FIVE

They walked out to the south gate to find Steven on gate duty. He came down from his perch to close the man gate behind them. "Bring me back some bacon," he joked as he undid the first lock.

"Ha," Sarah said as she pulled the door open. "I find any bacon, it's all mine." As she walked through the bus, the pry bar clipped to her backpack smacked against the metal of the seat back, clanging loudly. She always added it to her arsenal when she stepped outside the gates. Guns were still a last resort, due to the noise and dwindling supply of ammo. She really needed to give Paul's idea some thought. She removed the steel bar from the door. Using the key hanging on a nail beside the door, she unlocked the padlock and hooked it on the hasp. "See you later, Steven." She slipped thru the door, the rest right behind her.

Tony and Sully went immediately to their horses. Mick and Sarah stood in the street waiting for them. Mick was tense, his fears about Josey nearly overwhelming him. Sarah saw his discomfort. "It'll be fine, babe," she said softly. "Josey's going to love it."

"So Sully talked to you about Josey?" Tony led his horse over to where they were standing.

"Talked about what?" she asked.

"Giving Josey a ride on the horse."

"No way." Sarah's heart started to pound. She could fall off, get killed. Her daughter wasn't riding a horse.

"Why not?" Sully asked. "She'd love it." He was already mounted on his horse.

"Because." Sarah racked her brain to come up with an excuse. Any excuse. "She's – she's too little."

"She's not too little," Sully said. "My sisters were riding when they were younger than she is now."

"She'll fall off. She's very squirmy."

"I'll have her. I'll even wear Mick's contraption if you want." Sully stopped and looked up at the sky. "I'd just really like to show her how to ride, but if it bothers you that much, it's OK." He looked back at Sarah.

She saw pain in his eyes, pain and longing. She wondered if his sisters made it. Probably not. She looked over at Mick.

Mick gave her a slight smile. Now she knew how he felt. "If you're comfortable with it…" he said.

Sarah blew out a sigh. "Just for a little bit," she said to Sully, who rewarded her with a grin.

"I'll take great care of her," he said, moving to Mick. "Do you want me to wear the harness or whatever it is?"

Sarah laughed. "It's a carrier."

"It's a straitjacket," Tony said. "How do you get her out of there?"

Sarah undid a few straps, then motioned for Tony to take her. He looked tense. "I don't want to ride with her, Sully does. He can get her."

"I can't," Sully said. "You're going to have to hand her up to me." He mounted his horse.

Tony looked at Sarah. "You get her."

"I can't. I don't carry her when I'm armed. She knows that. I don't want to confuse her." Sarah couldn't hide her smile at the big, bad soldier afraid of a ten-month old baby.

Tony looked up at Sully, then back to Sarah. With a loud sigh, he reached for Josey. She squirmed and giggled, almost as if she was trying to make it more difficult for him. Finally, he pulled her from the carrier and handed her up to Sully, who laughed. "That wasn't so hard, was it?"

"Bite me, Sully."

Everyone laughed. "Thanks for not saying what you really wanted to say," Sarah said. "We're not swearing around her."

"Boy, I bet that's hard for you," Sully said. Sarah favored him with a smirk as she checked on Josey. Her daughter was sitting in front of Sully on the saddle, his right arm wrapped around her, his hand lightly gripping her side.

Sarah saw that Sully had a tight grip on her, but she was still worried. She'd let him carry her for a few minutes, then get her back on the ground where she belonged. She was aware Tony was saying something. "I'm sorry, what?"

"Do you want to ride? I can walk."

"No, walking is good. Keeps me in shape."

"Mick? Do you want to ride?"

"Noooooooo. I don't like horses." Besides, he was enjoying the freedom of not having twenty pounds strapped to his chest.

"Alright. Let me know if either of you change your mind." Tony boosted himself up in the saddle. "Ready to go?"

The soldiers moved down the road, Sarah and Mick behind them. "It's killing you, isn't it?" Mick asked.

"What?"

"Josey on the horse."

Sarah shook her head. "No, it's fine."

Mick grinned. "Liar."

"Shutty."

They walked at a brisk pace, the miles disappearing as they moved through the barren land. Every few minutes, Sarah thought about taking Josey from Sully, but when she looked,

Josey was laughing or Sully was talking to her, so Sarah thought to let them ride together a little longer. Just a little longer.

Tony regaled them with stories of the odd things they had seen on their journey, Mick laughing at the soldier's tales. They had all come a long way since their first meeting a year or so before. Sarah had been afraid that Tony and Sully would force them to relocate from their safe haven. She had lost too much to just give it up. Luckily, it was just an informal meeting, the remainder of the government of the United States reaching out to what was left of its citizenry. Tony and Sully merely took the names of the survivors back to their military base, to add them to the lists of those who were still alive. Everyone hoped to find a family member someday. Everyone but Sarah. She had already found her family.

Over the chatter of Tony and Mick, she realized that Sully had grown quiet. She quickened her pace to move closer to him. Josey was asleep in his arms. "How'd you do that?" Sarah asked.

Sully smiled. "It's the rocking of the horse. Puts them right out. My mom would have me ride my sisters around until they fell asleep. I always wanted to try it with my daughter." His smile faded.

Sarah knew. "How old was she?" She asked softly.

"She would have been three. My wife was attacked while she was still pregnant."

Sarah closed her eyes at the horror. "I'm so sorry," she whispered.

A slight shrug, not enough to disturb Josey. "We've all had losses." Sarah knew it was so much more than that. Sully cleared his throat. "We've made good time. Another couple of hours and we'll be there."

"We've travelled that far already?" Sarah looked behind her as if she could see their journey.

"We've been on the road about 3 hours."

"Damn," she said. "Certainly doesn't feel like it." Suddenly she could feel the tightness in her legs, the slight ache in her back. She shook her head. "Now it does. Thanks, Sully."

He laughed. "You're welcome, ma'am."

"Ass."

"Do you want to take a break or keep going?" Sully asked.

"We should keep going. We stop, she'll wake up, we'll never get her back to sleep." Sarah shrugged. "Besides, it's only a couple more hours."

The stretch of road they were travelling on was barren. Very few buildings existed there before the end of the world. Of those, both her group and the group at Kittington cleaned out anything useful ages ago. Now, even those few buildings were barely standing. Three years of weather with no maintenance had reduced them to rickety structures she wouldn't enter on a bet. One hard wind and they would tumble down.

Which is why she was surprised when she caught motion near what was once a farmer's stand. A groan let her know what she was dealing with. Without a word to the group, she unsnapped the strap holding her pry bar to her backpack and walked towards the creature. It used to be a middle-aged male, dressed in jeans and a quilted flannel jacket. It groaned louder as she approached and reached for her. As soon as she was in reach, she swung the bar, the curved end sinking into the temple of the zombie. It fell, her prybar pulling free with a slurping sound. Sarah looked down at the ghoul and shook her head.

She heard Mick come up behind her. "I think that's one of Evan's people," Sarah said, motioning to the corpse on the ground.

He studied the mangled face. "Yeah, it is. Mark or Martin. Something like that."

"Martin." Tony said from next to them. He had dismounted and stood beside Mick. "He was one of Evan's scouts."

"I don't see a bite," Sarah said. She used her prybar to move the corpse.

"Maybe he just died and came back." Tony sighed. "Mick, can you help me carry him back by the building? Evan might want to come back for him." Mick took his feet, Tony took his head and together, they carried the body to the side of the building. Tony wished he had something to cover the corpse, but there was nothing. "Let's get going. We're almost there."

Sarah looked at the body, hoping she wouldn't end up walking after death, shoved to the side of the building like an afterthought.

They kept walking, not talking much. The reality of the mutation finally hit Sarah. Her daughter, her baby, was infected. Mick was infected. She was infected. What she feared the most had the potential to happen. She could turn. She could become a zombie, trying to eat her family and friends. The thought put fear into Sarah. She couldn't let it happen.

Mick watched Sarah as they walked. He could see the thoughts passing over her face. He had made her promise that she would take care of him if he was bitten. He needed to make her the same promise. He wouldn't let her become one of those.

It started slow, but eventually Josey woke from her nap. She looked around, confused, then spotted her mother. She made her sound for "mama," her hands reaching.

"Hi, baby, you have a nice sleep?" Sarah said softly. She was hoping Josey would be content on the horse, but it wasn't to be.

Josey's face twisted into a frown. Her bottom lip started to quiver and Sarah knew what was coming next. Her mouth opened, she took a breath and Josey let out a scream.

"Sorry, guys, we're going to have to take a break. Josey needs to eat." She looked over at Mick. "Want to get her down? I'll start getting the gear off."

Sully stopped the horse, but he was still trying to bounce Josey out of her mood. It wasn't helping. He handed her down to Mick, who bounced her on his hip. "Just a minute, Josey girl. Mama needs to get ready."

Her cries were getting louder. Sarah pulled the cooler from her shoulder, shrugged out of her backpack and dropped it on the ground. She undid the holster and slipped her sheathed knife from her belt, setting them carefully next to the pack. She picked up the cooler and walked it over to Tony, who had dismounted along with Sully. "Why don't you guys eat? It'll take a bit for me to feed her." She handed him the cooler.

"Why'd you strip your gear off?" Sully asked.

"I told you, I don't hold her when I'm carrying." She motioned with her head to Mick and walked a few feet from the soldiers. She found a tree and sat, leaning against it. She unzipped her jacket and untucked her shirt, reaching up under to lift her bra. She took Josey from Mick, who had stopped crying, knowing what was coming. In deference to Tony and Sully, she tucked Josey under her shirt so she could nurse.

"Oh." Sully turned away quickly. "I didn't realize you breast-fed her."

"Formula's all expired," Sarah answered. "Believe me, I'd give her a bottle in a heartbeat if I could. She's got teeth."

Mick smiled as he walked back to the guys and took the cooler from Tony. "Anyone else hungry?"

CHAPTER SIX

Their break lasted 45 minutes, long enough for the sun to dip low in the sky. But at least everyone had eaten and Josey had a clean diaper. "We need to make up time," Tony said as Sully mounted up. "Mick, you can ride with me and Sarah and Josey can ride with Sully."

"Uh, I don't like horses," Mick said, an uneasy look on his face.

"They don't bite, Mick," Sarah said with a smile. "Much."

"Ha ha." Mick looked from Sarah to Tony. "Do I have to?"

Tony suppressed his smile. "Yes, you have to. It's getting dark."

"What do I have to do?" He was resigned to it, but he didn't have to like it.

Sarah watched with a grin as Tony mounted, then held out an arm to Mick. After a few attempts, he made it, sitting behind Tony on the saddle. He looked miserable. "It won't be long, babe," she said. "We'll shave the time in half." She handed Josey up to Sully, who situated the baby in front of him as before. She hurriedly put her gear back on and moved over to Sully.

"I can't pull you up," Sully said. "Not without letting go of Josey."

"You keep hold of my girl," Sarah said. "I'll get there myself." She gripped Sully's hard thigh, put a foot into the stirrup next to his and heaved herself up. And missed. She tried again. And missed. She heard Mick's laughter and cursed him under her breath. She shifted her position, dug into Sully's thigh until she heard him wince, then tried again. This time she made it. She looked over at Mick and mouthed "Fuck you." He laughed louder.

Troy and Sully pushed the horses into a trot. After a bit of a rough start, Sarah remembered her rhythm and moved with the horse, her hands loosely clutching Sully's jacket. She glanced over at Mick. He had a death grip on Tony's jacket and was bouncing in the saddle, every movement bringing a grimace of pain. She could only hope the ride wouldn't be too long. Otherwise, she'd have to find some other way to occupy her nights.

A little over an hour later, just as the sun was hitting the horizon, they approached the settlement of Kittington, housed in what was once Kittington Elementary School. Evan and his people had surrounded the building with box trucks parked end to end, leaving just a small area before the entrance to the school. At the rear of the school were hundreds of trees, apple and pear, more than enough to sustain their small group and trade for the supplies they didn't have. Sarah was counting on Evan needing supplies.

They waited in front of a pair of trucks until their sentry spotted them. "Tony? That you?" The sentry called.

"Me, Sully and Sarah and Mick from…" Tony turned to Sarah. "What is the name of your settlement again?"

"Thornville."

"Sarah and Mick from Thornville," Tony finished.

"Hold on, we'll let you in."

They waited about ten minutes; the sun nearly gone by the time they heard one of the trucks start up. After much maneuvering back and forth, there was a gap between the trucks just wide enough for the horses to walk through. As soon as Sully led his horse thru, stopping on what was once the parking lot for the school, the truck inched back into position. Sarah slung her leg over the horse's back and slid down off the animal. She stretched, stifling a groan. Mick wasn't so lucky. She heard him curse as his feet hit the ground, along with a sharp hiss. She walked over to him. "Rough ride?" She asked.

"I am not getting on that fucking animal again. I don't think I'm going to walk right for a month."

She smiled. "You'll be fine. Can you get Josey? I think Sully wants to get down, too."

Mick waddled over to where Sully sat with Josey. Sarah tried hard not to laugh. She almost made it. She stopped laughing when she saw one of Evan's people, George, headed their way. Where was Evan?

"Where's Evan?" Tony asked.

"Dead. Fucking zombies got him about two months ago. I'm in charge now." Sarah was dismayed. While Evan was condescending, he was still a decent guy. From what she remembered of George, he was misogynistic to the extreme. She hated the idea of talking with him about anything but she wanted to know what Kittington planned to do about the virus mutation.

"What do you want?" He asked brusquely, turning to Sarah.

"Wanted to talk. And I'm looking to trade," Sarah said evenly. "We're low on fruit."

"And you think we have tons to spare?"

"I think you have orchards right outside your doors and you preserve everything you don't eat," she countered. "So if you have some to trade, I'd appreciate it. If not, I'll just head back with what I've brought."

"What did you bring?"

She wasn't giving up that easily. "Do you have fruit?"

He turned away from her. "Tony, Sully, what brings you around?"

"We need to talk. We have some news." Despite all his time in the saddle, Tony stood straight, his military bearing not allowing anyone to see he was aching all over.

"Come on, then." George looked at Sarah and Mick, who held Josey in his arms. "I guess you can come, too."

"Gee, thanks, George," Mick said sarcastically. George snorted and walked away. The group followed.

They walked across the parking lot, up a set of concrete stairs. There was a skinny man at the doors with a rifle slung over his shoulder. He opened the door when George approached, holding it open until the whole group entered. Sarah saw a slight smile on his face when he saw Josey, but it was gone by the time she passed.

A propane lantern sitting midway down the hall didn't put a dent in the gloom. Sarah could hear murmurs of conversation as they walked down the hall. George stopped before a door with 101 painted on the glass. "You two wait here. I'll come back and see if we have anything to trade after I've talked with Tony."

Sarah rolled her eyes. She didn't bother to comment, just pushed open the door and stepped inside, Mick right on her heels. The room held nothing but a long table and a scrawny grey-haired woman sitting in the lone chair. The room had an odor of unwashed bodies and human waste. Sarah wrinkled her nose at the stench. One of the first things she did when she arrived at their settlement was to clean up the buckets of human waste that Annie and her people didn't have time to dispose of. They now had someone assigned every day to collect the waste for use in their gardens and greenhouses. It wasn't a fun job, but a necessary one. They made sure that no one did it twice in a row. Sarah even took a turn at carrying the shit.

"I know you," the woman said when Sarah entered. "You were a lot fatter last time I saw you," she cackled.

"I'm sorry, I don't remember your name," Sarah said with a pleasant smile.

"I'm Dina, George's wife." She held out a dirty hand, grime caked under her nails.

Sarah shook her hand once then dropped it, resisting the urge to wipe her hand on her jeans. "Sarah, from Thornville down the road. This is my husband, Mick and our daughter, Josey." She glanced around the room. She didn't remember it being this bad the last time they visited.

"Ooh, isn't she a cute one!!" Dina stood from her chair. "Can I hold her?"

"No, sorry," Mick said, taking a step back. "She doesn't do well with strangers. She'll start crying and won't stop for hours." He didn't want his daughter anywhere near these people. He was ready to jump back on the horse just to get away from them.

"Oh, that's too bad. I haven't seen a baby in years." She plopped back down in the chair. "What brings you folks here?"

"We're looking to trade. We came with Tony and Sully, the Army guys." Sarah looked around. "Is there somewhere else to sit?"

"No, we burn the chairs and tables for warmth." She pointed to a pile of broken boards in the corner.

Didn't help, Mick thought. The room was barely warmer than the outside. He saw a blackened patch of floor near a bundle of blankets. "You build fires inside the rooms?"

"Where else would we build them? Outside?" Dina stood up again and walked out from behind the table. "We just have a fire long enough to warm up near where we're sleeping. We don't have it all night." She looked at Sarah. "Go on, sit down. I can stand."

"No, I'm fine." Sarah wasn't sure what happened to Kittington. The last time she was here, before Josey was born, it was cleaner and better organized.

"What do you have to trade?" Dina asked, plopping back into the chair.

"Uh – depends on what you need."

Dina cackled again. "We need a lot."

"I can see," Sarah said in a measured voice.

"We ain't got much, but at least we have a roof over our heads." Dina sighed. "I used to have such a nice house. Had all stainless-steel appliances in my kitchen. Every gadget you could think of. Hell, we got a whole room full of that shit, totally useless now." She scratched her head. "Where are you from again?"

"We have a settlement about twenty miles down the road," Sarah said. She looked around as she spoke. "Used to be Thornville, so we kept that name." The faded pictures made Sarah think the room used to be a kindergarten. Sad to think it would be years, if ever, that a kindergarten classroom would be necessary.

The door opened. "Come on if you want to trade," George grumbled from the doorway.

"George, what are you going to trade for?" Dina asked. "Maybe some chocolates?"

"We don't need damn chocolates. Get the fire started. I'll be back in a bit."

Sarah and Mick followed him out the door. "Where are Tony and Sully?" Mick asked. He shifted Josey to his other hip. She tangled a small hand in his hair.

"They're around," George muttered.

Sarah glanced in the next room they passed. Four young women, looking at her with wide eyes. She gave them a small smile as she walked by. The next room was a mess of blankets, a foul stench wafting from the open door. She put a hand to her nose and tried not to gag. She coughed a bit instead. She averted her eyes quickly when she glanced into the third room, where two people were having sex. There was no privacy in this place. She resolved not to look in any other rooms.

She kept her eyes straight ahead until George opened another door and went through without a word. Sarah stepped in front of Mick and, with her hand on her gun, walked into the room. It was brighter than the hall, a battery powered lantern on a relatively clean table putting out light. There was a young girl in the room, probably not out of her teens. She cowered in the corner; her hands clasped together in front of her. Sarah nodded at her, then put her eyes back on George. He settled into an office chair and stared up at her. "What do you have to trade?"

Sarah looked around the room. It was cleaner than any of the others she had seen, but not by much. There were cupboards lining three of the walls and a large table pushed against the other. She could see signs of a fire in the corner between the table and the cupboards. She looked back at George. "Do you have fruit?"

"Well, that depends on what you have to trade."

Sarah sighed. "I don't need your shit, George. Just tell me if you have enough to trade. By the looks of this place, you probably don't."

"What the hell are you talking about? We have plenty!" George stood, hoping to intimidate the much smaller Sarah.

But she didn't intimidate easily. "This place is a dump. It smells. You build fires in the rooms, for Christ's sake." She kept her voice even. "I'm surprised you haven't all died of dysentery or something."

George took a step towards her. Mick tensed. He couldn't do much with Josey on his hip. Damn Sarah for bringing her along. "You think you're so high and mighty, don't you? Someone needs to knock you down, put you in your place where you belong."

"And you think you could do it?" Sarah stepped closer to George until they were nearly nose to nose. "You couldn't, even if you really wanted to." Her voice was low. "You can't even keep a dozen people clean and safe. You're pathetic." She raised her voice. "Let's go, Mick. I can't stand to be here another minute. We don't need fruit this bad."

She turned to go and George grabbed her arm. In a second, she had the gun out and pointed at him. "Touch me again and that girl in the corner is in charge."

He released her arm. She could see fire in his eyes, but he abruptly laughed, backing away. "Damn, you're touchy, girl! I was just kidding with you."

"I wasn't." Her voice was flat. "We're leaving."

"Wait!" George exclaimed. He looked over at the girl in the corner. "Get out." She ran from the room, the door gently closing behind her. "It's hard here," he whined. "Evan died and no one wants to listen to me. People don't want to do anything; they don't want to keep the place clean. I have a hard time getting people to go out and pick the goddamn fruit, let alone do any hunting. They're all a bunch of lazy shits."

"Please watch your language," Sarah said. "We're not swearing around the baby." She reholstered the gun, but she left the strap undone.

George made a rude noise. "Sorry." But she knew he wasn't. "I need to get some help. Some better people. Martin was my best man and he up and left a week ago. Was supposed to be scouting for supplies and just lit out for the territories." George missed the look between Mick and Sarah. "Can you loan me some of yours? Maybe send some here to live?"

Sarah shook her head. "It doesn't work that way. My people can do what they want. If they want to come live here, it's their choice. I don't own them. And truthfully, George, I can't see any of them wanting to live here."

"How 'bout I come with you, stay in your settlement?"

Sarah started. "What about your people?"

"What about them? They can find somewhere else."

"Your wife?" Mick asked, aghast at what he was suggesting.

"Yeah, I guess I'd want her to come along, too. And Candi, that gal that was just here."

Sarah barely repressed a shudder. She didn't want to think of what kind of relationship he had with Candi. "We'd have to take it to the council," she lied. "The council votes on all new members."

"Ask them," he said eagerly. "I can bring a lot of fruit with me." He smiled, his teeth grungy and yellow. "My contribution."

Sarah was saved from answering when Josey started to fuss. She turned to her daughter. "She needs changed," Mick said.

Sarah looked around. The table was the only clean area in the room. "Bring her over."

"You can't change her there!" George exclaimed. "That's where we eat."

"Her butt won't touch the table," Sarah said as she moved behind Mick to open the front pouch of his backpack. "And we'll wipe the table when we're done." She pulled out a changing pad, a diaper and a resealable bag full of wipes.

She moved to the table and laid out the pad. She held the diaper and wipes as Mick laid Josey on the pad and quickly changed her. The diaper was full, the odor adding to the miasma in the room. Sarah wrapped it up, trapping most of the stench inside. "We need to find somewhere to dispose of this." She folded the pad, then pulled a wipe from the bag and cleaned the spot where the pad rested. It was the cleanest spot on the surface. She held the soiled diaper as far away from her body as she could.

"There's a garbage pile in the hall." George pointed.

"Thanks." They needed to leave. Now. Sarah didn't care it was dark. If they moved fast, they could be home before midnight. "Where are Tony and Sully?"

George shrugged. "Around."

"Can you tell them we had to go? We need to get the baby home."

"You gonna ask your council to let me in?" George grinned again.

"I'll talk to them." Sarah couldn't wait to get away. She'd rather face down a herd of zombies than stay another minute with George.

"Here." George opened the closest cupboard. He pulled out two jars of apples. "A good faith gesture." He handed them to Sarah.

Awkward as it was, she took them both in one hand. She wanted a hand free in case she needed it. "Thank you. We'll see you later." She backed away out of the door, Mick preceding her.

When they were in the hall, Mick whispered, "Are you really going to let him in?"

Sarah opened her mouth, but she didn't know what to say. She closed her mouth, cleared her throat and said instead, "Tony and Sully didn't tell him about Martin?" She found the garbage pile George had mentioned and added the diaper to the smelly heap.

Mick shrugged. "I don't know, babe. And it's not our place to tell him."

"He acted like he didn't even know about the mutation. He just cared about getting out of here." Sarah shook her head. "I don't want him in our camp, Mick. But I feel bad for all these other people. That poor girl…"

"You can't save everyone, Sarah." Mick's voice was soft. "There's a limit to the number of strays we can bring home."

"I know, but –"

"Let's just worry about what we have right now," he interrupted. "We need to get back home and deal with our people."

"You're right." She sighed as they reached the door. She stopped. "And you were right about Josey. We never should have brought her on this trip."

"I'm right twice in one day, huh?" Mick said with a grin. "I need to write this on the calendar."

"Shutty." Sarah reached up to touch his face.

Josey put her hand on her mother's. "Da?"

"That's right, Josey. Da's right twice in one day." Mick's eyes twinkled. "What do you think of that?"

"Don't worry, sweetie," Sarah said with a smile. "It won't happen again." She pushed out the door, Mick's laughter following behind.

CHAPTER SEVEN

The same guard was at the door when they came out. He stood up straight from his slouching position against the railing, but when he saw it wasn't George, he relaxed. Sarah gave him a smile. "Do you know where Tony and Sully are?" she asked.

"I think they're around back. There's a little bit of hay back there for the horses."

"Thanks." Sarah started to walk past.

"Hey," he said. "How old's your girl?"

"Ten months," Mick said. And she feels like it, he thought, as he hoisted her back up on his hip.

"My granddaughter was about that age." He sighed. "I like them when they're young like that. They can't talk back."

Sarah nodded. "She's learning, though. She'll be sassing us before we know it."

The man smiled briefly. Then it faded from his face. "Do you have room where you're at?" He looked around and lowered his voice. "Just for a few people?"

"Are you not happy here?" Sarah asked.

"Not really. No one takes care of anything. George has me sitting guard duty when I should be out hunting. We can't live on pears and apples forever."

Sarah looked at Mick. He gave her a slight shrug. She turned back to the guard. "Our council has to approve new members. George asked about coming in, too."

"If you take him, you can take me," the guard said eagerly. "I'm a hard worker and a good hunter, when I can get out to hunt." He stepped closer to Sarah and she tensed. "I'll be a big help there."

"We have to get back now, but we'll send a rider out in a few days to let you know if the council's agreeable," Mick said. "What's your name?"

"Tom. Tom Christopher." He held out a hand and Mick awkwardly shook with his left.

"Alright, Tom. We'll send someone out, let you know." Sarah started walking down the steps.

"I worry about the other people here," Tom said, stopping her in her tracks. "The girls. Since Evan died, this place has gone to hell. Not all the guys are nice."

She turned back to him. "We'll do what we can, Tom." She motioned to Mick and they went down the steps together.

"I know that look," he said when they were out of earshot of Tom.

"What look?" Sarah kept her voice even, despite the fact that she was seething inside. What she thought she saw in there was true, if Tom could be trusted.

"You want to take them in. All the strays."

She turned to Mick. "If the girls are being mistreated, then yes. And you should, too."

"I do, babe. We just need to be sure that that's what's really going on." Josey was getting heavy. He'd have to put her in the carrier for the trip back.

"I had the feeling, Mick. When I was in that school, I felt that something wasn't right with those girls. They look beaten down, like Donna was in Sugar Creek. Like I could have been." She shook her head. "I can't let that happen."

"Let's just get home and we'll talk about it there, figure out what to do." He needed to talk her down before she went back in the school and forcibly removed the women. "It'll just be a day or two."

She blew out a sigh. "OK, you're right."

"Did you hear that, Josey? Three times in one day! A new record!"

Sarah felt her anger lessen. It was still there, but Mick always made things better. "Don't let it go to your head."

They walked around the corner of the building and saw Tony and Sully with the horses. "Did you get what you needed?" Tony asked as they approached.

"No. Evan, I could deal with, but George? George is being, well, George." Sarah brushed the nose of Tony's horse. "Did you talk to him about the mutation?"

Tony nodded. "It was weird, he didn't seem to care."

"Yeah, he's not caring about much," Sarah said. "He's let this place go to shit. We're heading back."

"It's late," Sully said. "You won't get home until close to midnight."

"Better than spending a night here," Mick said. "I wouldn't feel safe and I certainly don't want Josey here."

Sully looked at Tony. Tony gave him a slight nod. "We'll ride you back," Tony said. "We can stay at your place tonight, head out to Boyer in the morning."

"I'd appreciate it," Sarah said. "I wasn't looking forward to the walk back, but Mick's right, we can't stay here."

"That's four, Josey!!"

"Quit keeping track, Mick," Sarah said, rolling her eyes. "Because you'll never catch up to me." She grinned.

They mounted up in the same configuration they used on the last leg of the trip. Sarah watched Mick try to get comfortable on the horse. "Move with the animal," she said. "It'll be much easier."

"How the hell do I do that?"

Sarah thought a moment. "I don't know, I just do it."

He snorted. "Thanks for the advice."

They waited nearly 15 minutes for someone to come and open the gate. Sarah was ready to do it herself and fuck their wall, but finally a sullen-faced skinny man slowly made his way to the truck and moved it out of the way. Sully gave the man a sarcastic salute as they rode past.

They put the horses into a trot, hoping to make it back to their settlement in less than three hours. Over the clopping of the horses' hooves, Sarah asked, "Did you tell George about Martin?"

"Yeah," Sully answered. "He didn't seem overly concerned."

"He wants to join us in our settlement." Sarah told Sully. "Him and his wife and a girl, Candy. I think she might be his mistress."

"Candy? She can't be much more than eighteen."

"That's what I thought," Sarah said. "I don't think any of those women are being treated well."

Sully shook his head. "If you let him in your camp, you better watch your ass."

"I know."

They didn't talk much more on the way back. It was a long and tiring ride and Sarah felt herself starting to nod off at points. When they pulled up to their gate, Paul was on the gate. "I didn't expect you back tonight," he said as he unlocked the door.

"Me, either," Sarah said with a tired sigh. She moved thru the bus, every step a chore. Mick followed with Josey sleeping in his arms, Tony and Sully right behind him, their saddlebags slung over their shoulders. When Paul was locking up, Sarah said, "Make sure those horses are OK tonight. Tony and Sully are going to rest here before heading to Boyer tomorrow."

"OK. Bobby's after me, I'll let him know, too."

"We need to have another council meeting tomorrow," she said. "After breakfast."

"What now?" Paul asked, dismayed that his sleep would be disrupted.

"We'll talk tomorrow. I'm exhausted." Sarah walked on, Mick, Tony and Sully right behind. It took quite a bit of effort for Sarah to make it to Ash and up the two flights of stairs to their apartment. She saw a new deadbolt in the door, the keys stuck in the lock. "Bobby's been busy," she said to Mick as she turned the key and pushed open the door. She turned on the battery powered lantern next to the door as it was long past time for power.

"Wonder how many he got done?" Mick asked as he followed her in.

"We'll find out tomorrow." She turned to Tony and Sully. "Spare bedroom is in there, but there's only one bed. Queen-sized, but if you're weird about sharing a bed, the couch is pretty comfortable."

"I have no problem with it," Tony said.

"I'm cool. Where does Josey sleep?" Sully asked.

"She sleeps in our room." Sarah opened their bedroom door and leaned against the jamb. Mick slipped around her with Josey. "Kitchen opens at seven for breakfast, so make sure you eat before you go. If you want to leave earlier than that, tell whoever's in the kitchen to give you something for the road. I'm done in; I'm going to bed."

"See you in the morning," Sully said as he followed Tony into the spare bedroom.

Sarah moved into their room and closed the door. She began to unload her gear as she watched Mick try to undress Josey without waking her. It was a losing battle. She woke and started to fuss as he was changing her diaper. Sarah sighed loudly as she hurriedly removed the rest of her gear and stowed it in the lock box.

"I'll stay up with her so you can sleep," Mick said as he picked Josey up and held her to his chest, rubbing her back.

"You don't have the right equipment." Sarah kicked the box under the bed and reached for the baby. She plopped herself into the rocking chair near the bed and set Josey to nurse, hoping it would put her back to sleep.

Mick began undressing, his body aching from the ride. He gasped as he sat on the bed. "I'm getting too old for this shit."

"Take some ibuprofen. I think there's still some in the nightstand. It'll help a little," Sarah said as she rocked Josey.

"You want some?"

"No, not while I'm nursing." She hadn't taken so much as an aspirin since she found out she was pregnant. She lived with the aches and pains.

"Michelle said an ibuprofen or two wouldn't hurt." Mick found the bottle and poured three in his hand. "You should take some. You're going to be as sore as I am in the morning."

"I'm fine, Mick. Take those and get some sleep. I'll put her down as soon as she dozes off."

He crawled under the covers and lay with his arms folded under his head. "You need to start delegating more, babe."

"I know." And she did. But she knew she'd do it right.

"No more long trips out, especially not with Josey."

She looked at Mick over Josey's head. "You're right. She can stay in the walls for a little while longer."

"Thank you." He smiled.

"You're welcome. Now turn out the light and get some sleep." He dimmed the lantern until it was barely giving off illumination.

After a few minutes, she heard his steady, even breathing. He was asleep faster than she thought he would be. The trek really tired him out. Her, as well. She wanted to close her eyes in the worst way, but not until Josey was asleep. Instead, she thought about the newest problem.

She did not want George in their settlement. But she could not leave those women there unprotected. She knew what it was like to be under the thumb of a man, fearing she would be raped or worse. She actually had the worse happen to her. Would George agree to her taking his women? Probably not. So she would have to have George at the settlement as well. It was a catch-22. She didn't want him, but she wanted to help his people. He wouldn't leave his people, so she would have to take him. There was no good solution.

Josey stopped nursing; her eyes closed against Sarah's breast. She gently disengaged her daughter and laid her in the bassinet. She ran a hand over her back before she backed away. She looked at the door and let out a big sigh. She still needed to make her nightly trek around the town, to make sure everything was as it should be. Nothing ever happened, but Sarah felt better when she made sure. "Not tonight," she whispered. She undid her belt and jeans and pushed them down, stepping out of them and leaving them where they lay. She crawled under the covers and snuggled up to Mick's warm body. She was asleep in minutes.

Josey woke four hours later. Sarah was up immediately, moving to the bassinet to pick her up. She tried walking with her, talking with her, but she was still fussy. Since Mick was still sleeping off the hard day, she left their bedroom and moved into the living room. Turning the lantern on low, she curled up on the sofa, pulling a blanket over her bare legs. She set Josey to nurse again, rubbing her back as she fed.

The guest bedroom door opened and Sully stepped out, closing it behind him. "Hi," he whispered.

"Did she wake you? I'm sorry."

"No, I don't sleep much. You mind if I sit?"

Sarah indicated the end of the sofa. Sully sat and let out a breath. "Long day for her?" He asked, turning to face Sarah.

"Long day for all of us. I expected to stay at Kittington and rest up, not race back here. I didn't even get what I went there for and came home with a whole new set of problems." She winced as Josey bit.

"You need to be very careful with George," Sully said. "He doesn't like women. He wouldn't be happy with you running the place."

"Maybe I'm not happy with me running the place anymore." She rubbed her free hand over her eyes.

"Sarah, you're doing a great job here," he said, pulling his feet up on the sofa and turning towards her. "You have plenty of food, you have power, you have heat. You even have half-assed showers. Your people are content and it's all because of you."

"That really doesn't make it easier," she said, shifting Josey. "I barely have time for me, for Mick, for her. I get stuck with all the tough decisions because inevitably, the council's vote is a tie. I'm not even thirty years old, I shouldn't be doing this shit."

"None of us should. But you have to keep doing it, because you're doing it the right way. The way things should be done." Sully scratched at his beard. "You're keeping your people safe. They're happy and together and you're even helping others. You can't give it up. Who the hell knows how the next leader would do things?"

"Maybe smarter. They wouldn't fall in love. They wouldn't have a kid. They wouldn't get people killed." Her voice broke, thinking of Ryan.

"They would probably do worse." He reached over and touched the hand resting on her lap. "You do good, Sarah. Keep doing good."

She gave him a slight smile. "I don't know how much longer I can, Sully. I want to be a normal person."

He laughed. "None of us will never be normal, Sarah. Not after this." He leaned back on the sofa. "Hell, we probably weren't too normal before this shit."

"You're right." Josey had fallen asleep again. Sarah moved her out from under her shirt and held her to her chest. Josey squirmed around a bit, finding her most comfortable spot.

"She really is gorgeous," Sully said.

"She's going to be a handful. She my daughter and she's a ginger." Sully laughed. Sarah bit her lip, then continued on. "Would you want to join us here? I could use the help."

Sully shook his head. "I'd love to, but I don't think there's any mustering out of the Marines anymore. There'd be no one to take my place and it's already running on a shortage of men."

"How 'bout making this your home base? I can get you your own apartment." Sarah grinned. "I can even get you a girlfriend."

Sully's face grew red. "I can find my own girlfriend."

"Do it here. I'd love for you and Tony to be a semi-permanent part of our community."
"You'd have to give it a better name than Thornville first."

CHAPTER EIGHT

Sully fell asleep on the sofa. Sarah put the sleeping Josey in her bassinet in their bedroom, then covered Sully with the blanket she had been using earlier. With heavy steps, she headed back into their bedroom and sunk into bed, falling asleep almost immediately.

Tony and Sully didn't stick around for breakfast. They ate some old protein bars from their saddlebags and left town at dawn. But not before leaving Josey's doll on the sofa, sitting on the folded-up blanket.

Sarah and Josey were still sleeping when Mick awoke. He didn't think for a moment to wake either of them. They needed the sleep. He pulled on his jacket and headed to the community kitchen.

"Annie's upstairs waiting for you and Sarah," Donna said as Mick entered.

"Sarah's still home sleeping," Mick said. "It was a long night." He looked at the list of foods available. "What do we have today?"

"I made some scrambled eggs from the last of the powdered stuff you guys found last month. Those will be good for Josey."

"Sounds good. I'll head up and get some."

"Wait." Donna squatted down and opened a cabinet on her island. She came out with a plastic container and lid. "Take this."

"Thanks, Donna."

He left the kitchen, taking the stairs two at a time to the communal dining room on the second floor. Donna and her crew made two meals per day, breakfast and dinner. In the beginning, everyone ate together, but as more people came to town and schedules no longer lined up, people stopped showing for both meals. Dinner was still well attended, but breakfast was hit or miss. Donna made less food and what wasn't used was incorporated into that day's dinner. Nothing was wasted.

Mick stepped into the dining room, saw about ten people scattered about the long tables, which could hold 50. Just like the kitchen below, walls had been removed to make one large room. Six-foot long tables and folding chairs made the room seem more like a cafeteria than anything else. The tables along the wall, holding chafing dishes full of food, only reinforced the appearance.

"Mick!" Annie called.

He waved at her, indicating that he would be over to see her. Quickly, he moved to the buffet line and filled the plastic container with eggs. Damn, he missed cheese. Besides the eggs, there were tomatoes and canned oranges. He bypassed the tomatoes, but filled a plate with oranges. He balanced the plate on top of the plastic container and headed over to Annie.

"Where are Sarah and Josey?" she asked as he sat.

"Still sleeping. It was a long night." Mick looked around the room, nodding at some, waving at others.

"Paul said something about a meeting after breakfast. Are you going to tell us about Kittington or is it more bad news?"

"Kittington, mostly." Mick scratched at his goatee. It was getting a little messy. During his next shower, he would have to trim it.

"What time should we come over?"

"Give us about an hour." He stood up. "That should be enough time to get Josey fed and settled. Can you round up everyone else?"

"Sure, Mick." She looked up at him. "Can you tell me if it's more bad news?"

He shrugged. "I really don't know if it's good or bad, Annie. That's what Sarah wants to talk to the council about."

"OK. I'll finish up here, then collect everyone else."

"Thanks."

When he got back to their apartment, both Sarah and Josey were awake. "Why didn't you wake me?" Sarah asked as she finished changing Josey's diaper.

"You were up all night," he said as he set the eggs on the table. "You needed your sleep."

"I woke up when I heard you leave. So that extra ten minutes really helped."

"Shutty." He shrugged out of his coat and hung it on the chair. "Let's eat while the eggs are still warm."

"Eggs?" Sarah picked Josey up and carried her into the kitchen. She set her in her high chair, making sure to strap her in. Josey was an escape artist.

Mick pulled plates from the cabinet and flatware from the drawer and set them on the table. "Donna cooked up the last of the powdered eggs." He opened the plastic container and dished eggs onto the plates. "Do you want to feed Josey or should I?"

"I'll do it." Sarah sat at the table and pulled Josey's plate closer. She flattened the eggs on the plate so they would cool faster. Josey saw the eggs and began to coo, her chubby hands reaching for her plate. "In a minute, sweetie."

Sarah wasted no time digging into her eggs. "Damn, even powdered, they're great."

"We need to find chickens," Mick said as he put pepper on his eggs. "We need more eggs."

"Fat chance of that." Sarah judged the eggs cool enough. She took a small bit on a spoon and fed Josey.

"Annie was at breakfast. She's going to get everyone and come here in about an hour."

"Why so long?" Sarah asked.

"Because I wanted to eat a relaxing breakfast and spend some time with my girls." Mick smiled just before he forked up some eggs.

Sarah let out a breath. "I was thinking last night that maybe I don't want to do this anymore."

Mick's fork clattered to his plate. "Do what? Us?"

"No! No!!" Sarah shook her head. "Lead. I don't know if I want to be in charge anymore."

"Don't scare me like that!"

She giggled as she fed Josey some more eggs. "Sorry. It just seemed a natural progression in my mind. Us not spending enough time together is why I don't want to do this anymore."

He picked up his fork and resumed eating. "Yeah, well, I'm not always privy to the inner workings of your brain, babe." He took a bite of eggs, chewed and swallowed. "Sarah, you were made for this. You're the best at this. You just need to delegate some more." He took a drink of water. "Like yesterday. You didn't need to go to Kittington. You were going to send Alan, but decided to go yourself. Did it help for you to go? No. It just brought up a whole new set of problems."

She sighed. "I know. Which is why I think I shouldn't do this anymore. I don't want to deal with it anymore."

"So who would? Annie? Troy? Paul?" He shook his head. "None of them have the skill and strength to do it." He reached across the table and took her hand. "We're fine, Sarah. I won't complain about a little more time, but if you delegate, we will."

"It's just so hard. I want it done right and I know I'll do it right."

He shrugged. "You have to learn to let sh—stuff go. It's not going to be perfect. But it will be good. Because we're together."

They finished their breakfast, then spent the next half hour being a family. Josey was just learning to pull herself up on the furniture. They both marveled when she managed to pull herself along the sofa, from Mick to Sarah. She basked in the praise she received and so, giggling, she did it over and over. Mick looked at Sarah and shook his head. She was going to be trouble.

The council arrived and Josey had to show off her new-found skill. After she had received her share of accolades, Sarah picked her up off the floor and put her in the play pen with the doll Sully had left for her. It would keep her occupied for the few minutes it would take to bring the council up to speed.

"We took a trip to Kittington yesterday to ask for a trade and also to find out if Evan had any ideas on what to do with the new info on the virus," Sarah informed the group. "The trade didn't happen and neither did the discussion about the virus. Evan's dead and George is in charge. He wants to come to our settlement."

"Is there a reason not to have his people here?" Annie asked. "The more hands, the better, right?"

"There are a few reasons." Sarah leaned back on the sofa. "George didn't ask for his whole group to come. He asked for himself alone, then his wife and a girl we presume is his mistress to join us." She looked around at the group. "He also has serious problems with females, most particularly females in charge."

"He'd have a helluva time here," Troy laughed. "He may not be a good fit."

"True," Sarah admitted. "But I think the women in his group are being mistreated. Every female we saw there seemed very frail and frightened. One of his group, Tom, said he worried about the girls in their group. He insinuated that some of the other members of the group weren't kind to them. I think they're being abused."

April caught her eye. She was one of the few on the council that knew what Sarah went through in Sugar Creek. "Then we bring them here."

"I don't think George will let them go," Sarah said. "I want those women here, where they can be safe and protected. But it may be that we'll have to take George as well."

"We can make it clear that we don't condone that kind of behavior here," Paul said. "And make sure that George knows that you are in charge. If he doesn't like that, he can move on."

"Or we can just go in there and take the females and let George fend for himself." Bobby had a hard time in Sugar Creek as well. He bristled at the thought of another man who thought he had the right to mistreat those who looked to him for help.

"Believe me, Bobby, I've thought about it. It would be so easy. But the right thing isn't necessarily the easiest thing." Sarah took a sip of her tea. "I think we need to take the whole group and like Paul said, lay down the law when they get here. But I'll go along with what the council decides."

The vote was five to one to accept George and his group into their community, with Bobby being the only dissenting vote. "Bobby, I understand why you don't want him here," Sarah said. "But he will not turn into Bill. I won't allow it."

Bobby sighed. "I hope not."

"Couple more things, then we're finished," Sarah said to the group.

"What else is there?" Mick asked. He didn't remember them discussing anything else.

Sarah shifted on the sofa. Her butt was still sore from riding the horse. "Annie, Troy, I need to know who can go on an extended trip down to Kittington. I want someone to go there and tell them we'll accept them. Our people can wait a day or so, then lead whoever's coming back here."

"You're not going?" Troy asked.

"No. I'm delegating." She caught Mick's smile from the corner of her eye.

"I want to go to Kittington," Paul said suddenly.

"Why? You almost never go on runs," Mick asked.

"I want to make sure that George knows we won't take his bull. He will understand how we do things or I'll leave him there."

Sarah nodded. "That's fine by me. Troy, Annie, can you work it out?"

Annie nodded. "It won't be a problem. Should we consider this a supply run or scouting?" Supply runs always consisted of four people, scouting two or more.

"If there's a potential for trouble," Troy looked over at Sarah and saw her slight nod. "I'd treat it as a supply run. Four. Paul, Mark, Jenny and maybe Val."

Sarah shook her head. "Not Val. This might hit too close to home for her." Sarah and Mick were part of the scavenging team that rescued Val and Erin from raiders. "But Jenny would be a good choice. She's our toughest fighter."

"After you," Bobby said.

"Oh, no, I think she has me beat. She'll be formidable. George may think twice about starting trouble if she's around."

"I'll come up with someone else and work out the schedules." Troy closed his notebook. "Is that it?"

"I want to send a letter to George, spelling everything out in no uncertain terms. I think our people should give him the letter and give him a day to make up his mind. If he doesn't agree, they get the women out, at least those that want to come. George's wife will probably stay behind. There's a guy named Tom there who wanted to come with us as well. Then they head back."

"OK, Sarah," Annie said, rising from her chair. "Bring the letter down to the market when it's ready. We'll be getting them ready to go."

Sarah stood. "Thanks, everyone. I'll see you at dinner."

Mick took Josey to Missy's day care, since both he and Sarah had work to do in the morning. Sarah worked on the letter for George. She wanted to be firm, but not antagonistic. When she was finally satisfied, she geared herself up for the outdoors and walked to the market.

The crew consisting of Paul, Mark, Mandy and Jenny were already there, along with Troy and Annie. "Thank for doing this," Sarah said.

Jenny shrugged. "Gets me out of shit duty for a day." Jenny was a tall brunette, with a scar running down one side of her pretty face. She had been a bartender when the world went to shit, barely escaping with her life when one of her customers attacked her, thinking he wouldn't get prosecuted for rape and murder. She ended up scarred, he ended up dead. She swore she wouldn't be subjected to that again and trained herself to fight. Most people gave her a wide berth, but Sarah saw a kindred spirit. They weren't buddies, but they respected each other.

Mark and Mandy were recent additions to the community. They came in together, the last survivors of a survivalist compound that had been overrun. One mistake with a gate and thirty people were gone. Mark and Mandy barely escaped and were near starving when they stumbled across the community. Once Michelle and April had nursed them back to health, Sarah found their knowledge to be an asset and she used both of them to help shore up defenses. April and Mandy were now a couple.

"Give this to George," Sarah said, handing the envelope to Mark. "Tell him if he can't abide by what's written here, then he's not welcome. But make sure you get all the women out."

"If he won't let them go?" Mark asked as he shoved the envelope in his pocket.

"Get them out however you have to." Sarah looked at their packs. "You might want to take a small tent or something. You're not going to want to stay inside their building."

"We'll be fine," Jenny said, tightening the straps on her pack.

"There's a guy named Tom who wants to get out. He might be able to help you with the women."

"How many women are there?" Mandy asked as she slicked her dark blonde hair into a ponytail.

"Six, I think, including George's wife, Dina." Sarah shrugged her shoulders. "She may not want to come but make sure you get the rest of them out."

"We'll take care of it, Sarah," Paul said. "Don't worry."

"I'm not. I know you guys got this."

She walked with them to the gate. She pulled Paul aside after Mark, Mandy and Jenny had passed through. "Keep an eye on Jenny. She has a real thing about abused women."

Paul nodded. "We'll bring them back."

"You need to let them know about the virus, too. We're telling everyone else at dinner."

He nodded again. "I'll take care of it. We'll see you in a few days."

♦

The news of the virus mutation was not well received at dinner, much as Sarah expected. Some people were angry, some were upset, a few even cried.

"What does this mean?" Donna asked, her voice breaking. "Are we all going to turn?"

"As far as the scientists can figure, anyone who has been in contact with a zombie in the last six months is now infected." Sarah waited until the murmurs died down before she continued. "Additionally, if you're in close contact with someone who is infected, chances are you are also infected."

"So I'm infected because Ed goes out?" Ed's wife Bonnie asked.

"If Ed has been in contact with any of them in the past six months, then yes, that's what the scientists are saying," Sarah said.

"You know he was," Bonnie cried. "He came home covered in blood!"

"I'm sorry, Bonnie."

"Sorry? What does that help?" Bonnie's voice was ragged. "Nothing! My husband goes out and I end up infected. How is that right? How is that fair?"

"You realize that I'm infected, Bonnie," Sarah said, biting off her words. She was trying to control her anger. "As is my husband. And my daughter. All because Mick and I are constantly out there taking care of this group. You tell me how fair it is that my ten-month old daughter is infected."

"Well, it's not but –"

"But nothing, Bonnie. It's done. It's happened. We can't change it and bitching about it will not change it." Sarah cleared her throat. "We still have to go out and find supplies. And we will. That will not change. If anyone has a problem going out, we'll take it under advisement. But we're not going to stop. Not if we want to survive."

"But what do we do if someone dies?" Gabriel asked. He didn't talk much, but did everything that was asked of him without complaint. The most Sarah knew of him was that he used to sell real estate.

"Bobby and Chris will be installing new locks on every apartment door. All doors are to be locked every night."

"What if someone in the apartment dies?" Sarah turned her head to see who spoke. It was Joey, who shared his apartment with Blake and David. Blake looked uneasily at Joey.

"You have the option of locking the bedroom doors in the apartments, too. If you want additional locks, just let me or Bobby or someone else on the council know." Sarah looked around the room. "It's not an ideal situation, but there's really not much else we can do."

"Are they still talking about a cure?" Helen asked. Sarah noticed Helen's and Sid's clasped hands on the table.

Sarah shook her head. "I haven't heard anything recently." She waited for more questions. There were none, only muted conversations throughout the room. "We have a few other things to talk about. Mick?"

Mick handled the mundane – personnel changes, the newly acquired supplies, the items that were getting low, upcoming birthdays and anniversaries. As he talked, April whispered to Sarah, "That went better than I thought."

"Really? I thought it sucked." Sarah pushed her empty plate away and lifted her cup of water.

"I expected more anger, more lashing out. Everything they've known has been turned upside down once again," April said. "There's only so much a person can take."

"I know. I'm just about hitting my limit." Sarah watched the room as Mick spoke. A few listened, some looked shell shocked, but most were talking amongst themselves, trying to make sense of what Sarah had said. She could see anger, confusion, dread. Hopefully, they would soon realize that there was nothing to be done.

When Mick finished, Sarah nodded at Annie. With a smile on her pleasant face, Annie stood. "We expect to have an influx of new people soon," she said. "Kittington has decided to join us. I hope you'll make the newcomers feel welcome."

"How many new people?" Bonnie demanded.

"We're not sure how many will join us," Annie said. "We expect at least a half dozen."

"Where are you going to put them?" Someone called out.

"What about food? Do we have enough?" Another voice said.

Annie glanced over at Sarah. Pushing her chair back, Sarah stood. "We have plenty of empty apartments and plenty of food. Besides, they're bringing their supplies with them. Kittington was right next to a grove of apple and pear trees. They have plenty of fruit preserved and they will contribute it to our stores."

"What if they're sick? What if they turn?"

"Should we take on more people? Don't we have enough?"

Sarah zeroed in on the last speaker. It was Sid. "When we took you and Helen in, do you think we had enough people? When any of you joined our group, did we have enough?" She looked around the tables, seeing the faces she had always seen, people she thought were kind and welcoming. Fear does this, she thought. "April and Michelle will check everyone coming into our settlement. If they look ill, we'll quarantine them until we can be sure they won't die or turn."

She took a deep breath. "We fought hard to build this place. We've lost people. But we are still open to everyone that is willing to work and willing to be part of a community. We don't want people who are only looking out for themselves. If that's what you're feeling, that you can't welcome people who need help, then you can make your way to the other side of the gate. And don't expect to be welcomed back."

The room went silent. Sarah looked around the room, then nodded to Mick. "We're done here." She walked out, Mick behind her, carrying Josey.

When they were in the hall, Mick touched her arm. She stopped and turned to look at him. "I didn't think about Josey being infected." His voice was a soft whisper, filled with pain.

"I've been thinking about it since Tony told us. Since she's still nursing, most likely, she's infected."

"Damn."

"Exactly."

CHAPTER NINE

Two days after the announcement, Sarah was on the wall. Gate duty was one of Sarah's favorites. The good view, the peace and quiet. She'd do nothing but gate duty if she could. She could see for miles. Which is why she spotted the riders over a half hour before they got close enough to hear her. "Back so soon?" She called out to Tony and Sully as soon as they were within speaking distance.

"Boyer is gone," Tony said without preamble as they stopped the horses in front of the gate.

"What?" Sarah was dumbfounded. She was just there. No, it was over a year ago. She was still pregnant with Josey. It was her last trip out before she was born.

"Virus got them," Sully said. "It looked like it happened about a week before we got there."

"Jesus." Sarah shook her head. "Everyone?" She thought of Norm, who ran Boyer. He was lucky enough to survive the apocalypse with his granddaughter, Maddie, who said she couldn't wait to see Sarah's baby.

"Everyone." Tony sighed, shaking his head. "It was horrible. We had to…" He trailed off. They were people he knew, came to care for.

"We had to take care of them," Sully finished. "We placed them into a mass grave."

Sarah closed her eyes and shuddered. It can't happen here, she thought. I won't let it. She opened her eyes and looked down at her friends. "Do you guys need a rest? Just for a couple days?"

"No, we have to get back, make our report. We've been gone pretty long." Tony indicated his saddle bags. "We gathered up some of the supplies for you."

"There's more, but we couldn't bring them all," Sully said.

"I'll be right down."

Sarah met them on the other side of the gate. Sully handed her a duffel bag he had strapped to the back of the horse. Tony lifted a tote from his saddle pommel and handed it to Sarah. She could see some jerky, toilet paper and a box of tea bags inside. "Thank you." She looked up at Tony's face, seeing the exhaustion written all over his face. "Are you sure you can't stay, just for a little bit?"

Tony shook his head. "We've been gone too long already. Don't forget to send someone for the rest of the supplies."

Sarah nodded as she slung the duffel over her shoulder. "You guys be careful, OK?"

Sully nodded. "You be careful, you hear?"

She smiled slightly. "I'm always careful."

She watched them go, her heart heavy. For the brave men riding away, for the town lost to the virus, for her own family.

The next day, Sarah was working in the greenhouse mulching plants, when Troy found her. "They're back," he said.

Sarah stood up from her crouching position, brushing her hands together to remove loose mulch. She plunged her hands into a bucket of tepid water to get the rest of the dirt off, then dried them on a rag hanging from the bucket handle. "Where are they?"

"They came in the road by the garage."

"Let's go." Sarah waved at Steven, who was in charge of the greenhouse that day. He waved back. She grabbed her jacket from the hook by the door and shrugged into it as they walked out into the cold.

"How many? Did they get everyone?" She asked Troy.

He adjusted his stride to keep up with her. He had no idea how such a small woman walked so damn fast. "I don't know. They have two trucks. The bed of one was full of people."

"And the other?" Sarah nodded at people as she went past. She didn't make direct eye contact. She didn't have time to stop and listen to everyone's worries about the virus mutation. It was old news.

"Looked like it was packed with supplies. We only have 3 apartments ready. Do you think that will be enough?"

"It has to be. If not, someone gets a new roommate." She saw the two trucks just a block ahead, near one of their access roads. There were two secondary roads into town, barricaded with box trucks that were easy to move if they needed to get in or out. Every other road was permanently blocked with stacked cars, disabled tractor trailers or, in the case of the main road through town, buses and trucks. It was a good idea that had turned bad when Pete and his crew invaded town by using the movable barricades. But they needed the access points. Sarah had sentries check the roads every few hours to make sure they were still working as intended. Every night before she retired for the night, she walked the town herself. She could see that the box truck had been moved so that the two big pick-up trucks from Kittington could get through. Paul was in the process of moving the box truck back into place when she and Troy reached them.

Sarah spotted Jenny. "How did it go?" She asked as she looked up at the taller woman.

Jenny rolled her eyes. "A couple of them are lucky they made it here without dying along the way."

"That bad?" Sarah winced.

"Worse. You got some real assholes there." Jenny hefted her backpack on her shoulder. "Keep them away from me." She turned and walked away, towards her apartment.

Sarah sighed loudly. She really didn't need this shit. She walked over to Paul, who had finished moving the truck back in position. "How bad is it?"

"We got George, all the women, Tom and another guy named Chad. Two guys didn't want to join up, so we left them some food and headed here. There was a landslide on Route 88, so we had to detour. We'll need to remember that if we go back that way."

Sarah saw Mark and Mandy helping women out of the truck bed. George was in the cab of one of the trucks, sitting with the door open and his feet on the running board, just watching the action. "Did George give you much trouble?"

Paul shrugged. "He's an asshole. He read your letter and bitched and moaned and said he wasn't going somewhere where he wasn't in charge. I told him fine, send out all the women and we'd be on our way. A little while later, he said he changed his mind." Paul looked over at the man, who had jumped down from the truck and was looking around at the various buildings. "He's going to be trouble."

"He starts shit, I'll finish it." She saw Tom standing near a few of the younger women. "What about Tom?"

"He seemed fine. He was more than willing to come along. He hauled most of the supplies they brought."

"Alright. Gather everyone up and take them to the cafeteria. We're going to have a talk, then April and Michelle will check them out. Troy has the list of available apartments. They'll have to double up. We'll give them a few days to get used to us, then Troy will give them their assignments." Paul nodded. "What supplies did they bring?"

"Mostly fruit, some deer jerky and water, personal belongings."

"Troy, can you take the truck down to the market and find someone to unload the supplies?"

"I got it, Sarah. Lord knows, we don't want you to drive it." Troy smiled.

"You weren't even in the car at the time," Sarah laughed. "You don't get a say."

"I heard enough. I'll do an inventory of what they brought and get it to you this evening."

"No rush, Troy." Sarah looked over their new members. Not very clean, the women looked tired and beaten down. The men looked stronger, but still as dirty as the women. "Paul, I'll see you at the dining room." She turned on her heel and headed down the road.

♦

The stench of unwashed bodies was strong in the dining room. Sarah counted seven women and three men. Donna had put together a small snack to welcome the group and the plates were completely empty, not even a crumb remaining. Most of the women still looked scared, their bodies hunched over protectively. Only Dina, George's wife, sat up straight, her eyes flitting about the room. Of the men, Tom seemed content. Sarah noticed that he had only eaten half of his food, passing the plate down the line to the other women. Chad slouched in his chair, seemingly bored with the whole process. George, however, stared back at her, his arms folded across his chest, his face sullen. Paul was at her back, leaning against the wall, waiting for her speech.

"My name is Sarah Louis," she started. "I'd like to welcome you all here." She smiled. "We have a lot of people in town who are eager to meet you as well, but we'll give you a little time to settle in." She took a drink of her water.

"There are some rules for living here." She saw Dina roll her eyes. "First off, everyone works. It may not be all day, but everyone has to contribute to the success of the community. You'll meet with Troy today and let him know what your skills are. If you don't have any real skills, we'll find you something to do. There are some shit jobs, but everyone takes turns at them, including me. Everyone is equal in the eyes of Troy.

"Everyone stays in one of three apartment buildings, Ash, Shaun or Bub. Unfortunately, we only have three apartments for you. Chad, if you don't mind, I'd like to put you in with a couple of our people, Frank and Chris." Chad shrugged. "Tom, you're going to have to share an apartment with Ben." Tom nodded.

"Why does he only get one roommate and I get two?" Chad asked.

"Because that's where the openings are. I don't care who stays where, you two work it out, then let Troy know when you do." Sarah stared at Chad until he looked away. "George, you and Dina can have one of the apartments and you ladies can split up the last two. All apartments need to be locked every night due to the virus mutation." She could see the confused looks on most everyone's face. She looked at George. "Didn't you tell them?"

He shrugged. "I didn't see a need to."

She wanted to slap the smug look off of his face. "The virus has mutated. Anyone who has been in contact with a zombie in the past six months is now infected." The women gasped. Tom looked startled. "Infection can also be spread to someone you share close quarters with. So essentially, most of us are now infected. We lock the apartment doors at night in case someone dies during the night.

"Everyone coming into town has to have a medical exam. You will all be examined today after you meet with Troy." She wasn't used to talking so much. Her throat was getting dry. She took another drink of water. "We have the power on in Ash and Bub from 7:00 am to 9:00 pm. This building, Shaun, has power 24/7 because it's where we keep our food supplies and medical facilities. I ask that you keep power usage to a minimum. The generators work hard enough to keep us going as it is. We also have a shower in this building. Due to water restrictions, everyone can only shower twice a week, unless there's an urgent need. It's not the greatest, but the water is somewhat warm. You can all head to the shower after you've had your medical exam. I'll make sure there's enough water.

"We don't tolerate bullshit here." Sarah looked directly at George. "If you have a problem, you bring it to me or any other member of the council. You cause a problem; you get one warning. Second time, you're out. No exceptions. Does anyone have any questions?"

A hand rose. It was a young girl, no more than twenty. "What if – what if I don't know how to do anything? What happens to me?"

"We'll find something for you to do," Sarah said gently. "Whether it's working in the greenhouse or helping with the kids or helping Troy with inventory. Everybody will fit in somewhere. You don't have to do anything you don't want to do, but you have to do something." Sarah stared at George. "You won't be forced into anything, but you do have to contribute."

"Don't worry about us, Sarah. We'll get along." George's smile reminded Sarah of Pete, the man who killed Ryan. She suppressed the urge to shudder.

"Good," she said. "Any other questions?"

"Who's on this council of yours?" Dina asked.

"There's me, my husband Mick Cooke, Paul Schultz, Troy Smith, April Cullen, Bobby Stevens, and Annie Morris. You've met Paul, you'll meet Troy and April later. At dinner tonight, I'll be sure to introduce the rest of the council."

"How does someone get on your council?" George leaned forward in his chair; his arms crossed in front of him on the table.

"I really don't know. We've never had to replace anyone." Sarah cringed at the thought of having George on her council. "Now if there's nothing else, we'll go down to see Troy so you can get your housing assignments. He'll also explain the food rationing system." She heard groans from the group. "We don't actually ration, but we do make note of how much you take," she explained. "After you talk to Troy, you can come back here for the medical exams and showers. We hope you'll be happy here." She turned and left the room, Paul following her.

"We'll have to keep an eye on George," he whispered as they watched the group stand and gather the meager belongings they had brought with them.

"Don't worry, I won't put up with his shit. He'll be out on his ass if he tries anything." She pasted a smile on her face as the group filed past her and Paul.

Paul moved to the stairwell. "Come this way. This won't take very long, then you can head back here to get showers."

Sarah watched as they followed Paul. The girls huddled together, with the exception of Dina. She walked alone, ignored by her husband, shunned by the rest. Tom followed the women, with George and Chad bringing up the rear, their heads close together as they talked. Sarah walked behind them, her hand itching to rest on the butt of her gun. This was going to be trouble. She felt it in her bones.

CHAPTER TEN

People who hadn't been beyond the gates in the past six months were not all willing to go. The council decided not to force the issue, so Sarah agreed to go on the next trip out, to retrieve the reloading equipment Paul had found.

"I wish I could go with you. I feel better knowing I have your back," Mick said. He watched as Sarah rinsed the pump she had used to express milk for Josey to have while she was gone. She hated using the damn thing.

"You need to stay here with the Bug. She's teething again and we can't leave her with Missy. Besides, I'll be fine, babe. I'm not going out alone. It'll be me, Steven, Paul and David. And we're driving, so we'll be back tonight." She headed into the bedroom, to get her gear from the lockbox.

"What happened to delegating?"

"Mick, people are scared. They don't want to go out. I've been out, I have nothing to worry about. And maybe it'll make people realize it's not so bad." She strapped on her holster and knife. She picked up her backpack in one hand, the pry bar in another.

"Other people could go."

"You're right. But I want to go." Josey picked that moment to cry, saving Sarah from answering anymore. When Mick went to retrieve her from the play pen, Sarah walked quickly through the living room. "I'm going to go," she called. "I'll see you in a few hours." She left before he could answer.

She knew it was wrong. She should have talked to him about it. But she liked going outside the walls. She liked seeing what else was left. It had always been her favorite part of the post-apocalyptic books she used to love to read. Seeing what was left after the world ended, how people reacted. She stopped outside the apartment building and shrugged her backpack onto her shoulders. She knew, though, that she would have to stop. She was a mother now. She had a family.

She still had half an hour before she had to meet up with Paul and Steven at the second access road. She walked down the quiet street, her hands in her pockets, thinking that this would probably be her last run. She was so deep in thought, she almost ignored the soft cry. When she heard it again, she stopped, her ears straining for the source. She didn't hear another cry but she did hear a sharp crack and what she thought were muffled words. She followed the sound to see Chad and one of the girls from Kittington between two buildings.

She still hadn't learned all their names. He was gripping her arms and she could see a red mark on the girl's face. "You think this place makes you something special? You're nothing here, just like you were at home," she heard Chad say. "You're just a whore."

"No!" The girl cried softly. "I don't want to."

When Sarah saw Chad begin to unbuckle his belt, she felt the heat of anger fill her body. Gripping the prybar she didn't realize she was still holding, she walked over to the two of them, her steps silent. When he unzipped his pants, Sarah spoke, "I heard the word 'no,' Chad."

His head whipped around. "Hi, there," he said with a sick smile. "We didn't see you there."

"Obviously. She said no, Chad."

"Oh, no, she likes to pretend she doesn't want it, but she likes it rough." He turned his head to the girl. Sarah saw his grip tighten on her arm. The girl winced. "Don't you, Lyn?"

Lyn's eyes were wide with fear. "Looks like a no to me, Chad. Let her go."

"Or what?" He sneered.

"Or I take this pry bar and break your fucking hands," Sarah growled. "Then for good measure, I'll break your fucking knees. Let her go now."

Chad thrust Lyn away from him. She stumbled, falling at Sarah's feet. "Sure, no harm, no foul." He tried to zip his pants unobtrusively, but Sarah caught it.

Sarah watched as Lyn stood. Sarah motioned the girl behind her and Lyn moved quickly. "Wrong, Chad. This is most certainly a foul. This is your only warning. I catch you doing something like this again, I'll have your balls, then I'll throw you over the wall."

"Hey, it was just a little fun!" He protested, his voice a whine.

"The fuck it was. Consider yourself warned. Fuck up again and you're gone." She saw his eyes twitch, his hands form fists. "Go ahead. Try me. I'll break every bone in your miserable body." The anger wanted – needed – to be released. She wanted him to try something. Her hand gripped the bar so hard, her fingertips were white.

Chad held up his hands. "I'm sorry. It won't happen again."

"It better not. Now go." She motioned with the prybar. With a sneer, he moved from between the buildings and walked past her, so close he almost touched her. If he had, Sarah wasn't sure she would have stopped without killing him. When he was out of sight, she turned to Lyn. "Are you OK?" she asked the girl, who couldn't have been more than seventeen.

Lyn nodded, her eyes filled with tears. "Th-thank you."

"You should get checked out," Sarah said. "Let me walk you to the clinic."

Lyn shook her head. "I'm fine, he just slapped me."

Sarah gritted her teeth. This would not stand. She would get him out of the community, warnings be damned. "Are you sure?"

Lyn nodded. "I'm fine. I just – I just want to go back to my place."

"OK. If he touches you again, if he even looks at you funny, you let me know right away."

"I will. Thank you again." Sarah watched as Lyn jogged back towards Bub. Her hand was starting to hurt. She unclenched it, the prybar hot where she had gripped it so tight. She attached it to the clip on her backpack and began walking down the street.

Paul and Steven were already at the truck. Paul saw the look on her face. "Is everything OK?"

"Let's just go." She was still trying to get the anger to dissipate. She knew if she talked about it, it would build up to the point where she would get out of the truck and find Chad. And the results wouldn't be pretty. She slid out of her backpack and threw it in the back seat, climbing in after it.

"David sprained his ankle, so he can't come. We have to go to Troy to see who else is available to go." Paul leaned into the car, preventing her from closing the door.

"Let's just go." She repeated. She was barely holding onto her calm.

"We can't go. We need a fourth. Your rules." Paul smiled.

"Fuck the rules. I make them, I can break them. Let's go now." Her voice was a growl. With a shrug, Paul backed away as she slammed the door closed.

The roads were empty, abandoned and stripped vehicles pushed to the side of the road. Sarah didn't know where they were headed. She sat back in her seat and closed her eyes, hoping to erase the ugliness of the morning. She didn't speak and her travelling companions, sensing her mood, didn't speak to her.

Their destination was a former gated community. The guard shack was lying half in the road. Paul drove around it, steering the truck to the right. He stopped about four houses down. "This is where the reloading equipment is. There's a ton of other houses that we could check for other supplies."

"You two work on getting the reloading equipment. I'll check out the other houses." Sarah opened her door to get out of the truck, grabbing a handful of reusable totes as she did.

Paul stopped her. "No, we stay together. We haven't cleared all these houses."

She blew out an exasperated sigh. "That'll take too long. I don't want to be gone all day. I'll be fine by myself."

"You always tell us to go out in pairs," Steven said.

"Well, do as I say, not as I do. I'll yell if I run into problems." She hopped out of the truck and headed down the street.

Paul and Steven watched her go. Paul shook his head. "Come on, let's get this done quick so we can catch up with her."

"She's crazy, you know."

Paul smiled sadly. "I think she has to be a little crazy to deal with the shit she deals with."

Sarah didn't want help. If this was to be her last run, she wanted to do it on her terms. She headed to the first house, through the grass turned to weeds, onto the sagging porch. She unsnapped her prybar from the backpack and used it to tap on the door. She waited, but she didn't hear anything from inside. She tried the knob, surprised to find it unlocked. Slowly, she pushed open the door.

The smell was bad, but not as bad as some. She took shallow breaths through her mouth as she stepped further into the living room. She headed straight to the kitchen, not wanting to see the reminders of the people who used to live there. The back wall of the kitchen was nothing but windows, letting enough light in for her to avoid using her flashlight. Bypassing the fridge, she started opening cabinets, looking for food. She found some canned goods, a couple of jars of spaghetti sauce. She loaded a tote, then looked around the room. She saw a closed door and knocked. No answer, so she slowly opened the door, which revealed a staircase leading to the basement. She closed the door. No matter what might be down there, she didn't do basements. Not since Sugar Creek. She turned and moved through the kitchen to the stairs leading up. She dropped the tote at the base of the steps. Time to check the upstairs. Toilet paper and feminine products were worth their weight in gold.

The stairway was dim, so she pulled out her flashlight and clicked it on, looping the strap around her wrist. The smell grew stronger as she climbed, nearly overpowering once she hit the second-floor landing. When she passed the first bedroom, she saw the reason. Two corpses lay in the bed, unrecognizable as to sex. She could see the dried blood and brain splatter on the headboard and the wall. She didn't have the heart to disrupt the corpses, but they needed that pistol on the edge of the bed. Slowly, stepped into the room. "I'm sorry," she whispered as she slid the gun from the edge of the bed and backed out of the room. She popped the clip on the gun, saw there were only two bullets remaining. She slammed the clip back into place, flipped the safety on, and slipped the weapon in her pocket. She gently pulled the door shut, then continued on her way. The next door was the bathroom. She stepped inside, searching for supplies. She found a four rolls of toilet paper, but no feminine products. The medicine cabinet held various prescription bottles. She dumped them all in the tote, along with all of the over-the-counter meds. Before she left, she took the partial roll of toilet paper from the holder and dumped it in her bag.

She retreated from the bathroom and headed further down the hall. She stopped in front of a closed door and tapped it with her flashlight. No response, so she opened the door. It was a linen closet, blankets, sheets and towels filling the top three shelves. The last one held a jumbo-sized package of toilet paper. "Yes!" she exclaimed as she pulled it from the closet. Behind the toilet paper were boxes of tissues, disposable razors and some cleaning supplies. She pulled the tissue boxes and razors out, but left the cleaning supplies. Under the last shelf lay beauty supplies – a hair dryer, curling iron, electric razor – now completely useless along with a soft sided suitcase and backpack. She grabbed those as well, filling the backpack with the boxes of tissue and razors.

Her hands full, she kicked the package of toilet paper down the hall, then down the stairs. She set the pack of goods on the floor and went to check the final room. The door was open, so she just peeked inside, her hand gripping her poker. It was a simple bedroom, most likely a guest room. She opened the top drawer of the dresser and saw it was empty. She backed out of the room and headed back down the hall.

She picked up the pack she had filled and took the stairs two at a time, hitting the landing just beside the toilet paper. She opened the front door and pushed the toilet paper outside. She pulled a can of black spray paint from her backpack and marked an X on the door. Per their standard protocol, she put her scavenged supplies on the sidewalk in front of the house and moved onto the next house.

She found more food, cases of water, toilet paper, feminine supplies and, in one house, two boxes of diapers. She wanted to think that the toddler that the diapers had been meant for survived, but only if she ignored the blood on the toddler bed. She ransacked the dressers, taking all of the clothes. Adult clothes were easy to find, but baby and toddler clothes were harder to come by. She stuffed them into two sacks and added them to the stack of goods in front of the house.

She glanced down the street and saw Paul and Steven hauling what looked like a drill press to the bed of the truck. They didn't look like they needed her help, so she headed to the next house. Tapping on the door with her flashlight, she waited for a response. When she got none, she tried the door. Locked. She unclipped her prybar from the backpack. A weapon and a tool all in one, she thought as she put the end between the door and jamb and leaned on it. The door popped open and she stepped inside.

More food in the kitchen, including peanut butter and cans of soup. She found paper towels and napkins, which made good toilet paper. On the counter was an unopened box emblazoned with a medical supply company's address. That went straight into the tote. Surely there was something in there that April and Michelle could use. As the floor plans of all the houses seemed to be the same, she bypassed the door she believed to be the basement and trotted up the stairs to raid the bathroom. More toilet paper, more medications. This was turning into a profitable trip.

She left her haul in front of the house and moved to the next. It had become routine. Knock on the door, wait, open the door if there was no noise within. She cleared three more empty houses, leaving goods on the sidewalk. She wondered if the community had been evacuated. Some were, she heard, and this looked like the type that would have been.

She had travelled so far down the street that Paul and Steven were almost out of sight. All she saw was the top of Steven's head. They were still hauling things from the first house, so she moved on. She stepped up on the next porch, same as the seven houses before it. She rapped on the door, which was slightly ajar. No noise from within, so she stepped inside and quickly moved to the kitchen, barely even noticing the living room.

The kitchen was a wreck. Cupboards open, food spilled on the floor, blood splattered everywhere. Sarah backed up, figuring she could skip this house. She barely heard the groan, but she felt the arms wrap around her. With a cry, she pulled forward, the arms holding tight. She strained and the arms dropped away, her extra effort taking her two steps further into the kitchen. She slipped on some rancid food and went down, turning to her side at the last second so she didn't smash her face on the floor. Her prybar bounced from her hand. She flipped to her back and looked up at the zombie from her prone position.

It had once been a young man, maybe a college student based on the blood-stained tee shirt. A pair of headphones encircled its head, the cord hanging down to its waist. It had been there awhile, maybe since the beginning. The skin was stretched tight over the skull, dry and leathery looking, except for the mouth, which dripped infectious fluids. It reached for her and she kicked up, hitting it in the abdomen, her foot pushing through the decayed flesh. Guts and congealed blood rained down upon her and she cried out in revulsion.

She scrambled backwards until she could stand again. She looked around for her prybar but didn't see it in the debris on the floor. The zombie shuffled forward and Sarah took another step back, reaching to her belt and unsheathing her knife. She thrust the knife into the desiccated eye of the creature, pulling it out as it fell to the ground. She squatted down and wiped the knife on the zombie's pants before she sheathed it. She spotted her prybar, partially under the creature's legs. She slid it out from underneath him just as a sound caught her attention. She looked up to see a second zombie bending and reaching for her, the cord from this one's headphones tangling in her hair. With a grunt, she pushed the prybar up through the ghoul's forehead, nasty fluids dripping down on her face. "Fuck!" she screamed as she pulled the bar free and stood up. She kicked the second zombie as she stormed through the house to the front door.

Steven was on the sidewalk, ready to head up the walk to the house. "Jesus!" he exclaimed. "What happened to you?"

"What do you think?" She turned her back to him. "Dig in the front pocket of my backpack and get out the wipes." She felt him rummaging through the pocket, then his hand came around with a package of disinfecting wipes. She hooked the prybar temporarily on her belt and took the package. She ripped it open, pulling out a wipe to clean the gore from her face.

"How many?"

"Two. They were wearing fucking headphones." She turned and looked at Steven. "Is it gone?"

"Most of it."

Sarah crumbled the wipe and threw it to the ground. The solution stung her eyes, but better than the alternative. "Did you get the reloading equipment?"

Steven nodded. "I was just coming to see if you needed help. Paul went across the street."

"I have to get showered. We need to go." She unhooked the prybar from her belt and started up the sidewalk to the last house she had searched. "Get Paul and bring the truck around."

When Steven came back with Paul, Sarah could see him shaking his head. "You OK?"

"Fine, I just need to get this shit off of me." She could feel the gore drying on her skin.

"We'll load up what you got. Looks like a lot." Paul picked up the two totes from the curb.

"Seems like there's a lot of shit here," Sarah said, following behind. "We'll have to get another team out here."

"Not you?" Paul asked with a smirk.

"No, I'm done. This is my last run."

Paul shook his head. "Yeah, right."

"I'm serious," Sarah said. "I can't keep doing this. I'm a mother."

"You're also an adrenaline junkie. This is in your blood." Paul dumped the totes in the bed of the truck. Steven handed in a case of water. "You can no more quit this than those fuckers can quit biting us."

"I have to, Paul." Sarah pulled herself up into the bed of the truck. "I'll ride back here."

"Good idea."

CHAPTER ELEVEN

When they pulled into town, Christa was waiting for them. She had finally started to come out of her shell, over a year after they first met. "Sarah, Bobby needs you right away," she said when Paul stopped the truck. Sarah jumped out of the truck and Christa recoiled. "What happened to you?"

"Got a bit messy." She pulled her backpack from the bed of the truck. "I need a shower first; can you tell Bobby I'll see him in about 20 minutes?"

"OK." She started to walk away.

"Wait," Sarah called. Christa stopped and turned. "Can you get me a change of clothes and bring them to the shower?"

"Sure." The young girl walked away.

"Paul, can you guys take care of this? I really need to get this shit off of me."

"We got it." Paul motioned at the barricade. "Steven's already moving the truck back. I'll drive this down to the market and give it to Troy. Any idea where you want to set up the reloading equipment?"

"Wherever you think. You know more about that shit than I do." Sarah slung her pack over one shoulder. A little more gore wouldn't hurt it. "I'll see you later." As she headed down the street to Shaun, she hoped no one was scheduled to shower now.

Luckily, the shower was free. She stripped down, throwing the crusty clothes in a heap. There was no way she was wearing that shit again. Which sucked because the grey Henley was one of her favorite shirts. She stepped in the shower and turned the water on, quickly wetting down before pressing the button that slowed the water to a trickle. She soaped up, scrubbing hard with the wash rag to get the grime and gore from her skin. She turned the water back on and watched the pinkish water sluice down the drain. She had to wash her hair twice before the water finally ran clean. As she turned the water off, she hoped that Christa had retrieved clothes for her. Otherwise, she was walking home wrapped in a towel. She opened the shower curtain and stepped outside the tub.

Mick was leaning against the vanity holding her clothes in a bag. "Have a fun trip?" he asked.

She jumped, but just a bit. "Where's Josey?"

"She's with Missy. So, fun trip?"

"Not really." She reached for a towel and dried herself quickly. While the room was heated, it was still a bit chilly.

"What happened?"

She was briskly rubbing her hair. Her voice was muffled as she said, "Got caught by two of them. They were wearing headphones, so they didn't respond when I pounded on the door. I guess they saw me or smelled me or something."

"If I had been there, it wouldn't have happened."

She caught the undertone of anger in his voice. She stopped drying her hair and looked at him. "It might have," she said. "But probably not. I'm sorry."

"Sorry you snuck out while I was busy with Josey?" He handed her the bag of clothing.

She dropped the towel on the floor and took the bag. "Yes, I'm sorry. I just didn't want to argue about it anymore." She rummaged in the bag and found her panties and bra. She quickly put them on, then pulled a blue thermal from the bag. "I'm done with it, Mick. I'm not going out anymore."

"Why not?"

"Because I'm Josey's mom. I shouldn't be putting myself at risk like that anymore." She put the thermal on, then reached for her jeans.

"Is this about not wanting to run the place again? Because I thought we settled that."

"No, Mick, it's about me trying to do what I think is best for our daughter." Sarah slid her jeans up her damp legs and fastened them. "She deserves both her parents. I shouldn't go off doing shit that could get me hurt or killed or zombified."

"So that means I can't go out on runs anymore, either?"

"No! You can decide for yourself. I just don't think it's a good idea for me to do it anymore." She walked across the bathroom and stopped next to Mick, in front of the mirror. Someone had left a comb behind so she used it to pull the tangles from her hair.

"You know there's always risk, right?" He asked softly. "Even behind these supposedly safe walls. You could get hurt in here."

"I know that." She winced as she hit a particularly tough knot. "But there's a better chance out there. And I want to reduce the risk." She cursed as the comb got stuck in her hair. "I need to cut this," she muttered.

"No, you don't." Mick took the comb from her fingers. Slowly, he worked it through her hair until the knot was eliminated. He kept going, combing her auburn hair from the crown of her head to the midpoint of her back. Sarah nearly moaned, it felt so good. "Whatever you want to do, babe, I'll support you. But I know you'll be back on the road within a month." She opened her mouth to protest and he went on. "You can't stay cooped up in here. It's not in your nature. It's why we have what we have."

"Mick, I just want to be your wife. Josey's mother. I don't want to be like this."

"But you are. And it doesn't matter, because I love you anyway." He kissed the top of her head and handed her the comb. "Bobby's been looking for you almost since you left. Better get that hair braided and go see him."

About ten minutes later with her damp hair in its customary braid, Sarah set out to Bobby's garage. He was near tears when she found him. "What's wrong?" she asked.

"The solar panels. They're trashed." He walked further in the garage. Sarah followed. She saw the two panels he had been working on earlier. They were shattered, cracks radiating from various spots. A few pieces of glass had fallen out of one of them.

"What happened?" She asked. She didn't let her voice show the disappointment. She was really looking forward to solar power in Ash.

"I don't know," he said, running a hand lightly over a panel. "I thought I had them secured well, but apparently they fell during the night."

"It's OK, we'll find more."

"We might not. It took us a while to find these and even they weren't enough to power Ash full time." Bobby took a rag from his pocket and wiped his hands. "I'm really sorry, Sarah, I really thought they were secure."

"Bobby, it's OK. It's not the end of the world." She smiled. "We've already had that." He managed a small smile. "We'll find more."

Sarah, Mick and Josey spent the afternoon with Missy and Louis. The toddler showed no interest in Josey, despite the fact that she crawled after him wherever he went. It almost felt like they were a normal family, their kids on a play date while the grown-ups talked. If not for the weapons that Sarah had placed on top of the defunct refrigerator, out of the reach of grubby little hands.

During dinner, Troy handed Sarah a newly typed list of their supplies. "You hit the jackpot on toilet paper," he said as he ate the vegetable soup Donna and her kitchen helpers had whipped up for dinner.

"I was specifically looking for it." She scanned the list, nodding as she saw the wealth of supplies. "There are more houses out there and it was a pretty good neighborhood. Not a lot of them out there, either. We'll need to send another scavenging party." She set the list aside and picked up her spoon.

"Do you want to go back tomorrow?"

"I'm not going. If you have people that can go tomorrow, send them out." She blew on a spoonful of soup. "Make sure they check the basements, even the houses I hit."

Troy didn't know why she avoided basements; he just knew she did. It was one of her many quirks. "I'll send Joey, Phil, Susan and Chuck. They don't have anything else on the schedule tomorrow."

"Good crew." Mick said. He had Josey on his lap, feeding her smashed vegetables from the soup. Her face was smeared orange. "Maybe I'll come along."

Sarah's eyes flew to his. "Really?"

He smiled. "Just kidding."

"Butt." Sarah shook her head, but she was smiling.

♦

Sarah had been up and down with Josey all night. Her tooth was nearly in, but she was still having trouble sleeping. The both of them had just fallen back into an exhausted sleep when the walkie squawked on the nightstand. "Sarah!! Sarah!! We need you now!!!"

Sarah jolted awake, grabbing the walkie and stumbling out of bed to the doorway, away from the slumbering Josey's bassinet. "What? What is it?" she rasped.

Someone pounded on the front door. She turned her head to look at the door and two voices rang out, one from the door and one from the walkie. "We have a breach!"

In horror, she looked at Mick, who had awoken from the noise. Dropping the walkie on the floor, she ran to the front door and unlocked the deadbolt, flinging the door open. Blake was on the other side, his face a grimace. "We got a breach; I don't know what happened."

"I'll be there in five minutes, go!" She pushed him back out the door and flew into the bedroom. She grabbed her jeans and boots while Mick pulled the lockbox from under the bed and handed it to her. In order to not disturb Josey, she moved into the living room. Out of the corner of her eye, she saw Mick pulling on his jeans. "What are you doing?" she asked as tossed the lockbox on the sofa and yanked her pants up her legs.

"I'm getting dressed," he whispered. "I can't go out there in boxer briefs."

"You can't go out there, you need to stay with Josey." Sarah buckled her belt, then picked up the lockbox. She fumbled for the combination.

"I'll get Christa to sit." He sat on the bed to put his boots on.

"You're staying here," she said, finally remembering the combination. She flipped the top off the box and pulled out her gun and holster. She clipped it to her belt, then reached for the knife.

"I'm going out. You're going to need the help."

Sarah's eyes flew to his head, where in her dreams the bullet took his life. She jammed her feet in her boots. "You are not fucking going anywhere."

"Sarah, you're going to need the help," he repeated. "You don't know what's out there."

She grabbed her pry bar from the top shelf of the book case. "You won't be. Stay here." She opened the door and went through, slamming the door behind her.

"What the fuck?" Mick asked just as Josey cried out.

Sarah took the stairs down two at a time, racing out the front door. She heard a scream from the left so she took off running. She passed a corpse on the ground, the head nothing but mush, and put on an extra burst of speed. She saw half dozen zombies shambling around near the entrance they had used earlier that day. She repositioned the prybar in her hand and swung on the nearest one. It dropped and she trotted to Blake. "What happened?"

"Don't know." He turned to look at her, a bit of blood spattered on his face.

"How many are there?" She took a few steps and took down another one.

"I counted a least a dozen still moving and I took down three. April and Paul are out here, too."

Sarah moved closer to the barricade, Blake on her heels. She could see a small gap between the trucks, another zombie squeezing through the opening. "Get that truck moved back," she said, moving to take out the creature that had pushed through the trucks.

Blake jogged up to the truck and slid into the driver's side while Sarah watched the gap. No more zombies made it inside before he moved the barricade back into place. "Now what?" he asked as he jumped out of the truck.

"Now we get rid of the rest of them." Sarah squared her shoulders and set to work.

It took them less than a half hour to clear the zombies. Sarah stood in the middle of the street, surrounded by corpses, sweat drying on her brow. "Everyone OK?" she asked.

She got nods from the people surrounding her: Blake, April and Paul. They were all covered in gore, faces splattered with blood. "What the hell happened?" She turned to Paul. "Didn't you take care of that barricade today?"

"I watched Steven move it, Sarah. It was across the road," Paul said. He shook his head. "I don't know what happened."

"It's on a bit of a slope," Blake said. "Did he forget to put it in park? Might have drifted."

Sarah sighed heavily. "Maybe." She rubbed a hand over her forehead. "Anyone hurt?"

"No, we got them all." April knocked her bat on the ground, gore dripping from the spikes she had pounded into the end.

"OK, we need to get this shit cleaned up." Sarah wiped her prybar on the body closest to her and tossed it to the ground. She grabbed the legs of the corpse that she used to clean her tool and started dragging it across the road. She deposited it near the barricade, then went back for another one. The rest of the crew followed Sarah.

It took longer to clean the bodies from the street than it did to kill them. When they had finished moving the bodies, Sarah counted sixteen. She looked at the people before her, covered in sweat and gore and looking exhausted. "Do we have any big tarps? I want to cover these until tomorrow. I want Ben out here at first light to move them."

"I think there's one in Bobby's garage," Blake said.

"Go get it. And get some of those wheel stop things. Paul, April, go get cleaned up and try and get some sleep."

"You go, Sarah," April said. "You and Paul. You were both out on a run today and I'm sure you're exhausted. Blake and I will handle this."

Sarah thought of how angry Mick would be when she got home. She was in no way ready to face that. "I'm good, but Paul, you go. Try and get a couple hours of sleep before sunrise." She looked up at the dark sky. "Which is probably three hours away."

He shook his head. "I'll stay here and help."

"No, Paul, you and Blake should go. April and I can handle it." Blake came running back with the tarp and a pair of wheel chocks. Sarah took the tarp. "Go on, get showered and get to bed, both of you."

Sarah walked the tarp to the pile of bodies, April following. "I'll have Ben out here tomorrow," Paul said as he and Blake put the wheel chocks in front of the rear tires of the truck. When they finished, Paul slapped the younger man on the back. "Come on, you can have first shower." They headed off to Shaun.

"We need to have a council meeting tomorrow," Sarah said she handed an end of the tarp to April.

April made an agreeing sound as they opened the tarp. Then she asked: "So why don't you want to go home?"

"What? What are you talking about?" Sarah avoided April's eyes and she carried her end of the tarp to the pile of bodies.

"I can see it in your face, Sarah. I'm not stupid." They flicked their hands and the tarp opened; the flapping of the plastic loud in the quiet night. "What's wrong?"

Sarah's sigh was long and mournful. "I've been having this dream," she started. "Mick and I are trying to stop a bunch of zombies that came in through a breach in the wall. He gets shot by friendly fire."

"And you fought with him about coming out here to help tonight?" April asked softly.

"There was no fight. I told him he couldn't come. I left without waiting for his response." They tucked the tarp under the bodies and stepped away.

"Does he know about the dream?"

April almost missed Sarah's headshake. "I haven't told him."

"You have to, Sarah. He has to know why you didn't want him out here." April saw Sarah's shrug. "And you have to apologize for not letting him come out here."

Sarah looked sharply at April. "What?"

"You're wrong in this, Sarah. You can't control everything, as much as you want to," April said softly. "If something's going to happen to Mick, it will happen. You can't just forbid him to do anything you think might get him hurt."

"I know, I just…I just can't face the thought of losing him." Sarah's voice broke. "I never had anyone and now I have him and Josey and we've lost so many people. I just can't…" She trailed off.

April touched Sarah's arm. "Go talk to him now, Sarah. Before his anger has time to fester. Get this shit straightened out."

"He's going to be so angry at me," Sarah whispered.

"He loves you; he'll get over it." April smiled. "It's sickening sometimes how much he loves you. Go talk to him. Tell him about the dream."

Sarah nodded. "Thanks, April." She took a deep breath and blew it out. "Can you set up a council meeting for first thing tomorrow?"

"It can wait. Get some sleep." April smiled again. "After you talk to Mick."

♦

Sarah stood outside the door to their apartment. Not wanting to waste the water on another shower, she had cleaned her face and hands with baby wipes, getting the majority of the splattered blood and gore from her skin. Now she stood, gathering her courage to face Mick's wrath. She knew he would be angry. She deserved it. Taking a deep breath and biting her lip, she tried the door. It was locked. She let out her breath as she used the key left in the deadbolt to unlock the door.

Through the dim light of the battery powered lantern on the coffee table, she could see the bedroom door partially closed. Mick was laying on the sofa, an arm over his head. She gently closed the door and his eyes popped open. He shifted his legs off of the sofa, moving to a seated position, his hands pressed to the cushion on either side of him. He looked like he was ready to pounce. His eyes never left hers as she locked the deadbolt. The anger in his blue eyes scared her a little.

She leaned against the door and took a deep breath. Blowing it out slowly, she began. "I've been having a dream a few times a week. I'm still pregnant and you and I are trying to clear zombies because of there was a breach in the walls. I go into labor and you deliver our baby. Then you get shot." Her voice broke. "The last thing I see in the dream is you pitching over with a bullet in your head." She shook her head. "I can't…I can't…" She felt like she was going to hyperventilate.

"It's just a dream," Mick said. "It's not real." He looked down at the floor then back up to her face. The tears glistening on her cheeks almost made him stop. "You can't do that shit, Sarah. You can't bark orders at me like I'm the soldier and you're the general. I'm really fucking pissed right now."

"I know," she cried. "But I can't bear to lose you." She moved from the door and sat on the sofa. Her heart sunk when he shifted away from her. "All my life, I was fine being alone. But then you came along and now I don't know what I would do without you."

"So ordering me to stay here out of harm's way, treating me like shit, is your answer?" He shook his head. "Babe, I get what you're saying, but you're going about it the wrong way. Talk to me. Tell me what the problem is. Don't treat me like a fucking child. I don't do that to you."

"I know," she whispered. "I'm so sorry. I wish I could do it again, I would tell you."

He shook his head. "No, you wouldn't. You don't talk to me about shit like this. You keep it all inside until something happens, something like this. I love you more than anything, but this shit? Pisses me off." He stood up. "I know you're sorry, but I don't know if I can accept your apology right now. I'll sleep in the second bedroom." She watched with wide eyes as he headed into the spare room and closed the door behind him. Her hands covered her face and she burst into tears.

Mick stood with his back against the closed door. The sound of her sobbing nearly broke him. He rarely saw her in tears. He had never been the one to make her cry. With a heavy sigh, he scrubbed his hands over his eyes. He couldn't go out there. If he did, then everything he said would be disregarded. He had to make her understand. They were a partnership, in good and bad.

When he left the bedroom a few hours later, Sarah was sitting on the sofa nursing Josey. Sarah's red eyes followed him as he left the bedroom and moved into the bathroom. He splashed water on his face, hoping to hide his lack of sleep, then brushed his teeth. When he stepped out of the bathroom, Sarah was still staring at him. "I'm on the south gate this morning," he said, his voice even. "I'll see you later." He grabbed his jacket from the coat tree beside the door and unlocked the deadbolt, sliding through the door and shutting it gently closed behind him.

Sarah looked down at their daughter. "I really messed up, Josey." Her voice was a raspy whisper. "God, I hope I haven't messed it up for good."

To compliment the way she felt today, Sarah's morning assignment was hauling waste buckets. She took Josey to Missy's, ignoring her questions about why Sarah looked so bad, then headed to the nearest greenhouse to get the equipment. She avoided everyone as she grabbed the shit buckets, heavy gloves and respirator. Walking down the street to Bub, she tried not to think about what had transpired between her and Mick early that morning. But it was a losing battle. If she lost him, if he left her because of her own fuck up, she didn't know how she would survive in the same place as him.

The work was disgusting, but perfect for her mood. No one wanted to talk to the shit collectors. She just had to knock on the apartment doors, go straight to the bathroom, empty the chemical toilet into her bucket and move on to the next one. She didn't stop to socialize, just kept going until she finished the whole apartment building, filling two buckets. She carried the full buckets to the rear of the greenhouse and dumped the contents into the compost heap. At least she didn't have to mix it. That was someone else's shitty job.

She kept at it until she finished all three buildings, even though she was only assigned to do one. By the time she finished, her back ached, her shoulders ached, her arms ached and she smelled like an outhouse. She wasn't due for another shower, but fuck it, she was taking one. She stopped by Missy's to let her know she'd pick up Josey in a half hour, then back to her place to grab a change of clothes. Mick hadn't been home. She knew his shift had been up an hour previously. She wondered where he was. She wondered if he would come home.

When she got back to her apartment after her shower, Annie and April were waiting. One look at Sarah's face told April everything she needed to know. April smiled sadly as Sarah opened the door and ushered them both inside. "Does anyone want anything?" Sarah asked, her voice raspy. She cleared her throat.

Both ladies declined. "What are we meeting about?" Annie asked.

"Just a few things that need council input," Sarah said. "I'm going to put these dirty clothes in the laundry. I'll be back in a minute. Can you open the door for the rest?" Without waiting for a response, she headed to the small pantry where they kept their laundry. While there wasn't enough electricity to run a washer and dryer, Mick had found an old-fashioned wringer washer and Sarah used that to wash their favorite things. He had cursed profusely as he and Ben carried it up two flights of stairs, Sarah smiling behind her hand the whole time. Without a dryer, she hung their clothes on lines strung across the pantry. Many things, like socks and underwear, they just threw away and opened new packs. But even those were starting to get scarce. She was going to have to do a lot more laundry in the near future. For now, she just threw their clothes in the washer tub and added a little water so they could soak.

The time away from April and Annie let her regain her composure. April's sad smile almost made her start crying again. Her eyes already burned; her throat was already sore. She didn't need to add more pain. She just needed to know where she stood.

When she walked back to the living room, the rest of the council was there. Except Mick. She took a deep breath and sat in her usual spot on the sofa. Without Mick perched on the armrest, she felt lost. But she had to move on. "There was a breach last night and a bunch of zombies got in," she said.

"Shouldn't we wait for Mick?" Troy asked.

"He's been briefed," April said, looking over at Sarah, who looked away. "He'll join us if he can."

"How did it happen?" Annie asked, a touch of unease in her voice.

"Apparently, they got in through the access road by the greenhouse," Paul said. "We had used that earlier to bring in supplies. I'm positive Steven moved the truck back. There's a bit of a slope there, so maybe the truck rolled. We put wheel chocks in front of the tires to keep it in place."

"Was anyone hurt?" Bobby asked.

"No, we got them all before they even roamed too far from the entrance. I don't think anyone besides me, Sarah, Blake and April knew there was a breach. Ben knows, because we had him take the bodies out right before dawn."

"What do we do now?" Annie frowned.

"We need to make sure there are wheel chocks in front of the truck tires on both barricades," Sarah said. "We don't want a repeat of last night."

"I have more in the garage," Bobby said. "I'm not using them for anything. I'll put them at the other barricade."

"Thanks, Bobby," Sarah said. "In other news, I gave Chad his first and only warning. He was trying to coerce one of the girls from Kittington for sex."

"Forget the warning, he's out of here," Paul snarled.

"No, he gets one warning, Paul." Sarah shifted on her seat. Her hand moved to the armrest and unconsciously she began to stroke the fabric. "Those are the rules and we'll stick by them. But one more offense, any offense, and he's on the other side. So keep an eye on him."

Everyone nodded. Paul still looked angry. "Is there anything else?" Sarah asked.

Troy indicated his notebook. "We have a good supply of TP thanks to Sarah. A lot of canned goods, too. There's some medications for the clinic that you'll need to go through, April." April nodded. Troy glanced down at his note. "I sent Joey, Phil, Susan and Chuck back to where you found the stuff. I'm hoping they'll bring back more."

"Good." Sarah was starting to feel closed in. "Anything else?" There was nothing else. She stood. "OK, then, I'll see you all at dinner."

The council filed out until only April remained. After Paul had closed the door, April turned to Sarah. "What happened last night?"

"Nothing good." Sarah sunk back into the sofa and rubbed her sore eyes. "He was really pissed. He slept in the other bedroom. Didn't say much to me this morning other than to tell me what he would be doing."

April sat beside her. "I'm sorry, Sarah."

Sarah took a deep breath to calm herself. She wouldn't cry again. "So am I."

CHAPTER TWELVE

Sarah didn't see Mick again until dinner. She had picked up Josey from Missy's, despite Missy saying she would keep her for the day. Instead, Sarah took off her gear and threw it in a tote bag, then carried the bag and Josey back to the apartment. She spent the rest of the day with her daughter, laughing at her antics, soothing her boo-boos, and dreading the time when she took her nap. Without Josey to distract her, Sarah had nothing but time to think. And worry.

As soon as Josey woke from her nap, Sarah changed and dressed her and headed back out. With her gear in a cross-body tote, she took Josey to the makeshift school, held at Dominic's apartment in Ash. Dominic and Lucy, both former schoolteachers, taught the children in town ranging in age from 6 to 14. Sarah knocked on the door, waiting for a response of "Come in" before she opened the door.

"Hey, Sarah," Dominic said from his seat at the table in the middle of the living room. He had replaced his coffee table and loveseat with a table better suited to schoolwork. In his dining room was a second table and chairs. Due to the range of ages in the children, they were separated for schooling. Lucy, a former elementary school teacher, worked with Bryant, who was only 6, and Rachel and Lisa, who were both 7. Mikey and Elizabeth, who were 10, and Lily and Erin, who were 14 and 15 respectively, were taught by Dominic, who had more experience with older kids. He needed a lot with Erin. She was still traumatized from her ordeal before she entered their community.

"Josey!!" Elizabeth exclaimed, jumping up from her seat. Sarah could see a Fred Flintstone tee under her hoodie. Mick had given that to her years earlier, just days after they accepted the responsibility of Elizabeth from her former caretaker who had been bitten. It had become her security blanket.

"Elizabeth, we were in the middle of a lesson," Dominic said. She turned to look at him, her eyes wide and her lower lip trembling. He laughed. "OK, fine, we'll take a break."

Smiling, Elizabeth bounded over to Sarah and Josey. "Hey Josey girl!!" Josey held out her arms, babbling, and Elizabeth took her from Sarah's arms. She wandered away from Sarah, talking nonsense to the little girl.

Sarah sat down at the table, careful to avoid Dominic's outstretched leg. His leg was weak due to a childhood illness and he typically wore a brace to walk, but when at home he took the brace off. "Mikey, Lily, Erin, how are you?" Sarah asked the remaining students at the table.

"Glad for a break," Mikey said. He had shot up over the last few years, and now was taller than she was, just barely. Sarah was sure he would be taller than his brother, Jack, who at 20 was 6'3".

"Fine, Miss Sarah," Lily said in her quiet voice. She had always been quiet, ever since April and Jack found her wandering with Michelle, Christa and Steven near the cabin owned by Mick's uncle that they once called home. "Excuse me." She got up from the table and headed into the kitchen. Mikey followed. Erin never said a word, just favored Sarah with a rare smile before she followed the other two.

"And you, Dominic? Are they keeping you on their toes?"

"Always, Sarah."

"How's Erin doing?"

"She's getting a little better, but it's going to take time." He leaned back so he could see the dining room. "Lucy, take a break, come say hi."

Lucy pushed back her chair and came into the living room. "Sarah," she said.

Sarah had never warmed to Lucy. She flirted her way around the community, depending on which male could provide her with what she needed at the time. She got out of many of her chores by convincing others to do them until Sarah told Troy to permanently assign her to teaching. Since Dominic was in a relationship with Frannie, Sarah knew that Lucy wouldn't be able to seduce him into doing her job. "How are you, Lucy?" Sarah asked, not really caring.

"Everything's good. We could use more advanced school books."

"That's a priority on any run that's near a school," Sarah said. "Unfortunately, most are ruined or just plain gone."

"Well, do what you can," Lucy said then went back to the dining room.

Sarah raised an eyebrow at Dominic, who smothered a laugh. "Where's Mick?" he asked.

Sarah shrugged. "Around. How's things with you and Frannie?"

Dominic smiled. "We're really good. Happy."

"That's great." At least someone is, she thought. She glanced at the battery-operated clock on the wall and stood. "Ready for dinner, Josey?" She asked her daughter.

Josey strained in Elizabeth's arms, reaching for Sarah. "Da?"

Sarah swallowed. "Yeah, we'll see Da." She took her daughter and settled her on her hip. "I'll see you all at dinner."

"Can I come with you?" Elizabeth asked.

Sarah turned to Dominic. "Is it OK?"

He pushed back from the table. "Yeah, we're about done here."

"Get your things," Sarah said to Elizabeth.

The girl cleaned her work from the table, putting it into a divided section of the bookcase. She picked up her backpack and slung it over her shoulder. "I'm ready."

"No coat?"

Elizabeth shrugged. "It's not that cold. Besides, my hoodie is lined."

"OK, then, let's go."

Elizabeth chattered on their way to Shaun for dinner. Sarah nodded in the right places, made a few noncommittal noises. She was worried about what would happen when she saw Mick. Would he even talk to her? Would she beg him to forgive her?

"Sarah?" Donna called to her as they passed the kitchen.

"Go on up, Elizabeth. Save me a seat," Sarah said to the young girl. She nodded and bounded up the steps, full of energy.

Sarah walked into the kitchen. "What's up, Donna?"

"We lost a fridge," she said.

"What do you mean, lost a fridge?"

Donna walked to a battered white refrigerator. She tapped on the door. "It quit working. I salvaged some of the food, but I couldn't save it all."

Shit, Sarah thought. "How much did we lose?"

"The leftovers from yesterday's dinner." Donna walked back to Sarah and absently tickled Josey's foot. "I had the pork from that last wild pig in the freezer. I had to cook it for dinner tonight. I'm not sure it will be enough, though. I was planning to use yesterday's soup to accompany it."

Sarah sighed. "I'll get someone to get it out of here. Troy can tell us where we can get a replacement."

"We also lost milk and some venison. It puts us a little low on meat."

"OK, I'll let Troy know. Maybe someone can go hunting, look for another deer or something." Sarah rubbed her forehead. "Anything else?"

"No, I'd say that's enough."

Sarah trudged up the steps, Josey twisting with every movement. She knew it was dinnertime. And she was eager to see her Da. Sarah wondered how Mick managed to carry her all day, every day. She was heavy and she was squirmy. Just something else she needed to apologize to him for.

The dining room was full of talking and laughter, nearly every seat taken. Josey spotted Mick before Sarah did and started bouncing on Sarah's hip. "Da! Da!"

Mick turned from his conversation with Michelle. He smiled and excused himself, walking over to Sarah and Josey. "How's my girl?" he asked, taking her in his arms. As she babbled to Mick, he looked over her head at Sarah. "Hi."

Sarah bit her lip. "Hi." She had so much to say to him. But nothing would come out.

"I saved you a seat over here. Come on." He threaded through the tables until he reached two empty seats, both with plates of food in front of them.

"Thank you." Sarah sat next to him and folded her hands in her lap. "Did you – did you have a good day?" She couldn't come up with anything more original?

"Yeah, I did gate duty, then I was helping in the greenhouse for a while. You?"

How could he be so calm? She was screaming inside, wanting to beg and plead with him to forgive her. "I was on waste today." She watched him grimace. "I spent the rest of the day with Josey and stopped to see Dominic and the kids."

"Sounds like a nice day." He took a spoonful of peas from his plate and fed Josey. "You should eat while it's still warm."

She looked down at her plate with small portions of pork, peas and corn. She took the fork in her hand and drew a line in the peas. She had no appetite. She looked around and nodded at their tablemates – Ed and Bonnie, Grant and Jack, holding a spot for Mikey – then back to her plate. She couldn't live like this. What would she do if he never forgave her? If he left her?

"Sarah?"

Her head snapped up at his voice. "Sorry, I was woolgathering. What is it?"

He smiled slightly. "She's eaten all my peas and wants more. Can she have yours?"

"Of course." Sarah pushed the plate towards Mick.

"You haven't eaten anything," he said as he picked up a spoonful of peas.

"I'm not hungry." She dropped her fork on the plate.

Mick shook his head. "Sarah, you –"

"Sarah, heard we had a bit of a problem last night." George's voice ran over what Mick was saying.

Sarah looked up and saw George and Chad at the table across from hers. Also at the table was Chris, Candy and Dina. "There was no problem," she said evenly.

"Really? I heard there was a breach in the wall and zombies got in." His voice boomed over the room and it got immediately quiet.

"Where did you hear that?"

"Chad rooms with Ben. You had him out early this morning disposing of the bodies." George grinned.

"Is that true?" Bonnie asked. "Were there zombies inside?" Her voice rose with each word until she was practically screaming.

"Yes, there were zombies inside," Sarah admitted. "We took care of the problem before anything happened."

A dozen voices at once, asking questions, voicing outrage. "I thought it was supposed to be safe in here!" Helen said. "How could it happen?"

"We're looking into that," Sarah said. "Rest assured, it won't happen again."

"How can you be sure?" "This is ridiculous!" "How are we supposed to sleep at night?" "Why didn't you tell us?" Questions and comments came from all sides. Sarah fisted her hands and readied herself to stand up and tell them all to go to hell.

She felt Mick's hand on her arm. "This place is safe." His voice was loud and drowned out everyone else's. "My wife was out there in the middle of the night so that you didn't have to worry. And you don't." He looked around the room, catching the eye of everyone who voiced a complaint. "The situation was handled. Steps are in place to make sure it doesn't happen again." He captured George's smirking gaze. "If you no longer feel safe here, then you won't feel safe anywhere. We're doing what we can to keep the danger out."

"I just think that maybe we should have been told," Chad said. "Better than me finding out because my roommate snuck out this morning." There were mutters of agreement among some of the people. Others just shook their heads.

"I apologize for not telling you immediately," Sarah said, a hint of steel in her voice. "If it ever happens again, I'll be sure to wake each and every one of you with a full report."

"That's not –"

Sarah wasn't sure who was speaking, but she ignored them and kept talking. "We do the absolute best we can to make sure our town is secure." Her eyes found Lyn, huddled in the back of the room, sitting with the remainder of the group from Kittington. "I will do everything I can to make sure everyone is safe and no more trouble gets in. That's all I can promise you." She pushed her chair back. "Now if you'll excuse me, I need to walk the town and check for any potential problems." She moved through the tables, ignoring everyone, and headed out the door.

She was halfway down the stairs when Ben caught up with her. "I didn't tell him, Sarah, I swear." He was nearly out of breath from chasing her down.

"I know. He's a snake, him and George." She shook her head. "I never should have let them in this town."

"I'll keep an eye on him for you."

"Thanks, Ben. I appreciate that." She nodded down the stairs. "I better get going."

"Do you want some company?"

She shook her head. "Go back and finish dinner. Thanks, though." She turned and finished walking down the stairs.

Outside, she took a deep breath of the cold air. She blew it out slowly, hoping to blow away the anger she felt as well. She did everything she could, lost precious time with her husband and her child, and they still weren't happy. What else could she do? Maybe she really should quit. Let someone else deal with all the bullshit.

The door opened behind her and she turned, ready to pounce. Mick walked towards her, his hands in his pockets. "Hey," he said softly.

"Where's Josey?"

"She going to stay with Missy tonight. She was happy to have her. And when Josey heard she was going to be with Louis, she was pretty happy." Mick smiled.

Sarah shook her head. "She can't. She's still teething and she'll need to be nursed."

"She'll be fine. We'll get her first thing in the morning." He moved closer to her. "It'll be OK."

She nodded, then looked away. When she looked back at Mick, he was stunned by the raw pain in her eyes. "Are you – are we – are you going to leave me?" she whispered.

He closed his eyes and swallowed hard. Then he reached for her, enveloping her in his arms, tucking her head against his chest. "I will never, ever leave you," he breathed into her hair. "I love you." He felt her body hitch and she started to cry. He rubbed her back, murmuring nonsense words.

After a moment, she pulled away, her eyes and nose red, her cheeks wet with tears. "I'm so sorry," she said softly. "I was wrong, so wrong. And I was so scared you were fed up with me, that you would just go and it would break me, Mick. It would break me because I love you so much." She started to cry again and he pulled her close.

"Ssh," he whispered. "It's OK."

She stayed inside the comfort of his arms until her tears finally stopped. She lifted her head from his chest, suddenly self-conscious. She stepped back, swiping at the tears on her cheeks. He smiled and took her hands in his, then leaned over and kissed her. When he pulled back, she was smiling. "Thank you," she breathed.

"Let's walk the town, then we can go home." She pulled a hand free and wiped her face one more time, then they started walking, hand in hand.

CHAPTER THIRTEEN

They lay in bed, Sarah curled up on her side, her hand on Mick's chest, her legs entwined with his, as she told him everything he missed during the day. "I agree with Paul. Chad should be put out now," Mick said, rubbing her bare shoulder.

"I think so, too, but we have rules. We're all keeping a close eye on him."

"We're going to have to put him out, you know. Once a man starts that shit, he doesn't stop."

"If anyone knows that, Mick, it's me." She couldn't repress the shudder as she thought of Austin, how he took what he wanted by force. He didn't get it from her, but he did get something much more precious. Her unborn child. She still wondered if Mick would have had a son.

"I know, babe." He hugged her tighter. "We really need to keep a close eye on both of them. George is a sneaky fuck."

"I'm not worried about him," she said disdainfully. "I am worried about the meat supply. Losing that fridge wasn't good for us."

"I'm sure Troy is setting up a hunting party as we speak."

Sarah shook her head, her hair tickling his skin. "I forgot to tell him after George pulled his shit."

Mick shrugged. "Tell him tomorrow. We won't run out for a while."

"I'm worried the land around us will get over hunted. We need to –"

He hooked his arms around her waist and pulled her up so they were face to face. "Quit worrying. For one night." He lifted his head and kissed her and she forgot all about worrying.

♦

Early the next morning, they were at Missy's to pick up Josey. As soon as Josey saw Sarah, she started to fuss. "She's been an angel all night," Missy said.

"She wants to nurse." Sarah set the bag with her gear on the table and took Josey. They sat together on the sofa. "And I want her to nurse. Jesus, this sucks." She very quickly set Josey to nursing, sighing in relief.

Missy smiled. "I don't miss those days." She took a sip of her tea. "You look better than you did yesterday," she said to Sarah.

Sarah looked down at Josey's hair. "Well, it was a bad day." She smiled as she looked up at Mick. "But it's a better day today."

Missy laughed. "I'd like to think I had something to do with that."

Mick laughed. "You sure did. Indirectly, of course."

"You can leave her with me today, if you want," Missy said. "She's a doll."

"Maybe this afternoon?" Sarah said. "I think we need some family time." She looked at Mick, who smiled.

"Sounds good." A noise came from the other room. "The prince is awake. I'll be right back." Missy left the living room for the second bedroom.

"Family time?" Mick asked.

"Yeah, family time. I don't have anything on my schedule today and I think you're free, right?"

"Right."

He waited for it. "I just need to see Troy about the hunt." There it was.

"Sarah…" He trailed off, shaking his head. He snorted out a laugh. She wouldn't change. And if she did, she wouldn't be the person he fell in love with. "OK, we'll go see Troy."

They walked through town to the market. Many residents were up and about, heading to breakfast or their assignments for the day. Most smiled and waved. A few, however, avoided eye contact. "What do you think that's about?" Mick asked.

"George." Sarah shifted Josey on her hip.

Mick muttered a curse. "We should have never brought him in."

Sarah shrugged. "We did and it's done. We just need to figure out how to mitigate the damage he's causing."

Troy reached for Josey as soon as they walked in and Josey went to the big man with a giggle. She immediately began to pull on his beard.

"Why is it that she only yanks on your beard?" Sarah asked with a smile.

"It's different from everyone else's," he said. "Different texture for her little fingers." He winced when she pulled particularly hard. "What's on the agenda today?"

"One of the fridges in the kitchen broke down," Sarah said. "Do we have a replacement?"

"There are a few still in town that are easily accessible. I'll check my list and send a couple guys to haul one over." He gently untangled Josey's fingers from his beard and she promptly plunged them right back in.

Sarah hid a smile. "We lost some meat, so can you send a hunting party out?"

Troy nodded. "It may need to be an extended trip. I don't want to keep hunting right around here."

"Me, either," Sarah said. "Let me know who you decide to send."

"Chad said he had hunting experience."

"No!" Sarah said vehemently. "Do not send him out. I want all of those people where I can keep an eye on them."

"Those people?" Troy asked, raising his eyebrows.

"Oh, please," she scoffed. "You know what I mean. You saw the scene at dinner last night."

"Yes, I did," he said gravely. "That was ridiculous. You're right. Let's keep them together. Maybe on waste detail." His grin lit up his chocolate skin.

Mick laughed. "You're evil. I like that."
Troy shrugged. "Don't tick off the schedule maker."

♦

The next few days were uneventful. Until dinner on the third day. Donna made a turkey and vegetable stew that had very little turkey, due to the meat shortage. "I don't think I have a single piece of meat in this stew," Chad said loudly as he pushed his spoon through his bowl.

"I'm sorry, we're a little low on meat right now," Donna said hesitantly as ladled herself a small bowl. The dining room was full, the chatter of a couple dozen people quieting as Chad slammed his bowl on the table.

"How are we expected to eat this?" he asked, pushing the bowl aside, a bit of the gravy slopping over the edge to the table.

"With a spoon," Sarah said calmly. "A fork, if you're so inclined." She took another spoonful for herself and stared at Chad as she chewed the vegetables.

"You're kidding, right?"

"No, I'm not. If you don't like it, don't eat it. There are plenty of other people who would love to have more."

"What I like is meat," Chad said, slamming his hands on the table.

"We're low on meat," Sarah explained. "Which is why we sent a hunting party out a few days ago."

"How can you run low on meat?" This from Dina. "It's a staple of a normal diet."

"Are we living in normal times, Dina?" Sarah still radiated calm, but inside she was seething. How dare these people, who were living in subhuman conditions just a few weeks earlier, criticize what they were being offered? "Did you have meat with every meal in Kittington?" She raised her voice slightly so the whole room heard. "We lost a fridge, along with a vast amount of meat that was stored there. We have a hunting party out right now. We've been very fortunate up until now to include meat with virtually every meal. But as many vegetarians can tell you, it's not necessary."

"I bet you have meat for yourself," Dina said slyly.

"You would be wrong. I eat the same as everyone else."

"There's been some real issues around here lately," George said softly. He was sitting next to Dina, leaning back in his chair, looking completely at ease.

"Such as?" Sarah asked, her voice deceptively calm.

George shrugged. "The zombies, the food shortage. Wasn't there a problem with solar panels or something?" He sat forward in his seat. "Maybe you've not had your head in the game, spending so much time with your husband and your daughter."

Sarah looked around the room, at the faces of people she had known for months, some of whom she literally saved from the jaws of death. Not everyone would look at her. Some stared with openly hostile looks. She put her spoon back in her bowl and pushed it over to Mick. She stood up, clasping her hands in front of her. "If anyone feels like I'm not doing enough, I encourage you to speak to me and let me know your concerns."

"Maybe we should just have someone new in charge," Dina countered. "Someone older, more experienced."

Sarah tensed. She had been flirting with the idea of giving up the leadership, but she never really meant it. She couldn't leave these people to George. But what if that was what they wanted?

"There's an idea," Chad said. "Show of hands for a new leader?"

"Wait!" Sarah exclaimed.

"Are you afraid you're gonna get voted out?" Chad asked, his voice a sneer.

"No, actually, I'm not." Her voice was calm. "But if you want to take a vote, it should be just as it was in the past. Secret ballot, so no one can be coerced into voting for someone they don't really want to." She looked at George, who wore a smug smile. She wanted nothing more than to punch him in the face.

She turned her gaze back to the room, making sure to look into each and every face before she resumed speaking. "Tomorrow morning, everyone can go to the market and vote. Vote on if you want me to continue to lead you and if not, who you would like in my place. Troy will watch over the ballot box to make sure there's no tampering."

"Isn't Troy a member of your council?" Chris said from his spot near George. "One of your lackeys?"

Troy moved to stand, but Mick's hand on his arm stopped him. "She'll take care of it," he whispered.

"Troy is a member of our council. He's the guy who has made sure we have enough food." Sarah looked around the room, singling out the people who seemed to be siding with George. "He's made sure you get extra aspirin for your heart, Sid. He's made sure you have extra blankets because you get cold, Bonnie. He's no one's lackey. He's our friend." She brought her gaze back to George. "You can appoint someone to watch the ballot box with Troy to make sure there's no tampering."

"I'll do it," Chad said. "Lyn can keep me company." His look challenged Sarah.

"Lyn has a different assignment tomorrow." Sarah didn't know if she did or not, but she wasn't letting Chad use her. "You can manage yourself."

She looked around the room again, noticing that Helen was whispering harshly to Sid, Bonnie looking down at her lap. "Everyone who is so inclined to vote can do it tomorrow morning between nine and eleven. We'll count ballots at eleven. Thank you." She sat back in her seat, ignoring the murmurs of conversation.

"What the hell was that about?" Mick asked, pushing her bowl back towards her. Josey, sensing the tension in the air, was looking back and forth between her parents.

Sarah shook her head at the bowl of food. Her appetite was gone. "George trying to grab control." She rubbed her forehead, a sign of her stress, Mick noted.

"He won't get it," Troy said with confidence. "He doesn't have the support."

"He might." Sarah blew out a sigh. "We've had a run of bad luck. People have short memories."

A shadow fell over the table. Sarah looked up at Joey. "I've got your back, Sarah. Don't worry."

Sarah smiled. "Thanks, Joey, I appreciate it."

"Everyone here knows what you do for us. Nobody is going to vote you out." Joey twisted his hat in his hands as he spoke.

"We'll talk to people," David said from behind Joey. "We'll make sure they vote to keep you in."

"No, David, just let people make up their own minds." Sarah smiled again, her plain face transforming into something almost beautiful. "I really appreciate your support, though."

Many of the remaining diners came up to Sarah to pledge their support. She thanked them all, even if it made her feel like a politician. She wasn't a politician. She was just someone who wanted to survive and help others to survive.

Finally, the room was down to one table: Mick, Sarah, Josey and Troy. Val and Carole, one of the Kittington group, were cleaning up. "I guess I need to get a ballot box set up," Troy said. "Even though I think it's a stupid idea."

"It'll shut him up for a while," Sarah said. "And I could use the peace and quiet." She caught a whiff of something unpleasant. "And we need to go and get the little princess into a clean diaper." She pushed her chair out from the table and stood. Mick followed suit; his nose wrinkled against the smell. "We'll see you in the morning, Troy."

They walked home, Sarah returning the waves of some people, responding with a quiet "thank you" to anyone who spoke to her. Otherwise, she was silent. "The only people who vote for a new leader will be his cronies," Mick said to her. "You won't be voted out."

"I'm not worried about that," she said. "I'm worried that this is causing people to lose faith." She looked at Mick. "We have to have faith that this is going to work. We have to hope that things are going to be alright. If not, everything is going to break down." She sighed heavily as she waved at Mandy. "I like what we have here. I don't want things to change."

"It'll be fine, Sarah." He shifted his smelly daughter on his hip. "I have faith."

She looked at him and smiled. "Well, you gotta have faith," she sang.

He laughed. "Never pegged you for a George Michael fan."

"Yeah, well, you never pegged me for a George Romero fan, either." She grinned back at him. "Doesn't it suck to be wrong all the time?"

CHAPTER FOURTEEN

Once they got Josey settled for the night, they got into bed. Mick fell asleep almost immediately. Sarah, however, did not. She worried what the morning would bring. There were times, some quite recent, where she didn't want to lead the group any longer. She just didn't think she had it in her. But with Mick's gentle insistence, she began to delegate. She stopped micromanaging. And it was much better. She got to spend time with Mick and Josey and still take care of the group. She wanted that to continue. Not because she needed the accolades, but because she thought she did a good job. She was good for the community.

When the morning alarm, otherwise known as Josey's cries, sounded, Sarah had barely managed two hours of sleep. Throwing a robe over her tee and panties, she walked bleary eyed to the bassinet and picked up her daughter. Immediately Josey stopped crying, her hand clutching Sarah's breast. "I know, bug," Sarah whispered.

She carried her into the living room and curled up on the sofa to nurse her daughter. Mick walked out of the bedroom a few minutes later, his hair mussed from sleep. He rubbed a hand over his face and let out a huge yawn. "Tea?" he finally managed.

"Yes, please," Sarah replied. She leaned her head back on the sofa and closed her eyes. She was going to be useless today. At least she had greenhouse duty that morning. She didn't need a lot of brain power for that.

"Here, babe."

She opened her eyes to see Mick holding a steaming cup of tea. She reached for it with her free hand and brought the mug to her nose. Just inhaling the scent made her feel slightly more awake. "Thanks, babe." She took a sip, burning her tongue, but needing the caffeine.

He watched her as he sipped his instant coffee. The dark smudges under her eyes told of her sleepless night. "You don't have to worry, you know."

She smiled, but it was a strained smile. "I'm not." She shifted Josey's position, wincing when she dug an elbow into Sarah's side.

"Sarah…"

"Sorry. I am a little worried." She looked down at her daughter, then back at Mick. "I talked about quitting, but I didn't really mean it. I was just frustrated because we didn't have as much time together as I wanted. Now, I don't want to quit. I want to lead. I think I do good things. And I think I've finally managed to do both things, spend more time with you and Josey and lead our group. I don't want to give that up."

"You won't have to," he said softly. "No one will vote for him but his people. Maybe not even all of them."

She sighed. "I hope you're right." She looked back at Josey, who had stopped nursing and was staring at Sarah. "Let's go, bug. We have a busy day."

As they walked to breakfast, Mick with Josey on his hip because Sarah was geared up, she looked around the town, at all the work they had done. They had two huge greenhouses producing fruits and vegetables all year round. They had three open air gardens for the summer. The roads were free of abandoned vehicles, all of them stripped of vital components and pushed to the sides of the road. The buildings had all been cleared of anything useful, everything held in a central location. They had 3 apartment buildings with heat in the winter and power at least most of the day all year round. They had a shower, complete with warm water. They had a small school, a medical clinic, a cafeteria of sorts. While she didn't build it all, she was instrumental in getting everything started, much of it at a great cost. She devoted a lot of her time and energy to building a community. She had so much more to do.

They stepped into the second-floor dining area, the tantalizing smell one they hadn't experienced in years. "Pancakes!?!" Mick exclaimed.

"How'd this happen?" Sarah asked, leaning over the chafing dish and inhaling deep.

"I told you we found flour," Donna said as she walked in carrying bottles of syrup. "I had some baking powder that was probably expired, but I figured what the heck?" She put a bottle of syrup on each table. "I figured a good old-fashioned breakfast couldn't hurt our chances today." She smiled at Sarah. "Besides, if you get voted out, I'm never cooking again."

"Donna –" Sarah began but Donna kept talking.

"If it wasn't for you, I wouldn't be here. I don't like that George and his wife, and Chad reminds me too much of Austin. I won't work with them. I'll only work with you."

What Donna had done for Sarah while they were both in Sugar Creek still ate at Sarah. She didn't deserve Donna's loyalty. But it touched her just the same. "Thank you, Donna."

Donna just smiled. "I'm going to send someone with plates to whoever's on gate duty." She touched Josey's cheek. "I'll bet Josey will love those pancakes." She quietly left the room.

"You won't lose," Mick said. "There are too many people here who love you."

Sarah smiled. "I think you may be right." She looked down at Josey. "Want some pancakes, bug?" Josey clapped her chubby hands.

Mick took a seat while Sarah made their plates. Resisting the urge to pile her plate with pancakes, she only took two, putting four on Mick's plate since he would be feeding Josey. She added some strawberries to Mick's plate, the fruit small but apparently very tasty. She didn't know. She didn't like strawberries. She carried both plates to the table, then went back for cups of water.

Mick had already given Josey her first taste by the time she got back with the water. Sarah laughed at the look on Josey's face. Part wonder, part joy, she chewed her first piece and had her mouth open for the next. With a big grin on his face, Mick fed her another bite, then took one for himself. "They're good, but something's missing," he said.

"Eggs." Sarah sat next to him and cut her pancakes. "We don't have any eggs."

Mick quickly ate some more before Josey finished her mouthful. "We need to find chickens."

"I'll let you search for them." Sarah closed her eyes as the first taste of the pancake hit her tongue. She was never a huge fan of pancakes before, but damn, if they weren't fantastic now.

The room filled rapidly, the rumor of pancakes bringing everyone out for breakfast. Sarah heard lots of laughter and reminiscing as the community devoured the breakfast. When Donna came up to check the chafing dishes, she got a spontaneous round of applause. With a goofy smile, she dipped into a curtsy, causing the room to break into laughter.

"I think she's everyone's favorite person right now," Annie remarked. She had joined Sarah and Mick, along with April and Mandy, Paul and Bobby.

"Better her than George," Mandy said with a snort.

"He's not anything," Bobby said hotly. "I knew we shouldn't have let him in."

"He hasn't done anything wrong, Bobby," Sarah said. "He has every right to question the status quo, if he thinks he can do a better job."

"Well, he can't. He doesn't know a…a…darn thing." Bobby cleared his plate of his last bite of pancakes. After he swallowed, he continued. "He'll run this place into the ground if people vote him in."

"We don't know if people want him in charge," Sarah countered.

"Most people don't," Paul said. "I doubt he'll get more than a handful of votes."

"But even those handful of votes aren't good," April said. "It will give others ideas. They'll want to have elections, put other people in place."

"Maybe that's not such a bad thing," Sarah mused. Everyone turned to look at her. "We kind of have a dictatorship here. Should we have elections? Isn't that the first step to democracy?"

"Sarah, I know you didn't want this," Annie said softly. "But you have it. And you're good at it. We're all good at it. We have everyone's welfare in mind, not just our own. Can you honestly say that everyone else in the community will be like that?"

Sarah shrugged. "I don't know, Annie. But the way we have it set up, it looks like we're playing favorites."

"Once things calm down, we'll talk about elections, OK?" Paul said. "For now, things can stay as they are. And that means you are still in charge, Sarah." He stood up. "You need to remember that. Quit talking about change." He left, weaving his way around the tables.

"He's right," Mandy said. "You need to act like a leader and the people will see you as a leader. If you show doubt, or weakness, they won't believe."

"She knows what she's talking about," April said. "She used to work for politicians."

Sarah laughed. "I'll put you in charge of my campaign."

"You might have to campaign," Mick said as he bounced Josey on his leg. "If you want to keep the job."

Sarah looked at him. "Yeah, if I want to keep it." Her voice was soft. She looked around the room, at the people she had kept safe and warm and fed. Then back at Mick and Josey, the ones that mattered most. "Let's get a plate for Troy and go cast our vote."

As they walked to the market, more people passed them on their way to the dining area. "Are there really pancakes?" Jack asked as he and Mikey walked up to them.

"Better get them before they're gone," Mick said with a smile. "Josey ate three herself."

"No, she didn't," Mikey scoffed. "I can eat three, though."

"Have at it, kid," Sarah laughed.

They continued walking, surprised to see a handful of people milling about in front of the market. Sarah sobered her expression as she walked up to them. "Good morning," she said evenly. "Did you have a chance to have breakfast? Donna made pancakes."

"Pancakes?" Ed asked. He looked at his wife. "Did she say pancakes, Bonnie?"

"You're not deaf, Ed, you heard her." She looked at Sarah. "Can we eat before we vote?"

"Of course. Voting will be open until eleven." Sarah looked over the people gathered: Ed and Bonnie, Gabriel, Phil and Blake. "Everyone, go eat before they're all gone. You can come back when you're finished."

The small crowd dispersed and Sarah and Mick walked into the market. Troy was sitting in his usual seat. A six-foot table had been set up, a cardboard box with a small hole cut in the top dead center. Squares of paper and pens were next to it. At the other end of the table, straddling a chair, was Chad, a smirk on his plain face.

"Troy, Chad," Sarah said as she walked to the table. She put the covered plate of pancakes in front of Troy. "Your breakfast."

"You didn't bring me any?" Chad asked.

"I didn't know you'd be here." Sarah dismissed him and turned to Troy.

When Troy uncovered the plate, the sweet smell wafting through the room, Chad actually groaned. "Are those pancakes?"

"Yup." Sarah watched as Troy dug in, a smile on his face.

"Why don't you go get me some?" Chad asked, licking his lips. Sarah favored him with a withering glare. "Yeah, I didn't think so. Some leader."

"Get them yourself," Mick said. "We promise we won't stuff the ballet box." He gave Chad an insincere grin.

Chad snorted. "Fuck it, I don't need them."

"Don't curse," Sarah said. "I don't want Josey's first real word to be that."

Chad muttered something under his breath and turned away. Sarah looked at him a minute before she turned back to Troy. "Is it too early to vote? I have things I need to get done today."

He looked at his analog watch between bites of pancake. "Only 8:30. You have to wait."

"OK." Sarah found a chair behind the counter and pulled it out. She motioned for Mick to sit, knowing how tiring it got holding Josey. Mick shook his head, so she sat down. "What's happening today?"

"Jack, Claire, Jenny and Alan and going back to that settlement. The last group brought back lots of canned goods and water. But there's still a lot of houses to go through."

Sarah nodded. "How's the diesel holding up?"

"We're still good, but I'd feel a lot more comfortable if we had solar on the apartments." Troy finished the last of his pancakes. He looked down at the empty plate mournfully. "Those were good."

"Maybe we'll have them again," Mick said.

"No, the flour is better used for other things," Sarah said. "This is a one-time treat."

"Bribe, you mean," Chad piped up.

"Whatever you say, Chad." Sarah was surprised he guessed at Donna's motivation.

"You'll be listening to what I say soon enough," he muttered.

Sarah rolled her eyes. She'd leave before she listened to what that asshole had to say. She, Mick and Troy made small talk until his watch read nine. "OK, voting is open," Troy said. Almost immediately, people started coming in the door. The first person, Gabriel, looked at Sarah then Chad, then back to Troy.

Sarah understood his reluctance. "Troy, we'll be back in little bit to cast our vote." She stood and motioned to Mick. They slid by the people waiting, nodding at those in line.

"Why didn't we vote?" Mick asked as they walked towards their apartment.

"We were making people uncomfortable." She nodded at Chuck as he went past. "Let's just go relax somewhere. We'll vote later."

"You're the boss," Mick said innocently. She narrowed her eyes at him and he started laughing.

Sarah and Mick were the last to vote. Troy took their slips at just five minutes to eleven. But they didn't need to. George received only four votes. The rest were for Sarah. Chad insisted on tallying the votes after Troy, just to be sure. "The people have spoken," George said when Chad had finished counting. "I guess they're happy with the way you do things."

"I guess so," Sarah replied.

"If you ever need my help, or just want my advice, you don't hesitate to ask." George put his hand out.

Without showing her revulsion, Sarah shook it. "I will." On a cold day in hell, she thought.

"Come on, Chad. I think we're working in the greenhouse this afternoon." George turned and went for the door.

"Fucking great," Chad said, eyeballing Sarah as he followed George.

Once they had gone, Troy looked at Sarah. "He's not done."

"I know." She looked out the window and watched him and Chad walk up the street.

CHAPTER FIFTEEN

A few days after the vote, Mark, Phil and Frank came back from their hunt with a buck, two turkeys, and four rabbits. They were celebrated as heroes. To boost morale, Sarah asked Donna to use both turkeys and they had Thanksgiving in February. Donna even scraped together enough flour to make biscuits. It was as if all the unpleasantness of the past was washed away with turkey and gravy.

Sarah made a concerted effort to delegate more. She also started weekly updates to the community, letting them know what was going on. Things were running smoothly.

Sarah was on gate duty one bright sunny morning. Frank, his arm still in the sling, approached the gate. "Can I talk to you?" he asked, his eyes shifting left and right.

"Sure. Can you make it up here?" Sarah hadn't really spoken with him since she first introduced herself. She wondered what he wanted. A bigger apartment, maybe?

"Yeah, might take a bit. How do I get up there?"

Sarah pointed behind her. "Ladder's on the side of the building." She watched as he drifted around the store, only to appear about five minutes later on the roof. He walked gingerly, like he was afraid the roof would collapse beneath him. It wouldn't. They kept the roof clear of snow and other debris and Bobby inspected it once every quarter, along with all of the other roofs for the buildings they used.

"Wow, it's a nice view up here," Frank said as he stood next to her.

It was a nice view. There were clear sightlines down the road, which was rapidly becoming covered in grass and weeds. On the other side, the river was just visible, the water clean and clear without nearly three years of pollution.

"Yeah, it's nice." She nodded her head at Frank's sling. "How'd you hunt with that?"

He looked down at his arm. "I was stationary. I took it off."

As he looked down, Sarah slipped her hand closer to her gun. She wasn't sure she completely trusted Frank. "How's it healing?"

Frank shrugged. "I might have to have April rebreak it. I haven't decided yet."

"If it'll make it better, you should. So what's up?"

Frank shoved his hands in his pockets. He looked around, up, down, everywhere but at Sarah. "Chris is my friend. We've been together a long time."

Sarah knew this. "Yeah?"

"I don't feel right talking about him but…" Frank finally looked at Sarah. "He's been spending a lot of time with Chad and George. I think they've been messing with things around here."

This piqued her interest. "Such as?"

"He was talking with Chad and he was laughing, said something about Bobby trusting the wrong guy." Frank shook his head. "The next day, I was in my room and they were in the kitchen. Chad asked if Chris was sure no one saw him. Chris said no, then Chad asked him how he got them in."

"Son of a bitch," Sarah swore. "He moved the fucking truck, didn't he?"

"I don't know!!" Frank exclaimed. "Maybe?"

"Why'd you wait so long to tell someone?"

"Chris is my friend," he said again with a shrug. "I didn't want it to be true. I didn't want to rat on him. But this morning, George told Chris he'd be on the new council. And he could have all the – the women he wanted, only he didn't use those words." Frank shook his head. "I can't let that go. I've seen how Chad acts around women. Chris, well, he always took the path of least resistance and if Chad is promising him an easy time, he just might not do the right thing." He looked back at Sarah. "I thought you should know."

Sarah nodded. She knew they were up to something, but to intentionally wreck the solar panel? Let zombies inside? She needed to share this with the council. They needed to decide what to do about it. Could they exile them on hearsay? Who all was involved? The women? Just George, Chad and Chris? Frank was saying something. She turned to him. "I'm sorry?"

"I just asked what you're going to do? I don't want Chris hurt."

"The council will decide, Frank. Thanks for letting me know."

He knew from her tone that he was dismissed. He sighed heavily, then trudged across the roof to the ladder.

At dinner, Sarah stopped Paul on his way to the buffet of fish and potatoes. "We have a situation," she said softly. "We need to talk."

He could see from her face that she was worried. "I'm on the gate tonight," Paul said. "Do you want to meet me there?"

She thought a moment. "I think this is a whole council thing. Can we meet first thing tomorrow morning, after your shift?"

"That'll work." He searched her face. "How bad?"

"Pretty bad. Maybe." She shook her head. "We'll need to figure it out."

"OK, then tomorrow, 8:00."

"See you then." Sarah walked back to the table where Mick held Josey. Annie and April were already there.

"Is he OK to meet tonight?" Annie asked.

Sarah shook her head. "Tomorrow morning, after his shift on the gate. 8:00 at my place, OK?"

April nodded. "I wish you'd tell us what this is about."

"I still need to work it over in my head," Sarah said simply. "I need to figure out what we can do. It's not that cut and dried." She reached under the table and took Mick's hand.

"All right." Annie stood up. "I'll let Troy and Bobby know. We'll see you tomorrow." She nodded at Mick, smiled and Josey and took her leave.

"Frank was by to see me," April said. She took a drink of water. "He says he wants me to fix his arm."

"Can you do it?" Mick asked.

"Yeah, but he'll be out of commission for at least six weeks."

"Do it," Sarah said. "He's a good guy, he should have full use of his arm."

April nodded. "I didn't realize you knew him well."

"Well enough." She took a small spoonful of potatoes and fed them to Josey. "Take care of him, will you?"

"I was planning on it. I told him to come by after dinner." She ran a hand through her hair. "Our only problem is that we don't have any painkiller stronger than ibuprofen. Just whiskey."

"Use what you have to." All of the liquor was kept under lock and key at the medical clinic. It was intended to be used for medicinal purposes only.

"OK. I'll go get set up. See you three in the morning." April left, leaving Sarah, Josey and Mick alone at the table.

"You should tell them why we're meeting," Mick said softly. Sarah had filled him in when they were in the privacy of their apartment. "Maybe they can come up with a solution beforehand."

Sarah shook her head as she gave another bite of potato to Josey. "Bobby and Paul would throw them out without thinking about it. We need to think about it. Is this worth exile? When it's only hearsay?" She sighed. "I want them out, but is that right?"

"That's why we have a council, babe. So all the tough decisions don't rest on your admittedly strong shoulders."

Sarah laughed. She didn't get a chance for a retort as two women approached the table. It was Lyn and another woman from Kittington. Sarah thought her name was Ivy, but she wasn't sure. "Hi," Sarah said.

"Hi, I'm Lyn and this is Ivy," Lyn said in a soft voice.

"I remember both of you." Sarah smiled. "What can I help you with?"

"We – we just wanted to say thank you," Ivy said. She was a chunky blonde who was probably no more than 18 or 19. "For – for getting us out of there."

Sarah could see in her eyes some of the things she went through. Her gaze softened. "You're very welcome. Are you fitting in okay?"

"Yes, we're both permanently assigned to the greenhouses," Lyn said. "I used to work for a nursery and Ivy loves to garden."

"That's great! We need all the green thumbs we can to offset my black one." Sarah laughed.

"Your daughter is adorable," Ivy said.

"Thanks," Mick said. "But don't let her hear you say that, it'll go to her head." Ivy gave him a small smile.

"You're not having any more trouble, are you, Lyn?" Sarah asked.

She shook her head. "But I think he's been bothering Megan."

Sarah nodded. "I'll have a talk with him."

Lyn's eyes got wide. "Oh, please, don't. It'll make things worse. Ever since no one voted for them, he's been a lot meaner."

"Lyn, I have to. It's my job." She leaned forward. "It's my job to keep everyone safe. That means I need to stop problems before they happen."

"If – if you talk to him, don't tell him I told you, OK?" Lyn's voice was tremulous.

"Of course not. He'll never know you said anything."

"Thank you." She and Ivy walked away.

"More hearsay." Mick wiped Josey's face as he looked at Sarah.

"I know." She rubbed her forehead. "I can't think about this right now. Let's just go home."

CHAPTER SIXTEEN

Sarah didn't know what woke her. The click of the door being shut. The creak of the floor. The sound of a heavy footstep. A dim light where there shouldn't be one. She opened her eyes to see George standing next to the bed, holding their battery-operated lantern. She turned her head to see Chad standing over Mick, a knife at his throat. Mick's eyes were narrowed, his hands clenched into fists. She discarded her plan to jump at George. Her eyes flew to the corner of the room where Josey slept. Chris stood next to the bassinet. Dina was bent over it, cooing at the sleeping baby.

"What are you doing here?" Sarah asked, her voice low.

"What do you think?" George said. "Getting rid of the competition."

"Because your little tricks didn't work?" George cocked his head at her. "Sabotaging the solar panel. Letting zombies in."

"Don't forget the fridge," he said with a grin.

"Why?" She had to keep him talking. It would give her time to come up with a plan. The problem was, all of her weapons were locked up.

"Because I won't be led by a little bitch. I should be in charge."

"Yeah, 'cause that worked out so well for you in Kittington."

George snarled and moved closer to her. "What the fuck do you know? You weren't there."

"Thank God." Maybe she could roll over Mick, take out Chad. She relaxed her body, getting ready to make her move.

George's fist caught her on the side of her head. She winced, biting her lip. "Smart mouthed bitch," he muttered. He set the lantern on the nightstand.

"What do you want, George?" The lantern was now a potential weapon. If she was fast enough, she could hurl it at Chad, roll off the bed and take George down.

"You gone. Him, too. Your brat can stay. I told Dina she could raise her, teach her right."

"You touch a hair on my daughter's head, I will kill you," she bit off.

George laughed. "You won't be able to do shit. You'll be dead. Undead, actually." He pulled a knife from a sheath on his belt. "You're gonna slice your wrists. When you wake up zombified, you'll attack your husband. We'll be passing by and hear it and rush in here just in time to save your little brat."

"Couple flaws in your plan, George." Sarah kept her voice even. Inside, the fear was winning. He had a knife, Chad had a knife. She didn't know what Chris was carrying. All she had was the potential of a blunt object. "Why would I kill myself?"

"Because you had a fight with your husband. Maybe he thought you were a smart mouthed bitch, too." George's grin was terrifying. "What other flaws do you got?"

"Why wouldn't Mick get me help if I slit my wrists? And what would stop him from doing it once you leave? I'm sure you're too pussy to wait around for me to turn."

Another fist and her head snapped back. Through the pain, she heard Mick growl beside her. "You gotta watch that smart mouth, girl." George moved the knife in front of her face. He smiled when she shrunk back into the pillow. "You did it while he was sleeping. Of course, he'll be unconscious. A pillow over his face for a few minutes will take care of that."

Sarah took a shuddering breath. "If you think I'm going to let you cut my wrists, you're sadly mistaken. I killed a man who was trying to rape me, stabbed him in the thigh with a screwdriver. So if I wasn't willing to be raped, why the hell do you think I'd be willing to let you kill me?"

"Chris?" George said. Sarah's eyes flew over to the bassinet. Chris held a knife above Josey's sleeping body.

"George, you said I could have her!!" Dina exclaimed.

"Shut the fuck up!" George looked down at Sarah. "You do it or your daughter dies along with you."

"OK, I'll do it," she said.

"Sarah…" Mick's voice ended in a gasp. She turned her head to see Chad with the knife right up to Mick's skin, a thin line of blood trickling down his neck.

"It'll be OK," she said softly. Her smile wavered a bit. "I love you."

"How fucking touching," Chad snorted. "Can I put him out yet?"

"Not yet," George said. "Let's get her going, first."

Sarah shook her head. "Not here, let's do it in the bathroom." Her mind worked frantically. If she could get George alone, she just might be able to do something.

"Why? Here's just as good."

She shook her head again. "I wouldn't do it right here. If I was going to kill myself, I'd do it somewhere more private. That's the kind of person I am." She looked at George. "You don't want any questions, do you?"

George stared down at her, wondering what she was planning. "Keep an eye on her," he said to Chad. He moved to the bathroom and took a look around. The room was empty, with just a few harmless items on the counter and the chemical toilet on the floor. No weapons that he could see.

He stepped back into the bedroom. "OK, come on, then." He waved the knife at her.

Very slowly, she pulled the covers back and got out of bed. She looked around the room, noting the location of everyone in the room. Luckily, Josey was still sleeping. But goddamn if she wasn't going to kill Dina for daring to think Josey would be hers.

She stood beside the bed in her tee and panties, goosebumps breaking out on her legs. "Damn, she's got a pretty hot bod," Chad leered. "Too bad she's gotta go, I wouldn't mind a piece of that."

Mick lunged up and managed a glancing blow off of Chad's shoulder, catching Chad off guard. Chad pressed the knife against his neck and more blood trickled out. "Better watch, dickhead, before I slice your fucking throat."

"That would fuck up your plan, wouldn't it, asshole?" Mick hissed. He was breathing heavy, the anger coursing through his veins.

"It would, Chad, so just simmer down." George waved his arm towards the bathroom. "Shall we?"

Sarah glared at him as she moved past him into the bathroom. She took a deep breath, trying to center herself. If she went through with the plan that had formed, she knew she was going to have pain. But it would be well worth it. She sat down on the closed lid of the useless toilet, the chemical toilet to her right, and defiantly stared up at him. "Well?" She demanded.

"Hold out your arm." He approached her with knife in hand.

She took a deep breath and held out her left arm. He put the tip of the knife on the inside of her wrist and pulled it up her arm about two inches. The pain was excruciating. She bit back a moan as she bent over, holding her wounded arm to her chest as she felt the blood start to flow. Her unbraided hair hung down to the floor, shielding her movements.

"Damn, you're a tough one," George remarked, admiration in his voice. "Too bad we couldn't get along."

"Yeah," she panted, trying to get the pain under control. "Too bad." Her hands grasped the chemical toilet and she sprung up, smashing it into his face, dousing him with human waste. The knife clattered to the floor as he brought his hands to his face. Her left hand lost its grip as tendons snapped and the toilet slipped out of her hands. She pounced on the knife, taking it into her right hand. With a snarl, she lunged at George, burying the knife in his abdomen and slicing across. He screamed, his arms lashing out, a fist catching her on the side of the head again. She fell to her knees, the knife coming with her, ripping another large gash in his flesh.

When Chad heard the sound of the toilet hitting George, he took a step back from Mick so he could see into the bathroom. Mick clenched his jaw and pushed himself up from the bed, tangling his feet in the covers, but managing to stand in front of Chad. He raised a forearm and blocked Chad's knife hand. Mick's other hand went around Chad's throat and he pushed him against the wall. Chad struggled, but Mick was bigger and full of rage. He squeezed the smaller man's neck as he fought off his knife hand. Chad's face grew red, his arms flailing, the knife glancing off of Mick's arm and drawing a thin line of blood. Mick grabbed Chad's wrist with his free hand and turned it around, pushing the knife into the intruder's belly. Chad's eyes grew wide as Mick twisted the knife, then pulled it out, flinging Chad to the ground. "Sarah!" Mick roared.

Dizzy from the blow to the head and the loss of blood, Sarah stood slowly, shaking her head. George was leaning against the vanity, his hands gripping his abdomen, trying to hold his guts inside. "Motherfucker," Sarah growled as she pushed past him. He reached out with a bloodied hand and grabbed her left arm, squeezing the wound, the pain shooting through her. She turned and jabbed the knife up, catching him in the throat. She pulled it out, blood gushing, and she pushed him to the floor. She moved into the bedroom in time to see Mick thrust the knife into Chad.

She heard her daughter's cry. She turned to Dina and Chris, standing by the bassinet, looks of horror on their faces. "Get the fuck away from my daughter," she snarled, raising the blade in her hand.

Mick turned to see her and he gasped. Her face and tee were smeared red. But the worst was her arm covered in gore, blood sluicing down, a puddle forming where she stood. "Babe," he whispered hoarsely.

Sarah advanced slowly on Dina and Chris, a trail of blood following her. Chris dropped his knife and they both backed away, hands up. "Stop right there," she said. She risked a glance down to the bassinet to see Josey, crying but unhurt. Her mouth trembled as she smiled down at her daughter.

"Sarah." Mick came up behind her.

She closed her eyes briefly and leaned against him. She needed his strength. "Tie them up," she said. "I don't want them disappearing." She pressed the knife into his hand.

"We didn't do anything!" Dina whined.

"You stood by and watched as your husband and friend tried to kill us. That asshole there threatened my daughter. You did plenty," Sarah spat.

"Let me take care of that arm," Mick said.

"It's fine. Deal with them, then you need to get Josey. I can't lift her." She looked up at Mick, her eyes welling with tears. She was standing by sheer force of will. Her legs were weak and her vision was going in and out. She blinked rapidly and one lone tear crept down her cheek.

Mick brushed the tear from her cheek. "I'll be right back." He kicked the knife that Chris had dropped and it skittered under the bed. Mick advanced to where Dina and Chris cowered in the corner. "Turn around," he ordered. "Faces against the wall." He opened a dresser drawer at random and came out with a t-shirt. He notched a slit in the material with the bloody knife, then ripped it in half. Quickly, he tied their hands, first Chris, then Dina. "Sit," he growled.

While Mick was taking care of the remaining invaders, Sarah looked down at her daughter. She had stopped crying and was holding her arms out, wanting Sarah to lift her. "I can't, Josey girl," Sarah whispered.

Josey rolled onto her belly, her diapered butt in the air. Then she moved to a sitting position and held her arms out again. "Mama."

Sarah sobbed. It was the first time Josey had called her "Mama." She wanted to touch her, but her right hand was coated in George's blood, her left hand useless. She could barely feel her fingers. "That's right, bug. I'm Mama." Sarah's eyes fluttered and she tapped her left arm against the bassinet, the pain waking her up.

"Sarah?" Mick was beside her. "Let me see that arm."

"Get Josey," Sarah said. "She's scared."

"No. Let me see that arm." He had something in his hand, but she couldn't focus on it. Gripping the bassinet tight with her right arm, she lifted her left to his gaze.

"Jesus, babe!" He exclaimed. He brought his hand up, holding a white t-shirt. He wrapped it around her arm, tying it very tight. Sarah moaned. The fabric bloomed red immediately.

"Get – get Josey," she breathed. "She called me 'Mama.'"

"She'll be fine, I need to get April." Mick started for the door.

"No, Mick, take her." Sarah's knees started to sag and Mick turned back and caught her. "I don't know how long…how long I can stay awake with her…"

Mick gently eased Sarah to the floor, her back against the bed. "You better stay awake," he breathed as he held her head in his hands. "You need to stay awake."

"Get Josey," she whispered. "Bring her to me."

Mick swallowed the lump in his throat and went back to the bassinet. He picked up Josey, who wrapped her arms around him, her arm smearing the blood on his throat. He bent down so Sarah could see her daughter.

Josey reached for Sarah, her tiny voice perfect as she said "Mama."

Sarah sobbed. With supreme effort, she lifted her left arm. The stain on the fabric grew larger until nearly the whole makeshift bandage was scarlet. She touched Josey's soft cheek with her left pinky finger, the only one she could still sense on that hand. She left a streak of blood on her chubby cheek. "I love you, bug." She closed her eyes.

"Sarah!" Mick called. "Sarah, open your eyes!"

Her eyes slid open. "Yeah, just resting them for a minute. Not sleeping."

Her face was ashen, her lips nearly blue. "I'm going to get April. Keep your eyes open, do you hear me? Keep them open!!"

She nodded. "I love you, Mick."

His eyes filled with tears. "I love you, too, Sarah. Keep your eyes open!!"

She watched him stand and race through the room, Josey looking over his shoulder at her. Mick was safe. Her daughter was safe. She smiled as she took a breath. And closed her eyes.

BOOK TWO

CHAPTER ONE

Tony and Sully didn't recognize the man on the gate at the main entry to Thornville. Sarah must have brought in more people. Strays, she called them. They approached slowly, giving him time to see they weren't a threat.

"Can I help you gentlemen?" The sentry said from his perch on top of an old fast food restaurant.

"Staff Sgt. Anthony McGuire and Sgt. John Sullivan of the United States Marine Corps. We'd like to see Sarah or Mick, if she's not available," Tony said. The man cocked his head, an odd expression on his face. Tony smiled. "They know us."

"Just a minute." Tony and Sully watched as he unclipped a walkie talkie from his belt. He took a few steps back before he spoke quietly into the walkie. The only word they could make out was "Mick." After a response that they didn't hear, he clipped the walkie back to his belt and stepped forward. "Someone will be here to take you inside." He nodded towards the horses they both rode. "They can't come in."

"We know," Sully said. "Sarah usually has us tie them to that tree and whoever's out here watches over them."

The man nodded. "I'll keep an eye on them."

"Thanks," Tony said. They dismounted from the horses, leading them to the tree and securing them. "How long have you been here?" Tony asked.

"'Bout three and a half months."

"We must have missed you our last visit," Tony said as slid his arms into the straps of his pack. "We were here about three months ago."

"So you don't know then?"

"Know what?" Sully asked.

The man shook his head and looked over his shoulder. "Jack's coming. You know how to get through the bus?"

"Yeah, like we said, we've been here before." Sully shouldered his pack and moved to the nearly invisible door cut into the side of the bus that comprised half of the barricade.

"What's your name?" Tony asked as he joined Sully.

"Frank. Frank Dobson."

"Nice to meet you, Frank. We'll probably see you on the way out, we won't be staying long." Sarah will probably kick us out after we tell her why we're here, Tony thought.

The door popped open, Jack poking his head out. "Hi, guys," he said. He was tall and lanky, his hair long and curled against his collar, his beard practically non-existent. Tony remembered from his notes that he should be around twenty.

"Hey, Jack, how've you been?" Tony asked, holding out his hand.

Jack shook his hand, then Sully's. "Surviving. You?"

"About the same." Tony waved at Frank before he stepped into the bus, Sully right behind him.

Nothing had changed since the last time they had visited. Still the same metal bars welded the entire width, spaced a foot apart. Thick beams braced the bars in spots, making a very effective barricade to ward off an assault. As Tony and Sully moved through the door, Jack locked the entryway with a padlock, leaving the key in its slot, then slipped a steel bar over the entrance. Once they were all on the town side, he locked that door with another padlock and hung the key on a nail next to the door.

"Come on, I'll take you in," Jack said as he began walking towards the main area of town.

"We know the way, if you have something else to do," Sully said.

Jack shrugged. "I'm going this way, anyway."

They followed Jack through the familiar streets. They had visited many times before, but something seemed different. Even Jack seemed different. On their previous visits, he was more talkative, sometimes to the extreme. He had barely said anything.

"How are things going here, Jack?" Tony asked.

He shrugged again. "As good as they can, I guess." He started walking faster and Tony and Sully stepped up their pace.

"Tony," Sully whispered, pointing at the grassy area in front of an old war monument. Tony looked where Sully was pointing. There were now three crosses in the square instead of the two that were there the last time they had visited.

"Did you lose someone in the last few months?" Tony asked.

Jack barked out a short laugh that was not at all amused. "Yeah. We lost a lot." He walked even faster, as if he wanted away from the two soldiers.

Sully looked at Tony and shrugged. They moved even faster, not quite jogging, but close.

The streets were empty. Tony expected people to be outside. It was a nice spring day, the late afternoon sun warm on his shoulders. But the roads were quiet. They didn't see a soul as they moved past the side streets blocked with cars and car parts, past the buildings tagged with different colors of paint, faded after all this time. He never did find out what they meant.

Jack stopped abruptly in front of the building marked "Ash." "You can go up. Apartment 204," he said. Without another word, Jack jogged away towards the other gate at the far end of town.

"I guess we go up," Sully said. He shifted his pack on his shoulders and took the three steps in two strides. He pulled open the door and walked inside the dim vestibule. Tony looked around at the emptiness of the town, then followed Sully. He pulled his flashlight from his pack and flicked it on, dispelling some of the gloom.

"Didn't they used to be in a different apartment? 201?" Tony asked as they started up the stairs.

"I think so."

The light bounced off the walls, barely illuminating their path. Tony didn't know what it was, but he felt a sense of wrongness. From Frank at the gate to the walk through the town to Jack abandoning them, something was not right. He hoped that he was just imagining things.

Sully opened the door to the second floor. The ropes of LED lights were still fastened to the walls, making the flashlight unnecessary. Tony flicked it off and followed Sully into the hall. They walked around the corridor, passing one apartment that had a big red X on the door. The apartment they were looking for, 204, was two doors past that one. The key was stuck in the deadbolt, as in all the apartments they had passed. Sully looked at Tony and shrugged, then knocked on the door.

"Come on," said a voice from inside.

CHAPTER TWO

Tony opened the door and he and Sully stepped inside. The apartment was small, a living room that blended into a kitchen and two doors off the living room. One was open and they could see the edge of a bed. The other was closed, presumably the bathroom.

Sitting at the small kitchen table was Mick Cooke, a glass full of brown liquid in his hand. There was a half-empty bottle of whiskey on the table. His hair was disheveled, his goatee gone, a full beard taking its place. "I'd offer you one, but you're on duty," he saluted them with the glass before taking a long drink.

Tony looked at Sully, then back at Mick. "What's going on, Mick?"

Mick shrugged and took another drink. "I'm relaxing. Trying to, anyway. What do you want?"

"Where's Sarah?" Sully asked softly. He was afraid of Mick's answer.

"Gone."

"Gone where?" Tony asked.

Mick closed his bloodshot eyes and sighed. When he opened them again, they were filled with raw pain. "She's dead."

Sully cursed. Tony felt like he had been punched in the chest. "What? How? What happened?" He walked over to the table and sat across from Mick. Sully followed, pulling out a third chair and straddling it.

"Kittington," Mick muttered. "That fucking George."

"What did he do?" Sully asked, his voice a growl.

"He wanted to take over. He started sabotaging shit, pushed for an election, for fuck's sake." Mick took another long swallow of his drink. "When he lost the election, he snuck into our apartment with his fucking crew, threatened Josey. He – he took Sarah into the bathroom and sliced her arm, like she was committing suicide. The cut was too deep. She bled out before I could get April." He picked up his glass in a mock toast. "She killed the fucker first, though." He drained his glass and slammed it on the table. He reached for the bottle and uncapped it, filling the glass halfway.

"When did this happen?" Tony asked, leaning back in his chair.

"Sixty-two days ago."

"Just after we left last time." Tony shook his head.

"Where's Josey?" Sully demanded.

"She's with Missy. She keeps her most days now." He took a pull of his whiskey.

"Should you be drinking so much?" Tony asked softly.

"Fuck you, Tony." He took another drink, staring at his glass once he finished. "Getting this whiskey is the only advantage to being on the stupid council. Letting those fuckers in was such a goddamn mistake." He looked up at Tony, his eyes glazed. "Why are you here, anyway?"

Tony looked at Sully, who shook his head slightly. "We should probably take it to the council. Can you call a meeting?"

Mick drained his glass and stood up. "Fine by me." He walked carefully to the living room, where a walkie talkie was thrown haphazardly onto the sofa. He grabbed it, clicking it on as he brought it to his mouth. "Grant, this is Mick. Tony and Sully need to talk to the council. Can you get everyone together? We'll meet in the cafeteria."

"Sure thing, Mick." Grant's voice was layered with static.

Mick threw the walkie back onto the sofa. "Let's go." He headed to the door, stumbling just a bit before righting himself. He was through the door before Tony and Sully had even risen from their chairs.

♦

Mick walked to Shaun, slowly and carefully. Tony and Sully were right behind him, speaking volumes with just a few glances. The cafeteria was empty when they entered. "You want something to drink?" Mick asked. "I think there's water back there." He indicated the small kitchenette with a nod of his head.

Tony shook his head. "We're fine." They sat at one of the long tables across from Mick. "I'm really sorry about Sarah," he started. "She was one of a kind."

Mick snorted. "Thanks. It means so much." He folded his arms across his chest.

"How are things going here now, without her?" Sully asked.

Mick shrugged. "I don't know. I do my job; I take care of our daughter. I don't care about anything else."

"Is that what Sarah would want for you?" Tony asked.

Mick exploded out of his chair. "What do you know about what Sarah would want? And what the fuck does it matter? She's dead, she's gone. I'll never see…" He trailed off and swallowed hard. Without a word, he turned and headed to the kitchenette.

When he had disappeared, Sully spoke. "I don't know what to say to him."

"I don't think there's anything we can say." Tony shook his head. "He's lost the love of his life, the mother of his child. Someone like Sarah, you don't get over that easily."

"I guess you're right." Sully looked to where Mick had disappeared. "Should we go after him?"

Before Tony could answer, the door opened and Annie and April walked in. "Hi, Tony, Sully," Annie said in her soft voice. Her long grey hair was pulled back into a ponytail, not the typical braids she usually wore. April looked as she always did, her attention half on what was going on and half preparing for the next thing.

Tony and Sully stood when the women entered. "Hello, ladies. How are you?" Tony asked.

Annie smiled softly. "We're managing. How are things in the outside world?"

Tony grimaced. "That's what we need to talk to the council about. Is everyone else on the way?"

"They should be here in a few minutes," April said. She looked around the room. "Where's Mick?"

"He's in the kitchen."

April turned her gaze to Sully. "Is he drinking?"

Sully looked at Tony before answering. "He was. He's not now."

April shook her head. She turned to Annie. "I told you we need to move the liquor."

"We move it and he thinks we don't trust him. He'll find his way through this." Annie sat at the table and folded her hands in front of her. "He will."

April blew out a sigh. "Before or after he hurts himself? Or someone else? Someone who depends on him?"

Mick came out of the kitchen, a bottle of water in his hand. "I would never hurt Josey. I don't drink when she's with me."

"You say that now, but what happens when you forget?" April asked. "When you just need to take the edge off?" She walked over to Mick and touched his arm. She didn't miss his flinch. "We care about you, Mick. We want you to be well."

"This is as well as I'm going to get," he said, pulling away from her. "Where is everyone else? I want to get this done."

"So you can go back to drinking?" April demanded.

Mick was saved from answering by the opening of the door. The rest of the council stepped in. Troy walked in first. Bobby came in next, with Paul right behind him. Greetings were made all around, then the group gathered at the table around Annie. Mick stood, his back against the wall, waiting.

"We're starting to get overrun again," Tony said. "When the virus mutated, a lot of communities weren't aware and many were decimated." He looked at Mick. "We told you about Boyer last time we were here, how they were wiped out." Mick nodded once. "That's how it is in a lot of places now."

"What's this have to do with us?" Mick asked. "We're good here, we lock ourselves in at night so there's little chance of that happening here. There aren't many other communities around here to overrun us."

"Our numbers are down," Sully said. "Soldiers are dying or they're just tired and they're deserting. The government is asking for volunteers so we can clean them out again."

"Why should we volunteer? They haven't done a thing for us," Bobby said.

"Because you are still part of the United States of America," Tony answered. "It's your duty as a citizen."

"What about their duty to their citizenship?" April demanded. "I didn't see them volunteering when we were fighting for our lives."

"They couldn't fight everywhere," Tony replied. "Resources were stretched thin."

"So are ours," April countered. "We have no one to volunteer."

Tony sighed as he sat back in his chair. "Unfortunately, it's not a request. They are asking for two volunteers. If there are none, then the government will choose four individuals."

"So that's why you wanted a list of people," Troy said. He shook his head. "If I had known…"

"That was not the initial reason," Sully said. "But once the government realized the problem was back, they decided to use those lists to cull more recruits."

"How are you going to choose who to take?" Annie asked. "Will you leave us defenseless?"

"We won't choose," Tony said. He looked over at Sully. "We're not even supposed to be here. We came to warn you that it was coming."

"Thanks, I guess," Paul said. "We'll have time to talk to people, see if someone would be willing to go."

"I'll go."

CHAPTER THREE

All eyes turned to Mick.

"What?" Annie gasped. "You can't go, Mick."

He pushed himself off the wall and approached the table. "I can't stay here. Everywhere I look, I expect to see her." He looked over at April. "You're right. Eventually I won't be able to stop. And I'll hurt the only thing I have left of her." His gaze moved to Tony and Sully, sitting stunned at the table. "I'll go and I'll come back when my head is on straight."

"No, Mick. You can't. It's – it's not right."

"Maybe it is, Annie," April said softly. "Maybe this is what he needs to heal."

Annie looked around the room, looking for support. She found none. She looked back at Mick. "What about Josey? You can't leave Josey. She's not even a year old yet."

"You'll take care of her, won't you?" Mick looked around the room. "And you'll have help."

Annie tried one more time. "We need you here."

He smiled sadly. "I haven't been much use to anyone for the past couple months. You guys have been carrying me, I know it and you know it. This will be a chance for me to make things better, make them right." He turned to Tony and Sully, who still hadn't said a word. "Can we leave tomorrow morning? I can find another volunteer."

Tony cleared his throat. "You're supposed to wait for the others to come and make the formal request. We're not even supposed to be here."

Mick shrugged. "So we tell them you stopped by to check on us, mentioned the new threat and we just volunteered on our own." He ran a hand through his too long hair. "Just let me spend one more night with our daughter."

"Of course, Mick." Sully said. He stood and offered a hand to Mick. "Thank you."

Mick shook his hand. "I'd offer you guys to stay with me, but the apartment is way too small."

"Your old apartment is still vacant," Troy said softly.

Mick swallowed hard, forcing the memories down. "OK. I'll meet you guys here at breakfast, OK?" Tony nodded. Mick smiled at the remains of the council, then left the room.

As soon as he was out the door, Annie turned on the rest of the group. "We can't let him go. He's not thinking right. He's been drinking and he's depressed and – and…" She didn't know what else to say to convince them.

"I think he has to go." Bobby spoke for the first time. "I think he needs to. He's lost everything he's ever cared for, except his daughter."

"We've all lost, Bobby," Annie replied.

"But you had how many years with your husband?" Bobby retorted. "Mick had a couple of years with Sarah." His voice broke as he spoke the name of the woman who saved his life. "It's not nearly enough time."

"It's never enough time," Annie said softly. She sighed. "I don't agree with it, but I won't stand in his way."

"No offense, Annie, but I don't think you could."

♦

Mick walked out of Shaun, heading for Bub, where Missy lived. She kept Josey during the day so Mick could do whatever it was he did during the day, which was mostly drink and feel sorry for himself. No more. Despite downing more than half a bottle of whiskey since he left Josey with Missy that morning, he felt completely sober. He was finally doing something meaningful, something Sarah would be proud of.

The streets were empty. While the weather was nice, nobody seemed to want to take advantage of it. They all wanted to hide in their apartments. He blamed himself. He had been a miserable, morose motherfucker. His mood affected the whole town. He needed to get away, if only for the sake of everyone else's happiness.

He bounded up the stairs of Bub and pulled open the lobby door. Without turning on his flashlight, he moved up the four flights of stairs to the third floor. Remembering Sarah – always remembering Sarah – he knocked on Missy's door, waiting to hear her call to him to enter before opening the door and stepping inside.

"Mick!" Missy exclaimed when she saw him. "You're early." She put down the glass she held and walked to him, engulfing him in her embrace. It was a recent development, one he now realized started so she could check him for signs of intoxication. There were some days when he was just on the wrong side of sober and she made him sit and keep her company rather than take Josey right away.

"I'm fine, Missy," he said as he pulled away from her. "I'm not drunk." He smiled to soften the harsh words. "Where's my girl?"

"I'm not…that's not…" She trailed off, wringing her hands.

"It's OK, Missy. I understand. But I'm fine. Where's Josey?"

"I just put her in for a nap, but she's probably not sleeping yet. Let me go get her."

Missy left the living room to the second bedroom. She had cribs and toddler beds there, hoping that eventually her daycare would fill up. Right now, she only had two: her son, Louis, and Josey. The other children attended the rudimentary school that was taught by Dominic and Lucy with help from Christa. Missy had decorated the rooms with kids in mind, lots of bright colors and animals, nothing dangerous in the reach of small inquisitive hands. Mick felt Josey was safer here than anywhere else in town. Including with himself.

"Here she is!" Missy said brightly, carrying his daughter in her arms. Josephine Ryan Cooke was a bit sleepy eyed, but she perked up as soon as she saw Mick.

"Da!" She squealed, holding out her arms.

"Josey girl!" He reached for his daughter, cradling her in his arms, smelling her unique scent.

"Mama?" Josey asked, looking around. She had first said "Mama" on the day that Sarah had died. The first and only time that Sarah had heard it. Even three months later, she still asked for her, only the requests were getting further and further apart. Soon, she wouldn't even remember.

"No mama, sweetie. Just me." Mick kissed her bright red curls, forcing the pain down deep. "Are you ready to go?"

"Go! Go!" She squirmed in his arms and he knew she wanted down. She had just found her legs and was eager to walk.

"In a minute, sweetie." He turned to Missy. "Thanks for taking care of her, Missy. You've been a great friend."

"Of course. She's a doll." She looked hard at Mick. "Wait. You're not thinking of doing something stupid, are you? I won't let you out of here with her."

Mick laughed. "I've already done it, I think. I'm just going to spend the day with my best girl."

"Are you sure you're okay, Mick?"

He smiled sadly. "I'm better, Missy. I think it'll be awhile before I'm okay."

CHAPTER FOUR

Mick gathered Josey's things and carried her and the bag carefully downstairs. Josey knew they were headed outside and she would be able to stretch her legs. As soon as they hit the outside, she said "Down! Down!"

With a smile, he set her on the sidewalk, holding her hand as they walked slowly towards the market. He needed to get something for dinner, plus some supplies for his trip. She babbled happily and he responded in kind, even though he only understood 2 out of 5 words. She'd probably be talking in whole sentences by the time he came back. If he came back.

He shook his head of the morbid thoughts as he entered the market. Troy looked up from his desk, formerly the customer service counter. "Thought you might be by," he said.

"I need something for dinner for me and Josey and some supplies for the trip." He lifted Josey onto the counter and she reached for Troy.

Troy gathered the child in his arms and she immediately started tugging on his dark beard. "You'd think she'd grow out of that," he winced as she pulled particularly hard.

Mick laughed. "She's grown out of it for everyone but you." He moved the aisle where the preserved vegetables were kept. He marked his initials on the sheet that logged all of their produce. Once Sarah's job, it was now Annie's to determine what was needed based on the inventory logs. "What do we have that I can take with me?"

"You're determined to go?" Troy asked.

"I think I have to, Troy."

He looked at Mick's face, the pain that had been there for months. "I understand." Keeping a hand on Josey, he bent down and pulled a pack from the floor. "I've already packed this. Deer jerky, some dried fruits and vegetables and water. Should keep you for a bit." He slid the pack over the counter towards Mick.

"Can we afford to lose this much?" Mick asked as he looked at the bounty of food in the bag.

"We're good. We won't starve."

"Thanks, Troy. I really appreciate this." Mick held out his hand and Troy took it.

"Just come back, man."

♦

Mick and Josey had a quiet dinner of peas and potatoes, as quiet as it could be with a chattering toddler. Josey had a fondness for potatoes. They were lucky that she was already eating most solid foods before Sarah died. There was no longer a substitute for breast milk.

He took it all in, all her words and motions, her kisses and hugs. He would need it to sustain him for however long he was gone. He was wiping the peas from her face when there was a knock at his door. He gathered Josey in his arms and opened the door.

Donna stood there, wringing her hands. "It's not true, is it?" She asked. "You're not leaving, are you?" Her voice broke.

News travels fast, he thought. "Yes, I am."

Donna started to cry. "You can't go. You have to stay. What are we going to do without you?" Mick motioned her inside and shut the door. Josey, oblivious to the tension in the room, reached for Donna.

Mick let Donna take Josey. She held the girl tight, burying her head in Josey's curls. "I have to go, Donna. I'm afraid if I stay here, I'll go insane."

"We all miss her, Mick, but I know that nobody misses her as much as you." She bit her lip. "I never had a chance to repay her, for what she did for me."

"You repaid her and then some, Donna. You saved her from being raped. You became her sister." But Sarah had never thought she had done enough for Donna, the woman who was choked and raped in her place. She was always looking for ways to make it up to her.

Donna took a deep breath and looked Mick in the eyes. "What do you need from me? Food? Someone to take care of Josey? Whatever you need, Mick."

He smiled softly. "Could you sit with her while I get a shower? I probably won't have a chance again anytime soon."

"Of course."

Mick grabbed a change of clothes and some toiletries. He gave Josey a quick kiss on the top of her head before he left. He headed to Shaun, hoping the shower was free. He needed a fresh start.

His luck was in. The shower was empty. He showered quickly. What took the longest was shaving the beard he had accumulated since Sarah had died. He removed the excess hair in the shower, without a mirror, hoping he didn't screw it up too bad. When he finished and stepped out of the shower, he wrapped himself in a towel and headed to the mirror. "Not bad," he said to himself as he took in the slightly lopsided goatee. He cleaned it up in front of the sink until he looked almost like he had before. Just the hints of grey and pain in his eyes were different.

Donna smiled when she saw him. "Now you look like you."

Mick laughed. "It was past time."

"Will you come to the cafeteria? There are a lot of people who'd like to see you."

He shook his head. "I'd rather not. I just want to spend time with Josey."

She nodded. "I understand. I'll get out of your hair." She kissed Josey's cheek and got up from the floor where they had been playing. "Take care of yourself, Mick. Don't take stupid chances."

Exactly what Sarah used to say to him. He smiled sadly. "I won't."

♦

After Donna took her leave, Mick and Josey played games and read books, Mick trying to gather as much of her in as possible. He knew that he should stay for her, but he feared that if he did, he would do her more harm than good. He was getting her into her pajamas when there was another knock on the door. With a heavy sigh, he lifted her into his arms and opened the door. It was Tom, one of the refugees from Kittington. He was in his fifties, but still fit.

"I want to go with you," Tom said, not even bothering with a greeting.

Josey didn't want to be stationary, she wanted down. She squirmed in Mick's arms. "Come on in," Mick said as he set Josey on the floor. He closed the door behind Tom.

"Can I go with you?"

"Why?" Mick barely knew Tom, mostly just to make small talk. He used to seek out the new people, learn as much as he could about them. Since Sarah's death, he stayed within a select group of people, barely interacting even with them.

"I don't feel welcome here," Tom said. "Ever since what George and Chad did, everyone looks at me funny. Like I was part of it."

"But you weren't. It was them and George's wife and Chris. You warned us that George would be trouble."

Tom shrugged. "Maybe because I came here with them. I don't know. I just know that people barely talk to me; most avoid me."

Mick felt a twinge of guilt. If he would have sought him out, he would have shown people that he was a good guy. He knew he was a good guy. He remembered how he had cared for the women of Kittington. "I'm sorry, Tom."

"It's not your fault. You've always been good to me, but the others?" He shrugged again. "I heard they were looking for two volunteers and I want to be the second."

Mick leaned against the door. "You realize we may not be coming back." The words struck something inside him. He looked over at his daughter, babbling to the doll Sully had given her months before.

"At least I'll be doing something, with people who'll talk to me."

Mick nodded. "OK. We're leaving tomorrow morning. Head to the market and tell Troy you're coming with me. See what he has for you to take. Then get a good night's sleep."

Tom held out a hand. "Thanks, Mick."

"Don't thank me." Mick shook his hand. "I'll see you tomorrow."

♦

After Mick got Josey settled in her bassinet for the night – she would need a bigger bed soon – he decided to pack some clothes for his journey. He went to the closet where he shoved the few things he brought from the other apartment. As he was reaching for his backpack, he saw Sarah's shoved in the corner. He pulled it out and sat on the floor with it in his lap. He ran his hands over the fabric, remembering how the pack accumulated each and every stain and tear. With a lump in his throat, he opened the pack and turned it over, dumping the contents on the floor.

There was her hand sanitizer. Her pack of tissues. Her plastic bag of matches. A bottle of water. An antiquated box of raisins. Her zippo lighter. A bag full of bandages. A long-sleeved tee shirt. Under the shirt was a small piece of plastic that didn't look familiar. He picked it up and flipped it over to see a younger version of Sarah. It was her old college ID. She must have dumped it in the bottom of the bag in the early days and never bothered to throw it away. He stared at the laminated picture, wiping away each tear as it fell on the face of the woman he still loved.

CHAPTER FIVE

Since Sarah's death, Mick had barely slept at night. The only time he had managed more than a couple hours was when he drank a bottle and a half of whiskey and passed out, only rousing when Bobby and Paul came to check on him. Missy kept Josey that night, not letting Mick see her until he could prove he was sober.

On the night when he needed sleep the most, it was no different. He slept in fitful stretches of minutes at a time, waking constantly during the night to check on Josey, fearful that someone was hovering over her bassinet. He woke up gasping, seeing Sarah's ashen face as she lost her life's blood. He would start to doze, then second guess his decision to go with Tony and Sully and spend the next hour worrying about his choice.

He managed less than three hours of sleep. When Josey awoke at 6:30, he was right there with her, eyes wide open, staring at the ceiling. He turned on the battery-operated lamp on the nightstand and got out of bed before she could start to cry. "Be right there, Josey," he said to her as he headed into the bathroom.

When he finished, he came back out, smiling as Josey held onto the side of the bassinet and bounced up and down, eager to get out for the day. He picked her up, lifting her high in the air just to hear her giggle. He changed her diaper, put fresh clothes on her then, propping her on one hip, he picked up the lamp and headed into the living room. He set her in the play pen, leaving the light close. "Hang on a minute while I change, then we'll go get something to eat." She clapped her hands, delighted at the idea of food.

He went back into the bedroom and changed from his sleep pants and tee to a pair of jeans, another tee and a flannel shirt. He sat down on the bed and put on his boots, looking over at Sarah's sitting beside what should have been her side of the bed. Taking a deep breath, he stood and went to the closet, pulling a quilted hoodie from a hanger and shrugging it on. Then he picked up Sarah's backpack that he had filled with the supplies Troy had given him, clothing and ammo and a few other essential items the night before. He looked around the room, then headed back out to Josey. "Let's go get some food, Josey."

♦

As early as it was, the cafeteria was mostly empty. The only people there were the members of the council and Tony and Sully, all sitting around a table. He walked in with Josey on his hip and she clapped happily to see her "family."

"Come to me, Josey," Annie said, reaching for the girl. Josey immediately went to her. "I like the new you," she said to Mick.

"Not a new me, just a different me." He sat at the table across from Tony and Sully. "Tom is going to join us. He volunteered last night."

Tony nodded. "Did you get some sleep last night? You look like sh – crap." His eyes cut over to Josey, babbling happily to Annie.

Mick laughed. "I don't sleep anymore." He looked closer at the Marines. "What about you guys? You don't look so hot."

Tony grimaced. Sleeping in Mick and Sarah's former apartment wasn't the best idea. Once he and Sully saw the carpet in the bedroom, a three-foot square of pile markedly cleaner than the rest, neither of them got much sleep. "We slept enough."

Mick snorted. "At least I'm not the only one."

Donna walked in, carrying a tray covered in plates. Behind her was Candi, one of the women from Kittington. She also carried a tray full of plates. "I made a good meal to get you started, Mick," Donna said, placing a plate in front of him and a smaller plate next to it. Each plate held pork, a small helping of scrambled eggs, tomatoes, peas and pears.

"Donna, you didn't need to do this," he said. "You need to feed nearly fifty people once we leave."

Donna and Candi set plates in front of everyone else. "Yes, Mick, I did. You eat all of that, now." She smiled sadly at him before she left the room, Candi on her heels.

Mick shook his head, then gestured to Annie. "Give her over, I'll feed her."

"I can handle her, Mick," Annie said. Josey was already reaching for Annie's plate.

"I have a plate here for her and besides, I need to do it."

Annie nodded and passed Josey across the table. Mick sat her on his knee and began to feed her, taking a bite for himself in between. The door opened and Tom walked in, a pack on his back and a rifle in his hand.

"Have a seat and some breakfast," Mick said. Warily, Tom set his rifle in the corner and shrugged off his pack. He sat at the end of the table, next to Bobby, who slid a plate in front of him.

They made small talk throughout the meal, nobody mentioning why they were together or what would happen after they finished. Tom even made conversation with Bobby and Paul, feeling a little less awkward, but still eager to get out of town. When every plate was clean, Tony and Sully stood. "That was very good, Donna," Sully said to the woman who entered after everyone had started eating.

She smiled and ducked her head. "It wasn't much but thank you."

Tony nodded to Mick. "We should go."

Mick looked down at Josey, now full, resting against his chest. He stood slowly and turned to Paul. "I'm going to need some weapons and my knife." When his drinking started to get out of hand, Paul quietly removed all of the firearms from the apartment, along with the knife Mick used to carry. He now retrieved a large black duffel bag on the floor against the wall. Mick kissed the top of Josey's head, then said, "Daddy has to go away for a while, but I'll be back soon. You listen to Annie and April and everyone, OK? I'll be back as soon as I can, Josey girl." He kissed her again, then handed her to April before he started to cry.

Paul set the bag on the table and opened it. He began to pull handguns from inside and laid them on the table. His old Colt .45, a 9mm, a second 9mm. "I want that one," Mick said softly, ignoring the rest of the handguns inside the duffel. It was the gun they had taken from his neighbor's apartment all those years ago, the one Sarah had carried. Paul drew out a box of ammo and Mick popped the magazine on the gun. He slowly loaded it, remembering when he showed Sarah how to load it, how to use the safety. How his brother Ryan yelled at both of them. Once he loaded the magazine, he smacked it home, then slid it into the holster Paul had placed in front of him. He snapped the holster on his belt. His knife was next, shoved into the sheath already on his belt. His final weapon was a shotgun, the string Sarah had threaded through the trigger guard still intact. He fingered the string, smiling sadly. Without a word, he put the string around his neck and slid his arm through, the shotgun falling to rest by his hand. Paul silently slid extra ammo towards Mick. He gathered it and put it into one of the pockets of the backpack.

"I just need to grab a poker and I'm ready to go."

"We'll get it on the way to the gate," April said, standing with Josey in her arms.

"No, she stays here. I already said my goodbye." He reached in his back pocket and pulled out two pieces of plastic. He looked down at the top one, rubbing his thumb over the surface. "Show her these every so often, so she doesn't forget." He handed the pieces of plastic to Annie: Sarah's school ID on top and his old driver's license underneath.

"We will." Annie blinked back tears. "Be safe, Mick. Come back."

He didn't trust his voice. He nodded. He shook hands with the rest of the council, getting a hug instead from Troy. "Don't be stupid out there," Troy murmured in his ear. "I don't want to have to come looking for you." Mick had to laugh. Troy hadn't been out of town since they brought him in.

"Thanks, guys. Take care of my girl, OK?" Mick looked at Josey one more time before he left the cafeteria, Tony and Sully on his heels, Tom behind them. When he heard her soft voice say "Da?" he hesitated, but he took the next step. Then another.

♦

A small supply of melee weapons was kept at every building that was in use, one of Sarah's ideas. Even though the last breach was three months prior, and a result of George's sabotage, weapons were kept at hand just in case. Most people felt safe behind the barricades. Many never went beyond them.

Mick pulled a poker from the dust covered supply on the first floor. He stuck the tool through a loop at the bottom of his backpack. The metal brushed his thigh a few times while he was walking, a feeling that he would have to get used to again.

The four of them walked through the quiet town towards the North gate. Mick thought he had escaped without incident when he heard his name from behind accompanied by the sound of running feet. He turned and saw Mikey racing after them. He stopped, waiting for the boy to catch up.

At ten, Mikey was tall for his age. It seemed he grew a couple inches every week. At the rate he was growing, he would pass his brother, Jack. But now, he was still a little kid, his nose red, his cheeks streaked with tears. "You're leaving?" He asked once he reached Mick, his chest heaving from his run.

"I'll be back, Mikey."

"I don't want you to go." Mikey swiped a hand under his nose. "You should stay here, with us."

Mick smiled painfully. "I'll be back before you know it. I just need to go out and make sure things are safe."

"Promise you'll be back." Mick saw the glint of tears in his eyes.

"I promise I'll do my best to get back. You help look after Josey, OK?" Mikey nodded. Mick gave in to impulse and ruffled his dark hair. "I'll see you soon, buddy."

Mick turned and started walking, the sound of Mikey's sobs ringing in his ears.

The group of four made it across town to the North Gate without any other interruptions. Mick waved at Ben, who was on gate duty. "Can you lock up after us?"

Ben gave one quick nod. He turned away, heading across the roof to the fire escape.

Mick smiled. Typical Ben. He unlocked the door leading into the bus, hanging the lock in the hasp before following Sully, Tony and Tom through the bus. Sully had already unlocked the other door by the time Mick got there. They slipped through, closing the door behind them.

The horses nickered when they saw Sully and Tony. "You have horses?" Tom asked, walking to the animals.

Tony and Sully had checked on their mounts before they turned in for the night and first thing that morning. They could tell the animals were itching to get moving. "Yes, we still have a few mounts left." Tony walked to his horse, rubbing his side as he passed.

"Beautiful," Tom breathed as he stroked the horse's flank.

"Beautiful? You're crazy," Mick said

Sully laughed. "So I guess you're not going to ride?"

"Hell no. I had enough of that before, when we…" He trailed off, thinking of that trip with Sarah, when they went to Kittington.

Tony cleared his throat. "We'll walk them slow; you can just walk with us." He looked up at the sky. "For a while, at least."

"Tom, you want to ride?" Sully asked. "I can walk."

"Really?" His eyes lit up like a kid at Christmas. "I haven't ridden in years. I used to work on a small ranch and riding was my favorite part of the job."

Sully nodded. "Have at it." He moved to his saddlebags, where he shoved his dirty clothes. While the shower this morning was only lukewarm, it was still nice to be clean. Thornville was the only stop on their route where they could actually shower.

Mick looked around as Tony and Sully got their horses ready. He hadn't been outside in months. Nothing much had changed. There were still weeds growing up the center of the road, cracking through the asphalt. There were still the same abandoned buildings, slowly decaying after years of neglect. There were still the same trees, the leaves barely in bloom. Despite how everything had changed for him, the world stayed the same.

"You ready?" Sully asked.

Mick directed his attention to the soldier. “As I’ll ever be.”

CHAPTER SIX

The foursome started along the asphalt road, avoiding large potholes and weaving around the small trees that had sprouted over the years. Sully and Mick walked at their own pace as Tony and Tom rode ahead. The only downside was dodging piles of horse shit.

"Is that a bow on the back of Tony's horse?" Mick asked.

"Yeah, we're conserving ammo. Anyone who shows any aptitude for the bow gets one." Sully's eyes never stopped moving, checking their perimeter, looking for trouble.

"And you don't have one?" Mick asked with a smile.

"Like I said, you gotta show some aptitude. I couldn't hit the broad side of a barn with the damn thing."

Mick laughed. "Do they work? Can he really hit one in the head with it?"

"Yeah, but it's better when he can be prepared. Trying to pull it out, pull the string, load the arrow, it takes time. We mostly use it for food."

They walked a bit further, then Mick asked: "Where are we headed?"

"We have to make one more stop, then we'll head to our base."

"I thought we were the only community left in this area."

"The only community of any size," Sully answered. "The place we're stopping has only about five or six people."

"And you have to take two people from them?" Mick shook his head. "It doesn't seem fair."

"It's not. Our plan is to let them know, tell them to scatter." Sully glanced at Mick. "We thought maybe they could go to Thornville."

Mick stopped and looked at Sully. "Yeah, because it went so well with the last group that joined us."

Sully stopped. "This group isn't like them. They wouldn't cause problems."

"Famous last words." Mick shook his head and started walking again.

"Mick, they have to go somewhere. If they're still there when the orders come for volunteers, they'll lose two and they can't spare them."

Mick shrugged. "I don't care. I don't want them in Thornville. I can't lose anyone else."

They walked in silence for a good while. Then Sully asked: "How did you meet her?"

Mick smiled at the memory. "It was early on. She was with my brother and they were looking for me. I was holed up in my neighbor's apartment and Ryan bashed his way in. I flew out of there with a butcher knife, thinking it was a zombie." He smiled again, seeing Sarah up against the wall, her arms in front of her face, the first words she spoke to him. "She never let me forget it."

The smile faded as it hit him again that she would never tease him about their first meeting. She would never again tell him not to take stupid chances. She would never see their daughter walk. He felt the burning behind his eyes and he blinked rapidly. He wanted a drink.

Sully sensed his change in mood. He cleared his throat and asked, "What did you do before all this?"

"What?" Mick asked, his voice hoarse with unshed tears.

"Before this shit storm. What did you do?"

Mick blinked and cleared his throat. "I – I played guitar. I was in a band."

"Seriously?" Sully turned to look at Mick. "What kind of band? Were you famous?"

Mick laughed. "No, we weren't famous. We were just a bar band, but we were good. Played covers, some original shit. What about you? Were you in the Marines before this?"

"Yeah, I enlisted right out of high school. The plan was to stay in for one hitch, get out and go to college, paid for by Uncle Sam." Sully shrugged. "Turned out, I loved it. So I reupped, even though my girlfriend wasn't too happy about it."

"She dump you?"

Sully laughed. "No. She married me. I looked damn good in my dress blues, but she was so beautiful, she put me to shame. We had six good years together."

Mick knew the answer, but he had to ask. "What happened?"

"She died early on. She was pregnant with our first child. A daughter."

"Shit, I'm sorry."

Sully shrugged, but the pain on his face negated the simple gesture. "Take care of your girl, Mick. You don't know how precious she is."

Mick nodded. "Yes, I do. That's why I'm out here. I have to get back to who I was, someone Sarah could count on."

"I think you're still that man, Mick."

♦

They walked for hours, with only one brief break to have some lunch. As they walked through what used to be the business section of a small town, Mick was almost ready to get back on the dreaded horse when Tony pulled his horse around to where Sully and Mick were. "They're just up ahead," he said. He looked down at Mick. "They're skittish, so let us go ahead with the horses and you and Sully can follow behind."

"Do you want me to get down?" Tom asked. "Sully can ride in."

"No, this will be fine." Tony nudged his horse back around and they continued down the road.

"What does he mean, skittish?" Mick asked.

"Took them a while to warm up to us." Sully smiled at Mick. "Not quite as bad as when we first went to Thornville, but close."

"We really wouldn't have shot you guys, you know." He let a grin creep over his face.

Sully laughed. "I know that now, but damn, you guys were both pretty formidable."

They stopped in front of what was once a small bank. Tony slipped down from his horse and tied the reins to a parking meter. After a minute, Tom did the same. He then moved back to stand with Mick while Sully went to stand with Tony.

Tony stepped forward and banged twice on the door. "Danny! It's Tony and Sully!"

A few minutes went by. Tony looked at Sully, then banged on the door again. "Danny!"

No response. Sully undid the strap on his holster. Mick watched as Tony did the same. "Do you need our help?" he asked.

"No, we're good." Tony put a hand on the door knob and the door flew open. He stepped back quickly.

"Danny's dead." A skinny woman came out, her blonde hair short and choppy, like she took a pair of scissors and made random cuts.

"What happened?" Tony asked.

"He went out for supplies, got bit." She looked warily at Mick and Tom. "Who're they?"

"Mick and Tom, from a settlement down the road."

The woman turned back to Tony. "We don't have food; they can't stay."

"They're not," Tony said. "They're with us. We're going back to base."

"Guess you should come in, then. You're letting what little heat we have out." She turned and headed back in the door. Tony and Sully motioned for the civilians to follow as they walked into the building.

The lobby was strewn with dirt and old paper. Mick looked a little closer and saw that some of the paper was actually money – dollar bills, tens, twenties. He even saw a few hundred-dollar bills. He shook his head as he brought up the rear, everyone following the blonde woman around the counter to the back of the building.

They had turned the conference room into their all-purpose area. The conference table was in pieces in the corner. The middle of the room held blankets and sleeping bags. Against the wall were boxes half filled with canned food. Mick saw five people huddled together on the floor. He bit back a curse when they looked up at the newcomers. Three of them were kids. The fourth was a woman about his age, the fifth an old man.

"So why are you here? With these guys?" The blonde asked.

"The government is looking for volunteers to help fight."

The woman barked out a short laugh. "And they were stupid enough to agree to that?"

"It was either that or the government coming and taking four people."

Her jaw dropped as she looked at Sully. "Are you kidding?"

"No, ma'am. Two volunteers from every settlement or the government takes four."

"What the fuck am I supposed to do?" She ran her hands thru her short choppy hair. "I can't spare two people and I sure as shit can't afford four."

"You need to move," Tony said. "If they can't find you, they can't make you serve."

"And go where?" She directed a hand toward the door. "There's nothing out there. We're lucky we have this place." Her hand dropped and her shoulders sagged. "We can't go back out there."

"Jess, you don't have a choice," Sully said softly.

"They can go to Thornville," Mick said. Tony and Sully turned to look at him. "There's room."

"I thought you didn't –" Sully started, but Mick cut him off.

"I changed my mind." He looked at the woman, Jess. "Do you have a piece of paper and a pen?"

"I – yeah, hold on." She left the room and came back a few moments later with a strip of paper and a pen. She handed them to Mick.

He could see it was a withdrawal slip from the bank. He motioned for Tom to turn around and put the slip on his back. He turned the paper to the blank side and scrawled a short note along with a map. He walked over to Jess. "There's a map there. When you get to the gate, ask for Annie and give that to her." He handed her the note.

"You're letting us into your community? Why?" She clutched the note tightly.

He smiled slightly. "My wife liked strays."

CHAPTER SEVEN

They helped Jess and her group get their meager belongings packed for the trip. It amounted to two backpacks, carried by the women. The old man was too frail. Mick wasn't sure if he would make it to Thornville.

"We didn't see any on the way here," Sully said. "But keep your eyes open."

Jess nodded. "We'll keep watch."

They stood in front of the bank. Jess turned to Mick. "Thank you for this."

Mick shrugged. He hoped he was doing the right thing. He wasn't crazy about doing it, so that probably made it right. "We should get moving," he said to Tony.

"He's right." Tony looked at Jess. "Take your time, but don't dawdle. You don't want to be out here at night."

"I know, I know." She adjusted the pack on her back. She carried a piece of rebar in her gloved hand. "Thanks, guys." She turned and started walking, her group trailing behind her.

"That was a good thing, Mick." Sully clapped him on the back.

"I just hope it wasn't a mistake."

They resumed their trek. Tony and Tom rode while Sully and Mick brought up the rear. "We'll go a few more hours, then we'll stop for the night," Sully said.

"Your camp is that far off?"

"Settlements are few and far between. We have a large area to cover." Sully readjusted the rifle slung over his shoulder. "And there's not a lot of us anymore. People getting killed, deserting. So it's going to be even worse."

Mick laughed. "Thanks for letting me know earlier. I might have thought twice about volunteering."

Sully smiled sadly. "No, I think you would still be here."

♦

The walk was monotonous. The scenery barely changed – an abandoned house here, a burned out building there. Sully and Mick ran out of things to say. Mick was glad. He was breathing heavy from the exertion, every step felt like he was slogging through mud. The months of doing nothing but drinking were finally catching up to him. He just kept his eyes on his feet, watching each step, hoping that he could make the next.

"Mick!"

His head snapped up at Sully's call, seeing the zombie only four feet away. From the corner of his eye, he saw two more heading towards the soldier. Mick reached back, fumbling with the poker hanging from his pack as the zombie inched closer, its groans getting louder as it saw the food almost within its grasp. He backed up, switching to the clasp holding his knife to his belt. He finally freed the weapon, the zombie less than an arm's length away. Mick brought up the knife and pushed it down through the zombie's eye, drilling to the brain. The creature dropped at his feet, the knife remaining in his hand, gore dripping down the blade.

He turned quickly to see Sully dispatching the second of his two zombies, the first sprawled at his feet, its head a bloodied mess from where his machete chopped through. Sully looked over at Mick as the creature fell, seeing Mick's heaving chest, the sweat covering his brow. "You okay?"

Mick swallowed and nodded. "Fine," he rasped.

Sully shook the gore from his blade then slid it into the sheath clipped to his belt. He moved closer to Mick and whispered, "You in withdrawal?"

Mick shook his head furiously. "No. No!" He ran a hand over his sweaty face. "I'm just out of shape. I haven't done anything but sit on my ass and feel sorry for myself for months. I'll get it back."

"Don't hide it if you are. It'll just make shit worse."

The sound of the hoofbeats saved Mick from responding. "What happened?" Tony asked as he stopped his horse.

"They must have heard you going by, then stumbled out to find us," Sully said. He looked off the road, down the path the zombies had come from. "I don't see anymore."

Tony looked down at Mick. "You okay?"

Mick nodded. "Peachy. We stopping anytime soon?"

"Couple more miles. You want to ride?"

"Hell, no. Let's just get going."

Ten long miles later, just about an hour before dark, they reached an abandoned garage. Sully banged on the man-sized door and waited. When he heard no sounds from within, he opened the door and disappeared inside. A minute later, the garage door opened. Tony rode his horse inside with Tom following. Mick slowly brought up the rear.

He wanted nothing more than to collapse on the floor and sleep, but he knew there were things to be done to make the garage safe for the night. He looked around and saw that the space was clear, with the floor towards the back covered in straw and dead grass. Tony dismounted from his horse and led him to the back of the building. "Bring him over here, Tom," he said as he tied his horse to the leg of a work table. Tom led his horse to where Tony indicated.

Mick turned to Sully. "Is this an outpost or something?"

"Something like that. We usually break for the night here, unless we're too far away." Sully shrugged out of his pack. "Get comfortable. Firepit is over there." He pointed towards the front of the garage. "I'll round up something to eat if you can get a fire started." He headed to white cabinets mounted on the wall, now dingy and dusty with age. When he opened them, Mick saw food, water and other supplies stacked on the shelves.

"You leave your stuff here?"

"Why not?" Sully said as he pulled down four MREs. "We don't have to carry it and if someone comes by that needs it, they're more than welcome to it." He looked over his shoulder at Mick. "That's part of what we're supposed to do, help people."

Mick looked away. After Kittington, he didn't care to help anyone. But yet he did. Sarah still influenced his every action. He went silently to the fire pit and began crumbling the magazine pages that had been left there. He layered the kindling, then added a few slightly larger pieces. He slipped the pack from his back and dug inside for Sarah's Zippo. The paper went up immediately, tendrils of fire licking over the kindling before that caught. He added a few more pieces until he was sure the fire was going. His eyes followed the smoke up to a hole in the roof. They wouldn't be choking on the smoke all night.

"Thanks, Mick," Tony said as he came over, slapping him on the back. "Feels good."

"Yeah." Mick hadn't been cold; the hours of walking warmed him up. But as soon as he felt the heat from the fire, a chill settled in. He moved closer, warming his gloved hands over the flames.

"Why don't you sit down?" Sully said as he walked to the firepit. His hands were full of MREs. "You look like you're ready to drop."

"It was a lot of walking," Mick said.

"So take a load off. There's a bench against that wall if you want to slide it over."

Mick took an end of the bench and began to slide it across the concrete floor. Tom grabbed the other end and they carried it next to the fire. By the time they had it in place, Sully had placed a grate on the fire. He handed an MRE to Mick and Tom. Mick nodded his thanks as he took a few steps to his pack, picked it up with his other hand, then sat on the bench with a groan.

"Maybe next time you'll get on the horse," Tony laughed as he set an old-fashioned percolator on the grate.

"Is that coffee?" Tom asked eagerly.

"We can have a cup tonight and one tomorrow and that's it, the last of it," Tony said, using a poker to move the wood under the grate. "There should be more at camp. At least there was when we left."

"We save ours for special occasions," Mick said. "We haven't been finding much lately."

"Yeah, the last time we had coffee was…" Tom trailed off when he realized what he was saying. He looked at Mick, horror in his eyes.

"Sarah's funeral," Mick said softly.

"I'm sorry, Mick, I didn't think."

Mick shook his head. "It's OK, Tom. You can't watch everything you say." He looked around the fire. "Excuse me." He set his MRE on the bench, stood and walked away, towards the doors. He slipped out of the man-sized door, closing it gently behind him.

"I'm sorry," Tom said to the men around the fire.

Sully tore open his MRE. "There's nothing to be sorry for, Tom," he said. "Mick's right, we can't police everything we say. He's in a bad place and he's the only one that can get back out. We can help him, but he has to do it himself." He sighed. "Sarah was an exceptional woman. Hell, an exceptional person. It's going to take a while to get over her."

"I remember the first time I met her," Tom said, shifting on the bench. "Well, the first time I talked to her. I had seen her around when she visited Kittington, but I didn't talk to her until she came down the last time." He shook his head. "She was so petite, but damn, she had fire in her. I thought she was going to go and yank all the girls out right then."

"First time we saw her, she was on the wall, pregnant." Tony watched the coffee pot start to percolate. "We asked to see the leader of the group and she never let on it was her. Our fault, really, we just assumed it would be a man." Tony smiled. "She fooled us."

"And then she pulled a gun on us." Sully laughed. "She was fearless."

"And that was her problem," Mick said softly. He had walked back in after collecting himself to hear the end of Tom's words. "She did whatever she thought was right, no matter what the cost. And that's why I loved her. Why I still love her." He sighed and sat back on the bench.

Dinner was a quiet affair, the various MREs consumed and washed down with Tony's coffee. Mick pulled some of the dried fruit from his pack and passed it around for dessert. Tom volunteered to clean the dishes while Mick helped Tony and Sully set up bed rolls around the fire from the supplies they had left stocked.

"We should be at the base tomorrow afternoon, if we leave at first light," Tony said. "Mick, you and Tom should get some sleep. Sully and I will keep watch tonight."

Mick shook his head. "I can take watch."

"You've been walking all day. You have to be exhausted."

"I am, but I don't sleep much. Let me take first shift." Mick spread out the sleeping bag on the garage floor.

"Mick, it's our job."

"I get that, Tony. But I'll be up anyway. Why don't you just sleep?"

Tony looked at Sully, who shrugged. "Fine," he said to Mick. "Three hours and one of us will take over."

"Thanks."

"Why are you thanking me?" Tony asked.

Mick paused a moment. "I don't really know. Maybe for trusting me."

"We do trust you, Mick," Sully said. "We always have."

"Well, except for that one time…" Tony laughed.

Mick laughed. "Hell, I wouldn't have trusted me then, either. Go get some sleep."

"You want me to stay up with you?" Tom asked as he stood up.

Mick shook his head. "Nah, you get some sleep. I'll be fine."

"I'm sorry about earlier. I need to watch what I say."

Mick shook his head again. "No, Tom. You need to just say what you want. I need to learn to deal with it." He clapped Tom on the back. "Get some sleep. I'll see you in the morning."

It took another fifteen minutes, but soon the three men were wrapped in the sleeping bags, settled around the fire. Mick sat on the bench, staring into the flames. Damn, he really wanted a drink now. He hadn't faced a night without it since she had died. He sighed softly. He had to get his shit together. He had to learn how to live without her without the crutch of alcohol. He had to learn to live without her. Period.

CHAPTER EIGHT

The morning dawned cold and overcast. Mick managed about two hours of sleep after Tony had taken over watch. He didn't expect even that much. He felt sluggish but that was nothing new. He just needed to push past it.

They washed down some canned pears with the last of the coffee. Mick doused the fire as Tom rolled the sleeping bags and stored them back in the cabinet. Sully led the horses outside and since Tony drew the short straw, he cleaned up their droppings from the night. They were ready to go a half hour after the sun had risen.

"You sure you don't want to ride?" Tony asked Mick.

"Absolutely." He mock shuddered. "I don't want to be near that beast."

Sully laughed. "You and Tom can ride; I'll walk with Mick."

"No, I'll walk," Tom said. "I rode all day yesterday."

"You sure, Tom?"

"It's not much further, right? Besides, I should stretch my legs."

"OK." Sully and Tony mounted up, then led the horses away from the garage. Mick and Tom followed.

Mick and Tom talked at first, about little inconsequential things, nothing important, just trivial matters from the past. But after about an hour, the conversation waned and they just walked through the gloomy morning. Mick barely noticed the snowflakes that began to fall; he just pulled his hood up and kept trudging forward.

With nothing more than a quick break around lunch time for some beef jerky, they walked for hours. About eight hours after they left the garage, Mick spotted something off in the distance. He picked up his pace and moved between Tony and Sully. "Is that it?" he asked, his voice raspy from the cold.

"Yeah, we're about 20 minutes out," Tony said. "You doing OK?" He looked down at the man, bundled in a hooded fleece jacket, his hands jammed in his pockets, snowflakes stuck in his goatee.

"Fine." Mick slowed his pace to allow Tom to catch up. "We'll be there in about 20 minutes, Tony said."

Tom nodded. "Thank God. My balls are about frozen off here."

Mick chuckled. "Left mine about an hour down the road."

Mick nearly cried with relief when they approached the gates. They were solid, attached to what looked like shipping containers acting as walls. A uniformed man on top of the wall waved at Tony and Sully, then motioned to someone below him. The gates slowly started to open. Tony and Sully rode the horses in, Tom and Mick right behind them. The gates had barely opened enough to let them through before they shut again.

Tony and Sully dismounted, handing the reins to a young soldier who had run up to them, his fatigues too large for his skinny body. Another soldier approached, a clipboard in hand. "'Bout time you made it back," he said, holding out a hand for first Tony, then Sully.

"It's a big territory," Tony said.

"You'd know that if you ever left these walls," Sully added.

"Fuck that, I was out there enough." He looked over at Mick and Tom. "Who're these guys?"

"Vic, this is Mick and Tom, from Thornville. When we stopped to check on them, we told them about the problem and they volunteered to come help." Tony turned to Mick and Tom. "This is Sgt. Victor Bender."

Vic looked at Tony, then back at Mick and Tom. "They volunteered?" He laughed. "What a pair of dumb fucks. No one volunteers for this shit."

"We just want to help," Mick said.

"And you can't do that where you were?" Vic saw something in Mick's face. "OK, then." He turned back to Tony. "Major isn't going to be happy."

"He'll get over it."

"I'll need their weapons."

Mick looked at Tony. "I'll get these back? They were Sarah's."

Tony nodded. "You'll get them back."

Slowly, Mick took the shotgun from around his neck and handed it to Bender. He watched as Bender put it in a metal footlocker. He unsnapped the holster from his belt and handed it, gun included, to Bender. He started to unstrap the knife, but Bender shook his head. "Keep it."

"Thank you." He stepped back and watched Tom hand over his rifle.

"I'm going to find somewhere for them to bed down." Tony nodded at Bender.

"Nice meeting you." Mick held out his hand.

Vic looked at him a moment before he gave him a quick shake. "We'll see about that." He turned and walked away.

"Come on, we'll find you somewhere to get warm." Tony started walking, the rest of the group trailing behind, Mick glancing back at the metal box.

Mick had never been on a military base, so he didn't know if what he was seeing was normal or if the ZA had changed things. He expected metal buildings and lots of training areas. What he saw were normal brick buildings, with people scurrying about, most in uniform, but some in civilian clothing. There were tents in the training areas, with people huddled around fires. As much as he wanted to be there with them, basking in the heat, he hoped he wouldn't be assigned to a tent. There was a faint odor in the air, over the stench of unwashed bodies and port-a-potties. It was a familiar smell, but not one he could name.

He followed Tony and Sully to a large brick building, with nothing more than the number 3001 above the door. Sully opened the door and they walked inside. Mick shivered despite the warmth of the building, which was lit with low-level lighting. "Generators?" He asked.

"Yes, we have multiple generators out near the walls. The noise attracts the zeds and we have to get rid of them daily." Sully removed his cover and slapped it on his leg, removing the flakes of snow.

"Is that what we'll be doing?" Tom asked.

"Depends on the Major."

"Speaking of the Major," Tony said. "He can be a stickler for formality. Always refer to us and any other Marines by rank. And it won't hurt to address him as 'Sir'."

"I don't know your full names," Tom said.

"Staff Sgt. Anthony McGuire and he's Sgt. John Sullivan." Tony laughed. "I don't know your full name, either."

"Tom Christopher."

"Nice to meet you, Tom Christopher. Now let's head up and see the Major."

They walked up two flights of stairs before exiting into a dimly lit hallway. Tony made a left down the hall, stopping in front of a door with a frosted glass window. He knocked once, then opened the door. A uniformed man sat behind a desk, pecking at an old-fashioned typewriter on his desk. "Is the Major in?" Tony asked.

"Yeah, go on in." The guy looked up. "Who are they?"

"Volunteers," Sully said as they passed his desk and knocked on the door behind him.

Mick heard a gruff voice call out. Tony opened the door and stepped through, followed by Sully. He watched from the doorway as they came to attention and snapped off salutes to the man sitting behind the desk. "What did you find out there? You were gone long enough. Did you find me more settlements?" The voice said.

"No, sir," Tony replied. "We lost a settlement, actually."

"How do you lose a settlement?"

"They were gone when we stopped. It was one of the smaller ones, Camberton. Only seven people."

"It took you that long to figure that out?"

"No, sir, we stopped at the other settlements as well," Sully answered.

The Major finally noticed Mick and Tom standing in the doorway. "Who are they?" He demanded.

Tony stepped aside so that the Major could fully see them. "This is Mick Cooke and Tom Christopher. They're from Thornville. They volunteered to help."

The Major motioned them closer. Both Mick and Tom took one step forward. "You're from Thornville?"

"Yes, sir," Tom answered. He was straight up, his hands clasped behind his back.

"Had some military training?" The Major asked as he flipped thru the papers on his desk.

"Yes, sir," Tom repeated.

"Branch?"

"National Guard, sir."

The Major snorted. "Barely qualifies." He flicked his eyes from the paper to Mick. "You?"

"No, sir."

"You both look like strong men. That woman in charge there at Thornville, Sarah? She didn't mind you volunteering?"

All eyes fell to Mick. He cleared his throat. "She's dead, sir."

"Dead?" He looked at Tony. "You guys said she was good. I wanted her here."

"She was, sir," Mick said.

"Why'd you leave? Maybe you could have taken over."

"I didn't want it." He swallowed the lump in his throat. "She was my wife, sir."

The Major looked up at him and made a noise in his throat. "So your wife is dead and you came to me because you don't give a shit anymore?"

Mick drew back. Was that really the reason he came? "No, sir. I – I—"

"Then let's get you sworn in."

Mick shook his head. "I'm not here to enlist, sir. Just here to help. I'll be going back to Thornville."

He made that noise again, then looked over to Tom. "What about you? Are you going back?"

Tom looked over at Mick, then back to the Major. "I don't know, sir."

The Major pushed back his chair and stood. "Next time, McGuire, bring me people that want to serve."

"Sir, we're here to help," Mick said. "We don't need to be enlisted to do that."

"Why not enlist? We're short on men. Your wife is dead. Why are you so eager to go back to Thornville?"

"My daughter, sir. She's still there."

The Major made a disgusted sound. "You'll be dead inside of a week. You have an obvious death wish." He turned to Tony. "Find them a tent."

"Sir, there are no more tents," Tony said. "There is some room in 3090."

"They're civilians. They shouldn't be in barracks."

"They're civilians, but they volunteered."

The Major sighed heavily then shook his head. "Fine. Put them in 3090. They're your responsibility. If they fuck up, it's on you."

"Yes, sir."

"Get out of here." The Major dropped back into his chair and pushed papers on his desk. Tony motioned to Mick and Tom and they followed him out of the room, Sully bringing up the rear.

Once they were back in the hall, the door closed behind them, Sully turned to Tony and smiled. "Well, he wasn't as big an asshole as usual."

Mick laughed. "What? He was a dick!"

"He's usually much, much worse." Sully said, slapping Mick on the back. "Come on, we'll find you some space in 3090."

"Yeah, and don't fuck up. You'll make us look bad." Tony led them to the stairwell.

As they walked through the base, Mick studied his surroundings. Other than the fields full of tents, it looked like a typical town, with buildings, fast food restaurants, and a store, guarded by Marines. Most of the people he saw wore uniforms, but there were a few in civilian clothes, moving quickly through the streets. "Are there a lot of civilians here?" he asked.

"Yes, but most are women and children. All the able-bodied men were 'drafted'."

"Drafted?" Tom repeated.

"That's what they called it. Any men, and a few women too, that were in good shape were drafted into the service. Which essentially meant they got uniforms and had to put up with the Major's shit. Maybe a few extra rations." Tony shook his head. "But no training, no weapons, nothing. Most of them were killed pretty quickly."

"So why did you bring us here if there was a chance we'd be drafted?" Mick asked. He thought these guys were his friends.

"The Major was ordered to stop drafting men a few months ago. Now he just asks." Sully shrugged. "Surprisingly, most men take him up on it."

"Not me. I'm not staying. I'll help you out, then I'm back home to Josey."

"I've had enough of military life," Tom said. "I'll help, I might stay, but I'm not re-enlisting."

"Good choice."

Mick noticed a building with bars on all of the windows, a steel gate across the front doors and four Marines standing in front of the doors. "What's so important in that building?" he asked.

Sully looked over to where Mick indicated. "That's the labs. The scientists are in there."

"Are they trying to find a cure?"

"They're trying. They have zombies in there; that's why there's so much security."

"Zombies inside the compound?" Intellectually, Mick understood, but emotionally? He thought that was the worst idea ever.

"They're shackled, wear face guards like that Hannibal movie, and are locked up in cells. They're safe," Tony said.

Mick shook his head. "Famous last words."

Sully pointed to a building with 3090 above the door. "Here's where you'll be staying."

"Looks like a school," Mick said.

"It was. They repurposed it when the virus mutated," Sully opened the door and ushering them inside. "The classrooms were converted." It reminded Mick of their buildings, warmer than the outside, but not quite warm enough to remove a coat. They walked up two flights of stairs before emerging into a hall with soldiers moving back and forth. Sully led them to the end of the hall, where a soldier sat behind a desk, leafing through a magazine so old, the colors had started to fade. "Where do you have room?" Sully asked.

The soldier reluctantly dragged his gaze from the magazine to look at Sully. "For who?" He asked sullenly. "Those civilians?"

"First off, you were a civilian six months ago. Second, you show me some respect, private."

"Sorry, sir," he muttered.

"What?"

"Sorry, sir!" He shouted as he sat up straight.

"Better. Now find me two spots right now."

"Yes, sir!" He pulled a sheet of paper from a drawer and ran his finger down the list hand printed on it. He scrambled from behind the table and walked down the hall to his left. He stopped at a door, waiting for them to catch up. "There are two bunks in this room."

He opened the door and they walked inside the former classroom. Hastily built walls portioned the original space into two small rooms, each with a locking door, the key sticking in the lock, just as they did at home. A three-foot wide hallway allowed access to both rooms. They could see from the open doors that each room held two sets of bunk beds and two tables, with not much room for anything else. They went to the furthest room and stepped inside. There was a smell of unwashed flesh, old blood, and dirty socks. Mick coughed into his hand as he stopped just inside the door.

There were two Marines in the room, each warily eyeing the newcomers. Mick nodded and turned to the empty bunks.

"These will do," Tony said. "Go back to your post."

The bunks were on the far wall, away from the windows. Mick shrugged off his pack and threw it on the thin mattress on the bottom bunk. "I don't see any other civilians," he said quietly to Tony. "Is that going to be a problem?"

Tony shrugged. "Watch your ass and it shouldn't be." He looked at his watch. "Chow is at 1100 hours. We'll be back to pick you up, show you around after we eat."

Mick nodded. He heard Tom's quiet thank you as he unzipped his pack and pulled out a bottle of water. He sat on the bunk and opened the bottle. Taking a long drink, he studied the room and its two inhabitants. Mick raised his water bottle to the most blatant of the observers.

The man who had been staring stood and stared down at them. He was about Mick's height, but bulkier, his hair and beard light brown. "Who the fuck are you?" he asked, stopping in front of Mick.

"I'm Mick. Who the fuck are you?"

There was a ghost of a smile before he spoke again. "I'm Campbell. Sgt. Campbell. What are you doing here?"

Mick shrugged. "This is where the Major put us."

"I mean, why are you in this shithole of a camp?"

"We volunteered, me and Tom." Mick indicated his friend. Tom lifted a hand.

"Why the fuck would you do that?" Mick shrugged again. Campbell shook his head. "You must be fucked in the head."

"Not the first time someone's told me that." Mick smiled briefly.

Campbell leaned against the bunk beds. "Seriously, why would you volunteer?"

"Personal reasons."

Campbell grunted. "You looking to die? Because I need someone who's willing to kill the fuckers around me, then die to save me."

Mick couldn't help but laugh. "No, I'm not looking to die. Sorry to disappoint."

Campbell shrugged. "What about you?" He directed his words to Tom.

"No, sir."

"Don't sir me," Campbell said absently as he looked around the room. "You came in with Sully and McGuire?" Mick nodded. "Good guys. Listen to them, stick with them.

Don't trust any of the other assholes around here." He stood straight up. "Including me." He walked out the door.

Tom watched him go. "What was that about?"

"I don't know, but I will follow his advice." Mick swung around on his bunk and laid down. "Wake me in an hour." He closed his eyes.

CHAPTER NINE

Mick didn't sleep. He just lay with his eyes closed, listening to the babble of noises around him. The room wasn't soundproof, so he heard all the noises of the hall and some from nearby rooms, as well as the room he was in. He heard what sounded like an argument coming from the hall, but he couldn't make out the words. He felt it when Tom walked away for a few minutes, then settled back on his bunk. While sleep would have been preferable, the rest helped. He sat up on his own just under an hour after he closed his eyes.

"Let's get out of here," he said to Tom.

"Tony and Sully said to wait here." Tom looked at the wind-up watch on his wrist. "It's only 10:00. They probably won't be here until closer to 11."

"So let's find them." He stood up and shrugged into his backpack. "I'm tired of sitting around."

Tom shook his head as he stood. "I don't know how you do it."

Mick smiled sadly. "Neither do I."

They shouldered their packs and left the barracks, venturing back outside into the cold. The snow had stopped, but small patches still remained. Mick returned the few acknowledgements they received. Mostly, they got stares and glares. He didn't understand the animosity. They had volunteered to come help. You would think people would be grateful.

The base was like a mini-town. Barracks or the equivalent for the single men, housing for the married men. Although the housing was mostly occupied by Marines with few women in sight. There was a movie theatre, with a marquee that read "Cancelled by the apocalypse." He spotted the fast food restaurants again and realized they were shuttered. The MCX was still open, but the entrance was guarded by four Marines. A few smaller stores received the same treatment.

"Let's check out those tents," he said to Tom as he crossed the street towards the former training field.

"Is that a good idea?" Tom jogged after him.

"Probably not," Mick admitted.

They walked down the sidewalk before stopping at the entrance to the field. The grounds were covered with tents of all shapes and sizes. Campfires dotted the grounds, with some people just sitting around them while others cooked. They saw mostly women, but a lot of children and teens moving around the grounds. By unspoken agreement, they didn't walk into the middle of the camp but skirted the edges, trying to determine how many people the field held. As they walked, the sounds of the generators grew louder and louder until they were in front of a mid-sized building that bled sound. But over the sounds of the generators, they could hear the zombies, groaning and growling. Mick motioned for Tom to stay as he got closer to the building, then climbed a short ladder to peer over the brick wall that protected them from the outside.

There were zombies almost as far as he could see. The sounds of the generators were like a dinner bell and they were all hungry. His eyes followed the brick wall until he saw a larger group of zombies about 300 feet from the generators. He jumped down from the ladder and began to follow the brick wall, Tom right behind him. He saw the reason for the mass of creatures. The brick wall ended, with just a pair of fences separating the zombies from the civilians in the field. There was a tall, heavy wrought iron fence and about five feet away from that, a thick chain link fence. Nobody walked near the chain link fence, but the zombies still sensed there was something beyond, something they craved.

"Can you fucking believe this?" Mick spat. "Why the hell don't they have a brick wall here?"

"It doesn't look good," Tom said. "Those fences won't hold up forever."

"And the first to go would be these poor people just looking for shelter." Mick shook his head. "This is ridiculous." Mick headed across the field instead of skirting the edges, walking past tents and fires and multiple people. He registered that the people didn't even acknowledge him. He supposed he looked like just another refugee to them.

Tom followed him out and they ended up back at the barracks. They were heading back inside when Sully jogged over to them. "Where were you?" he asked.

"Looking at that poor excuse for a wall you have there," Mick said angrily. "Those people have no fucking chance if those fences are breached."

"We clear out the zeds on a daily basis. That's all we can do."

"You can extend the brick wall! Give those people some safety!"

"It's been suggested, Mick. Multiple times. The Major would rather use the labor for other things."

"What the hell is more important than keeping those things out?"

"Supply runs, grave digging, keeping them off the wall."

Mick snorted. "Yeah, that makes sense. Keep them from the sturdiest part of the barrier. Your Major is an idiot."

"Many of us agree," Sully said quietly. "But there are many who don't. And those that agree seem to disappear, so keep your mouth shut."

"Thanks for bringing us here, Sully."

"You volunteered, Mick. So shut up and let's get some chow."

They joined Tony at the mess hall. They stood in line, the only civilians among the soldiers. They received two small pieces of some form of meat, a small scoop of rice and a small scoop of broccoli that was so overcooked, it was almost grey. A cup of water completed their meal. Tony and Sully introduced them to some soldiers, ignored others. There was a barely noticeable division between the two groups, with very few soldiers not included in either group. Mick noticed that Sgt. Campbell was one of those who didn't take a side. He nodded at him when he walked past. Campbell didn't respond.

"When do the civilians eat?" Mick asked as he sawed at his meat.

"They have food sent out to them," Tony said.

"They don't come inside?"

Tony shook his head. "The cooks take food out. They get the same as us, but a little less."

"Less than this?" Mick motioned to the small portion on his tray.

"They get enough, according to the calorie charts. Men get a bit less than this, women a little less than the men."

"And if they need more?"

"They barter among themselves and with some of the soldiers."

"What do they barter with?" Tom asked, staring at the broccoli in disgust.

"Whatever they have." Tony took a bite of his rice.

"What would they have?" Mick wondered. Tony and Sully both looked away. Mick understood. "You're fucking kidding me." Tony and Sully wouldn't meet his gaze. "And you're okay with that?"

"No, we're not," Sully bit out. "But what choice do we have?"

"Put a fucking stop to it! Sarah almost died in a place where that's all women could do. How the fuck can you let that go on?"

"There's only so much we can do, Mick." Tony pushed his tray away. His appetite was gone.

"Mick, we're trying," Sully said softly. "There's a group on the way to headquarters to see if we can get another commander, one who actually cares about the civilians. But it takes time."

"And we have to do everything under the radar," Tony added. "The Major isn't very forgiving."

"Jesus, it's like I walked into Colonel Rhodes' outfit in 'Day of the Dead.'" Mick ran his hand through his hair. "What can I do?"

"Nothing. You're already under scrutiny because you're a civilian volunteer and you've been housed with us. Just do what you're told and keep your head down." Sully looked him in the eye. "You can do that, right?"

Mick shrugged. "For a while, anyway." He leaned in towards Sully. "But if this takes too long, if I see one woman being forced to do something she doesn't want to do, all bets are off." He finished his water then pushed his empty tray to the side. He leaned back in his chair and glared at Tony and Sully.

After they all finished eating, Tony and Sully led them back outside. As they walked down the street, Sully said, "You've been assigned to wall clean-up. We have to go back out, so can I trust you two not to get into trouble?"

Tom nodded. Mick shrugged. "I told you I'd give you time, but if I see someone being abused, I'm not going to stand by and watch it." Sarah never did.

"Fair enough," Tony said. He stopped in front what looked like a garage. "You get your tools in here." He stepped in the door and the rest of the group followed.

There was a truck up on a lift, a work light shining into the undercarriage. Various tool benches lined the walls, along with a couple tool chests. They stepped past the truck towards a bright light at the back of the garage. There was a welder in the back. He was bent over a vise that held a long length of pipe. It looked like he was welding spikes on the end. Tony waited until he pulled the torch away from the pipe, then he banged on the metal cabinet, getting the welder's attention.

The welder shut off the torch and lifted his helmet as he turned his head. "What, Tony?"

The welder was a thin female with her glossy black hair pulled back into a ponytail. She had a slight Asian cast to her face.

"I need a couple spears."

"You see I'm working on them, right?" She indicated the pipe she had been welding.

"You don't have any ready?"

"I got one. I need a dozen." She looked past Tony at Mick and Tom. "Who are those guys?"

"Mick and Tony. They're on the wall and they need the spears. How soon?"

"Where'd they come from?" She stripped off her gloves and threw them on table next to the vise.

"Thornville. They volunteered to help out."

She barked out a short laugh. "Why? Are they stupid or something?"

"No, we're not stupid. We just wanted to help." Mick held out his hand. "I'm Mick."

She ignored his hand. "I'll have the rest of the spears in a couple hours. Bring these jokers back then." She flipped the helmet down and started welding again.

"Gee, everyone is so nice here," Mick said as they left the garage.

Sully flashed a brief smile, then said, "Laurel is a bit prickly, but she's a damn good welder. Unfortunately, it means everything falls on her shoulders."

"She the only welder?" Tom asked. "I've done some welding."

"No, but she's the best, so everyone wants her to work on their stuff. She doesn't get a lot of rest." Tony nodded at a Marine walking past.

"If you can weld a strong line, you could probably be assigned there instead of on the wall," Sully said.

Tom looked at Mick. "Don't look at me," Mick said. "If you want to weld, then weld. I don't need a babysitter." He cocked his head. "That better not be why you volunteered."

"No, it's not," Tom spat out. "I just wanted to be somewhere else. Somewhere where people didn't treat me like the plague." He turned to Sully. "I can weld pretty good. I'd like to work there."

"I'll check with the Major when we get back, but it shouldn't be a problem." Sully glanced at Mick, who had a chastened look on his face. "Come on, let's go check in at the wall. I'm sure there are spears there."

They walked towards the wall, through the tents, not speaking. Mick knew that Tom didn't come to watch over him, he knew how much it bothered Tom that Thornville was not welcoming. Why did he have to be an asshole?

They stopped at a small shack where a group of Marines stood in a loose group, listening to another man in fatigues. There was a buzz of the generators filling the air, not very loud, but loud enough so that Tony had to raise his voice. "The Major wants these guys on the wall," Tony said to the tall Marine with his back to the group.

The Marine turned and Mick saw it was Sgt. Campbell. "They have weapons?" Campbell asked.

"Laurel's still making them. Do you have any here?"

Campbell sighed. "Yeah, we have a few, but they're shit. That's why she's making more. I guess they can use them." He turned his head. "Bates, Salina, give these guys your spears."

Two men came up with battered and bloody spears. They were about five feet long, with a ring of spikes welded on one end. The opposite end was wrapped with fraying electrical tape. Mick grimaced as he reached for his.

Campbell laughed. "You know which end to use, right?"

"I think I can figure it out," Mick said with a slight smile.

"We need to head back out, can I leave these guys with you?" Tony asked.

"Why don't we trade places and I go out? I haven't been out of this place in months."

"And there's a reason for that, Campbell," Tony said. "We'll be back in a couple weeks." He turned to Mick. "Remember what I said."

"You remember what I said," Mick countered. "Take care of yourself out there."

"We'll be fine," Sully said. He gripped Mick's arm. "You be careful." Mick nodded. He watched as they said goodbye to Tom, then walked away.

"See what volunteering gets you?" Campbell was saying. Mick turned to him. "The second shittiest job in the place."

"So what's the first?"

"You'll see. Dump your gear there." Campbell pointed to the shack. Mick and Tom took off their packs. Mick rummaged inside for his gloves, then set his pack just inside the door, beside Tom's. Campbell started walking and Mick and Tom followed.

He led them down along the wall. Mick could hear the groans of the zombies just a few feet away. Campbell stopped at a ladder and motioned to it with a wave of his hand. Mick shifted the spear to his left hand and began to climb. At the top, he stood onto the wall, staring down at the zombies milling below. He looked to his right and saw two soldiers about 50 feet away, standing on the wall, spearing the zombies, whooping with each kill.

"What are you waiting for?" Campbell asked. "You do know how to kill them, don't you?"

"What happens when the bodies start stacking up?" Mick asked, ignoring his question.

"The shittiest job in this place. Start killing them, don't worry about anything else." He pointed down the wall. "There are shifts of two man crews every 50 feet. Do your job, don't worry about anything else."

"When is my shift up?"

Campbell laughed. "When I decide it is." He clapped Mick on the back hard enough to make him stumble. "Have fun." He disappeared down the ladder. A few moments later, Tom came up.

"So this is what we volunteered for?" Tom asked, peering down the wall at the creatures reaching and grasping for them.

"Yup." Mick lifted the spear in both hands and brought it down thru the skull of the closest zombie. It dropped and he did it again. And again.

♦

Four hours of nothing but mindless killing. Mick's arms were quivering from the strain, but the zombies never stopped. Their pile of kills stretched nearly to the other crew's post, corpses stacked atop each other, yet the zombies never stopped. Mick was covered in sweat and splattered fluids and the spear had lost a few spokes, still, the zombies never stopped. When Campbell popped his head over the wall, Mick dropped the spear to his side and just stared at the man.

"Come on, take a break," the Marine said, climbing back down the ladder.

Tom descended the ladder first and Mick followed. When he hit the ground, he stumbled a little, unnoticed by anyone but himself. Campbell handed him a bottle of water and he uncapped it, drinking half the bottle before stopping. "Thirsty?" Campbell asked with a smirk.

Mick bit off the obscenity he was considering. He dropped to his ass, leaning against the shack and closing his eyes. The faint vibration from the generators felt good. It was all he could do not to sigh in pleasure. He sensed someone sitting beside him. By the huge sigh, he thought it was Tom.

"Hey, Cooke." Mick opened his eyes to see Campbell sitting across from him with an MRE in his hand. He tossed it over and Mick caught it. "You did real good up there."

"Thanks." Mick removed his gloves and tore open the MRE. The first thing he grabbed was vacuum sealed crackers. He ripped the package open and started eating, not caring that the crackers were dry and crumbly. They were food.

"You know there's some jalapeno cheddar spread in there for the crackers."

Mick shrugged. He just wanted the calories. He glanced over at Tom as he shoved another piece of cracker in his mouth. Tom was squeezing an orangish paste on his cracker before he took a bite. Mick chewed and swallowed, then asked, "Does it taste any better?" Tom shook his head and Mick laughed. Mick finished the crackers and rooted in the MRE pouch. He came up with a chicken pasta dish. He opened the package and dipped the spoon inside.

"You can heat that," Campbell said.

"Don't need to." He'd eaten them cold before and he was too hungry to care.

"So what's your story?" Campbell directed at Mick.

"No story." Mick shrugged. "I'm just here to help."

"Everybody has a story, Cooke. Why would you leave a flourishing place like Thornville?"

"You been checking up on me?"

Campbell shrugged. "I like to know who I'm working with." He drank some water from his camelback. "You were some kind of big shot there, weren't you?" Mick didn't answer. "What are you running from? Did you kill someone? Did you lose someone?" Mick looked away. "That's it, you lost someone. Who? Mother, brother, sister, lover?" Mick wouldn't meet his eyes. "You lost your lover, is that it? What happened?"

"I don't want to talk about it," Mick muttered, his appetite gone. He sat the chicken dinner on the ground next to him.

"We've all lost someone, Cooke." Campbell sat forward, his hands hanging over his knees. "You just need to get over it. Move on with your life."

"You think I don't know that?" Mick hissed. "I'm not the only one who's lost these past years, hell, ever, but you don't get to tell me to 'get over it.' I'll do whatever the hell I want." He tossed the rest of his MRE on the ground and stood up.

"Where are you going?" Campbell stood quickly, unsure as to Mick's intentions.

"Back to work." Mick grabbed the spear from where he had propped it against the shed and climbed back up the ladder. They could hear his grunts as he killed the creatures straining against the wall.

"It was his wife," Tom said softly. Campbell looked over at the man still on the ground, calmly packing his food back in the MRE pouch. "She was murdered. Almost lost his daughter, too." He packed Mick's food back in his pouch, then set the two of them just inside the shed door near their packs.

"He has a daughter and he's here?"

Tom stood and brushed off the seat of his pants. "He's doing what he has to do. I'm going to go join him. Thanks for the food." Tom grabbed his spear and climbed the ladder.

CHAPTER TEN

They worked into the night, dispatching any creature that ventured into their designated kill zone. When dusk was upon them, strategically placed flood lights kicked on, giving them just enough light to see the zombies below. Mick felt he had been on the wall for years. Slamming the spear down into the brain, twisting it to remove it, pulling it back out. Over and over until his mind was totally empty. When he felt the tap on his shoulder, he turned quickly, the spear coming up, blood splashing from the gory tip to splatter Campbell's uniform.

"I said you're done for the night." Campbell stepped back from the spear. "Let's go."

Slowly, Mick descended the ladder. When he got to the bottom, a Marine waited with his hand out. Mick handed him the battered spear and walked gingerly to where Tom waited. "You okay?" Tom asked softly. They hadn't spoken all night.

"I'm fine. Sorry about earlier."

"Not a problem, Mick." He stretched, bowing his back. "Damn, I could use about twelve hours of sleep."

"Me too, but after a long shower."

"Sorry, boys, no showers." Campbell walked up to them. "We shower once a week and my squad showers on Tuesdays."

It was Saturday. "We can't go to bed like this," Mick said. Both of them were covered in splattered blood and brain matter and sweat.

"I'll show you where you can wash up. Come on. Grab your stuff."

Tom and Mick grabbed their packs, shoving the uneaten MREs inside before strapping them to their backs. They followed Campbell as he walked through the civilian area. Most of the tents were dark, a few were dimly lit by flashlights or lanterns. There were a handful of low fires with a few men standing around them. Mick noticed the sullen looks when Campbell passed by. He kept his face neutral, remembering what he had told Tony and Sully. He wouldn't engage unless he had to.

Campbell led them to a low brick building. "Showers are in here, but like I said, once a week. There's a bathroom with water for washing up." He opened the door and took them down a hall to a musty smelling room with barrels of brackish water.

"How many people have washed before us?" Tom asked, looking at the murky liquid.

Campbell shrugged. "It gets changed every week or so."

Mick sighed. He had to get this shit off him. He pulled off his gloves and dropped them to the floor. He shrugged off his pack and opened it, rummaging inside until he found his bottle of hand sanitizer and a clean cloth. He poured some sanitizer onto the cloth and began to wipe the gore from his face. It stung as he found cuts and scrapes on his skin and he was reminded of wiping Sarah's face after an encounter with a zombie. He breathed deep until the ache in his chest disappeared.

He finished cleaning his face, then handed the rag to Tom. After pouring a good dollop of sanitizer into his hand, he passed the bottle as well. As he worked the liquid into his hands, he looked at Campbell, who watched him with a smirk. "Too good for our water?"

"Too good to catch whatever fucking diseases are lurking in it."

Campbell laughed. "I like you, Cooke."

"Gee, thanks." He took the rag back from Tom, who had wiped his face, and began brushing crud from his jacket. "Where's the rest of your squad, anyway? Don't tell me we're it."

"They're already at the barracks. They're not as eager at killing them; they don't get so dirty." Mick slanted a look at him. Campbell chuckled. "Seriously. They've been doing it so long, a quick wipe of the face is all they need. You'll get there eventually."

"My goal in life." Mick got the worst of the crud from his jacket and shoved the rag in his back pocket. "Right after I get some sleep."

"Come on, then. I'll take you back to the barracks."

"We can find our way back." He had hoped to do a little exploring. He picked up his gloves from the floor and shoved them in one of the outer pockets of his pack. Then he picked it up and slipped it on his shoulders.

"Civilian curfew is 21:00 and we're already past that. We need to get you back there now. Come on." Campbell turned. After a glance at Tom, who shrugged, Mick followed.

Mick hadn't noticed when they were walking from the wall but he noticed now. The streets were virtually empty. He saw but two Marines scurrying somewhere, but no civilians. A few dim lights illuminated the streets. The streets were silent, only the generator in the background, sounding much louder than it did during the light of day. Campbell reached the barracks and opened the door, ushering them inside as he watched the streets.

It was even quiet inside. "What time is it?" Mick asked.

"22:20," Campbell said after a quick glance at the watch on his wrist. "You two get extra time out because you're on my crew. Shift is from 12:00 to 22:00." He walked up the dim stairwell. Mick and Tom followed behind.

At Mick's quizzical look, Tom said, "Noon to ten p.m."

"But the other civilians have to be in by nine?" Mick asked. "What about those guys by the fires?"

"Most of the Marines ignore them. They're not causing any trouble and they know who reports to the major, so they can duck into their tents when they see them. You're with me, so you're OK."

"And what's the penalty?"

Campbell shook his head. "You don't want to know. Go up, get some sleep. You need to be back at the wall at 12:00 hours."

Mick stopped outside the door to their quarters. "What's the penalty, Campbell?" Mick needed to know.

Campbell sighed. "Confiscation of all property and banishment."

"Jesus Christ," Mick breathed.

"Cooke, just do what you came here to do, whatever it is, and go back to your kid. Keep your nose clean and you'll be fine."

"I can't do that anymore, Campbell. I can't sit around while people are being hurt."

Campbell shook his head. "You better learn how. Go to bed. Morning chow starts at 0630." He pushed past Mick to enter the room.

"Am I wrong, Tom?" Mick asked his friend.

"I'm not the one to ask, Mick. Remember, I just let George and his assholes do whatever they wanted in Kittington. But if I had to do it again, I wouldn't let it happen." He clapped Mick on the back and walked through the door, closing it softly behind him.

Mick sighed as he leaned against the wall. This place has not been what I expected, he thought. I'm going to get in trouble here. He let out another sigh before he opened the door and stepped through.

♦

Mick and Tom kept working with Campbell's crew. They killed the zombies, then dropped into bed each night. Mick managed more sleep than he had been, but it was still less than five hours a night. When he woke and couldn't sleep any longer, he laid in bed, waiting until the curfew was lifted and he felt safe moving around. Some nights were very long.

Mick was glad that Tony was still with him rather than welding. He would lose him soon enough, but it was good to have someone to talk to. The Marines, while cordial, still viewed them both with suspicion. He caught many odd looks from the other members of the squad before they wiped them clean with insincere smiles. His smiles weren't quite so sincere, either.

They discovered the worst job on base. While they were taking a break, Mick watched as heavily fortified bulldozers came to the wall and scooped up the corpses of the zombies that had been dispatched. They carried them to a pit and dumped them in. Marines dressed in hazmat suits overlaid with body armor used pitchforks to shift the bodies in the pit, then shovels to level the dirt once the pits were filled. Mick hoped he never pissed off the Major enough to be put on that detail. He didn't know how the Marines handled it.

They had been working together just over a week when Campbell called him off the wall. "You know where the welding shop is?" The Marine asked.

"Yeah, Tony and Sully showed me."

"Take this spear back, tell her we need more now and to weld them better." He handed him a spear with just one point left.

"Considering what we do with these, I'm surprised they last as long as they do."

"Forget the commentary, just get moving."

Mick snapped off a half-assed salute before he turned and headed to the garage that held the welding shop. He wasn't sure if he should knock before he entered, but since Tony and Sully didn't, he decided not to as well. He stepped through the door, closing it softly behind him. The same truck was on the lift, maybe the work light was in a different position. He didn't see the light from the welder at the back of the building. He wondered if Laurel was even here. He headed back, figuring he'd wait for her.

He saw them against the wall, a fatigue-clad man pressed against a woman he assumed was Laurel. Not wanting to interrupt their privacy, he began to back away. Then he heard her say "Stop!"

Without thinking, he dropped the damaged spear and moved to the couple. He grabbed the man's arm, yanking him away from Laurel. "Get the fuck away from her," he growled.

The man stumbled, the righted himself. "What the fuck's your problem?"

"You, asshole." Mick held his hands fisted at his side. He gritted his teeth, telling himself that no matter how good it would feel to pound this asshole's face in, he couldn't.

"Who the hell are you?" The guy was shorter than Mick, muscles going to fat, like an aging football player. Mick saw the name Watts on his breast.

"The guy who's going to kick your ass if I see you near her again. Get out of here." Mick glanced behind him at Laurel. Her eyes were puffy and it looked like her lip was swollen. He took a deep breath and clenched his fists tighter.

"You ain't shit," Watts said. "Nothing but a fucking civilian." He pointed at Mick. "You'll get yours, asshole." He walked past Mick, shouldering him aside. Mick watched until he left the building, then he turned to Laurel.

"Are you okay?" He asked softly.

"I'm fine," she said sharply. "You shouldn't have interfered." She ran a hand over her face, wincing when she touched her lips.

"Seriously?" Mick asked. "Did you want him to touch you?"

She looked away. "No, but sometimes it's just easier to give in."

"You don't have to put up with that shit. No woman does."

She laughed harshly. "What dream world are you living in? Women have always had to put up with that shit and it's only gotten worse since those things started walking."

Mick sighed heavily. "You're right. I'm sorry. My wife had the same thing happen to her and it really killed me that I couldn't do anything about it."

"You're married?"

He grimaced. "I was. She's – she's gone now."

"How did your wife handle it?" Laurel moved over to her welding table and started shifting around pieces of metal.

Mick laughed. "She killed the fucker. Stuck a screwdriver in his thigh and watched him bleed out." His smiled tapered off. "She ended up having a miscarriage, though."

Laurel winced. "I'm sorry."

"Me, too."

"Thanks for your help. But you better watch yourself. Watts is a real asshole."

Mick shrugged. "I've dealt with them before." He cleared his throat. "Campbell sent me for some more spears." He bent and picked up the one he had dropped. "And to get this one repaired."

She shook her head. "I keep telling him that I need to take more time with them to make them stronger." She reached for the spear in Mick's hand. "I have a couple done, but not many. You can take them with you."

"Would it help to have another welder?" While Mick hated to lose Tom on the wall, Laurel needed him even more than he did. "Not only with the welding, but with the – the other?"

Laurel inclined her head. "Do you weld?"

"No, but my friend Tom does. He mentioned it to Tony and Sully and they were going to ask the Major if he could help out here."

"The Major probably wouldn't approve. He likes to come down every so often." She looked at the floor.

"Fucking asshole," Mick spat.

She shrugged. "At least he makes sure I enjoy it, not like the rest of them."

"And that's supposed to make it okay? He's the fucking leader here. He should be setting an example."

"No, it doesn't make it okay. But what else can I do?" She walked across the shop and set the broken spear against the wall. She took a few steps to the right and grabbed three fresh ones. "Take these back; tell Campbell I'll have more in a couple hours."

Mick took the spears. "Let me know if I can do anything to help. Anything at all."

She nodded. "Thanks again. And I'm really sorry."

"For?"

"You lost your wife and your baby. I'm sorry."

Mick smiled. "Thanks." He tipped the spears to his head like a salute.

♦

"What took you so long?" Campbell asked when he made it back to the wall.

Did Campbell know what was happening to Laurel? Was he one of the ones who visited? The only people he could truly trust were Tony, Sully and Tom. "She was just finishing one up. Said she'd have more in a couple hours." Mick handed him the three new spears.

Campbell looked closely at him. "OK," he finally said. "Get back up on the wall."

Mick climbed the ladder with his spear and took his place next to Tom. When he was sure they were alone, he whispered, "You need to get to that welding shop."

"What? Why?" Tom stabbed down, watched another zombie drop.

"Laurel needs help. We have to figure out a way to get you there." He poked the spear through the head of a zombie clad in fatigues. He wished it was Watts.

They worked through their shift, stopping for a quick dinner break before it was back on the wall. Mick still hadn't thought of a way to get help to Laurel. Maybe something would come to him as he slept.

Campbell called them off at the end of the shift. Tom gestured for Mick to go down the ladder first. Once Mick was on the ground, Tom started down. Suddenly, his foot slipped and he twisted his body to avoid the hard fall. He cried out as his foot got caught in the ladder. Mick rushed to his side to help him down. "You OK?" he asked.

"Yeah, just twisted it." Tom set his weight on his foot and winced.

"What's wrong?" Campbell asked.

"Twisted my ankle," Tom said. "I'll be fine." He winced as he limped away.

"You sure?"

"Yeah, Campbell, I can sleep it off."

But the next morning, his ankle was worse. "I'm sorry, Campbell. I can't put much weight on it. I won't be able to stand on that wall." Tom sat on his Mick's bunk, his leg straight out in front of him.

Campbell cursed. "You have to. You can't sit around here or the Major will have my ass."

"Is there something I can do seated? Just until it heals a bit?"

Campbell shook his head. "There's nothing. You're gonna have to try the wall."

"What about welding? I've done a lot of welding in the past and I don't have to stand to do that." Tom caught Mick's eye and winked.

Mick covered his mouth to hide his smile. He coughed lightly. "It'll suck losing you on the wall," he said.

"It sure will, because you'll be solo," Campbell said. "Let me find you some crutches and we'll go to the welding shop."

After Campbell had left, Mick turned to Tom. "So you're not really that hurt?"

Tom shook his head. "You said she needed help. This was the only way I could think of. It won't be permanent, though."

"Maybe when Tony and Sully get back, we can have them talk to the Major, make it permanent."

"For as long as we're here," Tom reminded him.

"Yeah." What would Laurel do when they were gone?

Campbell came back with a beat-up pair of crutches. "Here." He thrust them at Tom, who stood gingerly and positioned the crutches under his arms. "Let's go."

They hobbled over to the welding shop. Campbell walked in, yelling Laurel's name. She came out from a room in the back of the shop, wiping her hands on a dirty rag. "I don't have any spears ready. Casey took what I had."

"I'm not here for spears. Tom here is going to work with you for a while. He hurt his ankle and can't stand on the wall. He can sit here and weld."

Laurel looked at Mick. He kept his face impassive. "Did the Major approve?" Laurel asked.

"I haven't had a chance to talk to him, but you need help and he needs to work. I'll clear it with him tomorrow." Campbell pointed towards the back of the shop. "He can work there. Just make sure he's back in his barracks by 2100."

"OK. Thanks." Laurel looked at Mick, who gave her a slight nod of the head.

Mick was exhausted when he got back to the barracks. He collapsed on his bed, not even bothering to remove his boots or even wipe his face. He sighed heavily, hoping sleep would come quick.

"Mick?" Tom whispered from his upper bunk.

"Yeah?"

"I know why you wanted Laurel to have help."

Mick groaned as he got up and stood at the end of the bunk. He looked around to make sure their small room was still empty. "Did something happen?" he asked softly.

Tom propped himself up on his elbow. "I had to go in the back and when I came out, a guy was messing with her. When he saw me, he backed off."

Mick nodded. "Thanks."

"Can't we tell someone? Like Campbell or the Major?"

Mick shook his head. "I don't know Campbell well enough and she said the Major comes to visit, too."

Tom muttered a curse. "What do we do? I can't stay there forever."

"We have to keep you there until Tony and Sully come back. Maybe they have an answer."

"I'm not hopeful, Mick."

Mick sighed. "Neither am I."

♦

Mick continued to work the wall solo while Tom helped Laurel in the welding shop. With two welders in the shop, the spears were coming faster, allowing Campbell to keep more creatures from the wall. He never checked with the Major about the new assignment.

Tom had been working with Laurel for four days when the Major came in. He stopped when he saw Tom. "Who are you and why are you here?"

"I'm Tom, sir, from Thornville."

"Why are you here?"

"I hurt my leg, sir, and couldn't work on the wall. Campbell said I had to keep working, so I volunteered to help weld. I have experience."

"Why wasn't I notified?"

Tom looked at Laurel, who was standing against the wall, torch in hand. "I'm sorry, sir, I don't know."

"Get back on the wall. They need you there more than here."

"Sir, he's been very helpful here," Laurel said softly. "We're making twice as many spears and he has some mechanical knowledge, too. He helped get the supply truck running."

The Major grimaced. "I should have been told that he was here. He's not supposed to be here. He has to go back on the wall."

"Sir, with all due respect, I think I can help more here. We're making twice the number of –"

"On the wall," The Major interrupted. "Now."

Tom looked at Laurel. She looked down at the floor, resigned to her fate. He reached for the crutches he had never really needed and slowly placed them under his arms, grimacing as he stood. "Sir, I really think –"

"One more word and you go in the stockade." Tom nodded and slowly hobbled away. He heard the door lock behind him.

♦

"What are you doing here?" Campbell asked when Tom approached the shed where they kept their equipment.

"Major threw me out." Tom spat on the ground. "He put me back on the wall."

The Marine cursed. "I forgot to check with him. We were doing so good…" He blew out a sigh. "Can you handle the wall?"

"Yes, but I'd rather be back at the welding shop."

Campbell laughed. "Wouldn't we all?"

"Seriously, Campbell. Wasn't it better with two of us welding? More spears were done, repairs were quicker."

"Yeah, but if the Major wants you on the wall, you're on the wall." Campbell shook his head. "Jesus, I hope I don't get shit for putting you there temporarily."

"Campbell, can you at least talk to him? See if I can work there? It would be –"

A yell came from the wall. "Help!! Mick's on the other side of the wall!" Campbell and Tom took off, Tom's crutches dropping to the dirt.

♦

"So this is what you do?" Mick turned his head to see Watts climbing up the ladder. He yanked the spear out of the zombie's head and held it loosely.

"This is where I've been assigned, yes." Mick was wary. Watts had a grin on his face that didn't quite meet his eyes.

"Doesn't take much to do this, huh?" Watts had made it onto the wall and was looking down at the creatures reaching for the living.

Mick shrugged. "It needs to be done and I can do it." He held the spear out to Watts. "Want to try it?"

Watts laughed. "Nah, I do my own thing. Just like you should do your own thing. Not put your nose where it doesn't belong."

Mick pulled the spear back and held it in front of him. "My own thing is the right thing. And that's what I do. What you were doing was not right and you know it."

"Just keep your nose out of my shit." Watts moved closer, his finger pointing at Mick. "I do what I want and I don't need some civilian asshole telling me otherwise."

"I thought Marines were supposed to be honorable."

"Fuck you, man." His arms shot out and pushed Mick. Mick stumbled and righted himself, then Watts pushed again. Mick went over the wall.

CHAPTER ELEVEN

Mick fell onto a mostly clear spot of ground, with just two creatures crumbling beneath him. He lost his spear in the fall, but still had his knife on his belt. As he lay on his back, on top of the squirming bodies, he unsnapped the leather holding his knife in the sheath and pulled it out. He rolled to his left and brought the knife up, driving it into the skull of first one, then the other zombie. He got to his feet, scanning the ground for his spear. From the corner of his eye, he saw a mass of creatures headed his way. He spotted his spear about three feet away and rushed to it, scooping it up and holding it in one hand as he slid his knife back into the sheath. He grasped the spear with both hands and readied himself.

The first one was old, barely keeping itself together. He gave it a quick jab to the forehead and it went down. The second was slightly fleshier, but still easy to dispatch. He heard someone calling his name, but he couldn't get distracted. Three more were almost upon him. He stabbed the first one in the eye, then swung to his left to get the next one. That left the third, a much fresher specimen, still looking almost alive. He jabbed the spear at its head, but lacked the force to push it thru. He pulled back and tried again, this time poking it through the thing's eye and into its brain.

He rolled his shoulders, waiting for the next. And the next. On the third kill, the spear shaft snapped as the zombie fell. "Shit," he muttered as he pulled out his knife. He turned his head quickly to check the wall, wondering how he was going to make it back up there. He saw a group of Marines banging their spears on the top of the wall, yelling obscenities. Most of the zombies headed that way. He looked forward again. There were still three approaching. He tightened his grip on the knife and slammed it into the skull of the first one. It pulled free with a spray of goo as the zombie dropped and he turned to the second. Underhand, through the bottom of the chin up through the brain. The third one lunged forward and grabbed his arm as he was pulling the knife free.

He yanked the knife out and shoved it down as hard as he could into the top of its skull and it fell, pulling on his arm. He dropped to one knee and, leaving the knife protruding from the corpse, he pried the fingers from his arm, glancing up to see two more lurching towards him.

"Mick! Get over here!" Mick looked back towards the wall and saw Tom and Campbell holding a ladder on his side of the wall. He worked harder to free his arm from the death grip. Finally, the fingers loosened. He yanked his knife from the zombie's head and sprinted to the ladder, climbing it with the knife still clutched in his hand. Tom grabbed his arm as he approached the top and yanked him over. He collapsed on his back, breathing heavy. He saw Campbell lean over the wall and heard the ladder fall to the other side.

"What the fuck happened?" Campbell yelled.

Mick sat up. He saw a group of guys walking along the wall towards him. Watts was in the lead. He waited until they were close enough to say "I tripped." He looked directly at Watts as he spoke. He kept his eyes on Watts as he moved down the ladder.

"You tripped?!" Campbell shook his head. "How the fuck did you trip?"

Mick shrugged. He nodded at the guys sliding past, tapping him on his shoulder. He thanked them for their help as they walked by.

"Take a break. Get your shit together." Campbell turned. "Tom, you were moving pretty good, get up on the wall."

"Wait, why is Tom here?" Mick asked as he stood. He vaguely remembered seeing him earlier, but pushed it from his mind in his fight for survival. "Why isn't he at the welding shop?"

"Major sent him back here."

"Fuck!" Mick swore. Campbell looked at him, an eyebrow raised. "You need to get him back to the garage. He needs to be there."

"Major says no. I'm not going up against the Major."

"Campbell…" Mick trailed off. He didn't know how much he could trust the man. Hell, he warned Mick himself not to trust him.

"Get down and take a break. Tom will be fine up here."

"It's not Tom I'm worried about," Mick muttered as he descended the ladder.

"You okay, Mick?" Tom asked as Mick stepped onto the ground.

"Yeah. How's Laurel?"

Tom grimaced. "The Major showed up and kicked me out. Threatened me with the stockade if I didn't leave."

"What are we going to do?"

"I don't know what we can do, Mick. Maybe Campbell can help."

Mick shook his head. "He won't go against the Major. We're going to have to get her out of here."

"We'll do it." He clasped Mick's arm. "How'd you trip up there?"

"I didn't." Mick walked away.

He sipped a bottle of water as he rested against the shack wall. Getting Laurel out was going to be a problem. They had to figure out a way around the curfew and he wasn't even sure he could get them to open the gates. He hated to wait until Tony and Sully returned, but he didn't see any other way to do it. With their help, he and Tom could protect her.

"What happened up there?" Campbell asked as he walked up to Mick.

"I tripped." Mick didn't know why he was protecting Watts. Probably because people would believe a Marine before they'd believe him.

Campbell dropped to the ground next to him. "I thought you were a goner, man, but damn, you really handled yourself out there."

Mick shrugged. "Had to learn to survive."

"Would you be willing to teach others how to do that?"

He shrugged again. "It's not something I can teach. It's just something we did."

"You and your wife?"

"Yeah." Mick smiled briefly.

"Tom told me what happened. I'm sorry." Mick nodded. "I just don't understand why you're here if you have a daughter at home."

"Because I needed to get away for a while." Mick picked up a stone and tossed it across the ground. "I'm going back. I just couldn't be there right then."

"Just hope the Major lets you go. He hasn't been getting a lot of recruits."

"He won't stop me." Mick scratched his cheek. He needed a shave. "What do you think of him? The Major?"

Campbell shrugged. "He's a Major. Most of them are assholes. I just keep my head down and do my job."

He'd be no help. Mick stood up. "I'm going back on the wall."

"You sure?" Campbell asked from the ground. "You can rest a little longer."

"I'm good." Mick brushed off the seat of his jeans and headed back to Tom and the wall.

After morning chow, Mick headed to the garage. Laurel was alone, finishing her breakfast, staring off into space. "Laurel?" Mick knocked on the door frame before he walked in.

"Hi," she said softly, pushing her plate across the table.

"I'm going to get you some permanent help," he said, leaning against the door jamb. "Either that, or I'm going to get you out of here."

"How are you going to get me out of here?"

"When we leave, you can come with us. We have a good settlement and we could always use a welder."

Laurel laughed. "You think you're going home? There's no way the Major will let you leave." She tucked an errant strand of hair behind her ear. "There's no new bodies coming in and plenty are disappearing. You've enlisted, whether you believe it or not."

Mick shook his head. "I'm not. I'll get out of here if I have to break down the gates. And I want you to come with me. Somewhere safer."

"Nowhere is safe."

"Our place is."

Laurel tilted her head and peered at him through her unusual eyes. "Didn't your wife get killed there?"

Mick felt the blow in his gut. "She did," he rasped. "But before she died, she made our place safe. Safe for everyone, but especially for women. I'd really like you to come with me when I go."

She shrugged. "What's the difference? Sure, if you go, I'll come with you. But you won't be leaving."

He wasn't going to argue with her. He was not staying in this shithole of a camp. "We're going to talk to the Major, get Tom back here."

"I already asked the Major, he said no."

"Well, we'll ask again. It can't hurt."

She smiled sadly. "Yes, it can." She stood up from the table, picking up her plate and glass. "Go do your thing, Mick. I'll do mine." She walked into the back room where, thanks to Tom, he knew that she lived. With a heavy sigh, he turned and left the shop.

After his showing on the other side of the wall, the Marines were much friendlier to Mick. While he enjoyed the new camaraderie, he still didn't trust them. So while they joked and laughed, Mick kept a close eye on them all, hoping to discover someone who was against the Major and on the side of good. Watts still kept his distance and Mick made sure he knew where he was whenever he was on the wall.

He and Tom took turns stopping at Laurel's and hanging out for a few hours before their shift. It still left her unprotected for a good portion of the day, but neither Tom nor Mick had a better idea.

They had been at the camp over a month. Tony and Sully were way overdue to report in. When Mick mentioned their absence to Campbell while they were eating their dinner next to the wall, the Marine laughed. "They're the Major's pets. They come and go as they please. Hell, they're probably hanging out in some settlement with some hot chicks that dig uniforms."

That wasn't the Tony and Sully that Mick knew. They never stayed at Thornville longer than a day and were never anything but professional when they were there. Donna always showed interest in Sully and he never showed her anything but respect. "Why don't you go out?" Mick asked.

Campbell gave him a wry smile. "I don't have the temperament for it."

"You don't like it beyond the walls?"

"I like it too much. Last time I was out, they had to drag me back." He shrugged. "So I am no longer permitted to go beyond the walls."

"Sorry, but that sucks. You should be able to leave if you want to."

"I signed a contract," Campbell said.

"When is your contract up?"

"Three months ago."

Mick looked at the man. "Why the fuck are you still here, then?"

Campbell shook his head. "Just because my contract's up doesn't mean I can leave. No one leaves." He took a swig from his water bottle. "About a month after the shit went down, the President enacted a little-known law discontinuing all military discharges. After he got eaten, the next President recalled all veterans back to service, since so many guys were lost." He signed heavily. "This latest President, Conrad, she rescinded both orders because so many were deserting anyway. She authorized additional pay for those who elected to remain. The Major ignored both orders. He won't let any of us leave, he hasn't authorized any additional pay – not that we're getting paid – and he tries to strongarm everyone that walks through the gate." Campbell laughed. "There wasn't anyone for months until you showed up."

"So leave," Mick said. "Walk out and don't look back. You won't be court martialed; you're officially done."

"And go where? Your community?"

Mick shrugged. "Sure, why not? It's a good place."

"So good that you left."

"I didn't leave because it was bad." He felt a headache coming on. He lifted a hand to rub his forehead and immediately Sarah came to mind. He was hit with a sharp feeling of longing – for her, for Josey, for home. He dropped his hand to his side. "I left before I did something stupid." He gathered his dinner refuse. "I'm going back on the wall."

"Just when it was getting interesting." Campbell smiled.

Tony came back then from his visit with Laurel. She had made three new spears. They hadn't stopped trying to get him assigned with Laurel permanently, but Campbell was reluctant to ask the Major. Mick kept working on him, though. He didn't know how much longer he would be able to wait. The idea of Laurel's mistreatment wore on him.

"How's she doing?" Mick asked as Tom handed him a spear.

Tom shrugged. "She acts like it's no big deal, but I can see it in her eyes. We need to do something, Mick. She's going to break."

"I'm trying, Tom. Worse comes to worse, we'll just leave, take her with us."

"If we're allowed to leave."

Mick grunted. He had already said his piece. He would not be held behind the walls.

♦

A week later, Mick and Tom were on the wall when Watts and his buddies sauntered over. They stood below him, chattering among themselves until Watts looked up, a smirk on his face. "Your buddy is back," he said.

Mick stabbed a zombie through the eye, then turned to Watts. "Tony and Sully?"

Watts shrugged. "What I heard. One of them didn't make it."

"What? What are you talking about? Who didn't make it?"

"How the fuck should I know?" He looked at his group. "Any of you know which one's dead?" With the same smirk Watts wore, his friends murmured their denials.

"Assholes," Mick muttered. He turned to Tom, who looked shocked. "I'm going to find Campbell," Mick said before he walked along the wall, looking for Campbell.

He found him a few feet away, shaking the muck from his spear. "Cooke, why aren't you in position?" he asked as soon as he saw Mick.

"I have to go. Tony and Sully are back."

"You have a job to do," Campbell said. "You can see them later."

"Watts said one of them didn't make it. I need to know."

Campbell sighed deeply. "Go ahead. Take your dinner now." Mick turned and started jogging back along the wall. "Just you, make sure Tom stays at his post." Mick waved his compliance as he headed back to where his partner waited.

"I'm going to see what's going on," he said to Tom. "I'll let you know what's happening."

"I hope that asshole's wrong," Tom said.

"Me, too."

Mick headed to the elementary school that was serving as their barracks. He didn't know where else to look for them. He took the steps two at a time, heading to the room Tony had pointed out as theirs. When he got there, he saw Sully sitting on the bed, his head in his hands. "Sully?" he said softly.

Sully lifted his head. His eyes were raw. "Mick. Hey."

Mick could see in his eyes that Watts' taunt was true. "What happened?" Mick asked.

"We were overrun." Sully's voice was barely a whisper. "We were walking down the road and we just stumbled into a herd." He shook his head. "We never heard them; we never saw them until they were right in front of us." He looked down at his hands, still smeared with blood and gore. "We got through the first wave, but the second…" His voice trailed off.

"I'm sorry, Sully." So inadequate, but what else could he say.

"He's not one of them," Sully said with anger. "I shot him in the head before he could turn. He was still alive…"

"Fuck," Mick whispered. He could only imagine how hard that had to be. He never had to do it shoot someone who had been bitten but was still alive, but Sarah did, when Becca was bitten. It ate at Sarah until the day she died. "You did the right thing, Sully," he said to his friend.

"I know, but that doesn't make it easier."

Mick gripped Sully's shoulder. "Try and get some rest. I'll be back to see you later."

"Can't." Sully blew out a breath, then stood. "Major wants me back out tonight."

"What?" Mick was stunned. "You just got back! You just lost your partner! He can't give you time to mourn?"

"Two other patrols haven't returned. Probably deserted. There's no one else that can go out right now."

"What's so important that you have to leave right away?" At Sully's shrug, Mick moved closer. "What about the guys that went looking for his replacement?" he whispered.

"They're one of the patrols that haven't returned. I'm supposed to go look for them."

"Jesus." Mick shook his head. "Sully, this place is bad. We have to get out of here, take Laurel with us."

"He won't let her go. He may not let you go."

Mick shook his head again. "With or without you, with or without his blessing, I'm leaving. And I'm taking her with me. Campbell, too, if he wants to go."

"Good luck. You'll need it." Sully gathered his pack and moved past Mick into the hall.

Mick left the barracks, heading towards Laurel's garage. Between Sully's apparent surrender and the death of Tony, he had a lot to deal with. He wanted to talk to Laurel, see if she had any thoughts on how to leave the base. He and Tom had visited enough that they no longer knocked before entering. He just called out her name as he walked through the door, past the Jeep on the rack.

When he stepped through the doorway to her welding area, he stopped. Watts was there, bending over a prone Laurel. Mick watched as he pulled his arm back and slapped Laurel across the face. She cried out and Mick clenched his fists.

He crossed the shop in three strides, digging his hands into Watts' shoulders and yanking him away, throwing him across the room. Watts smacked hard into the wall, knocking tools from their pegs. "I told you to stay away from her," Mick snarled as he advanced on Watts.

As Watts shook his head to clear it, Mick slammed a fist into his gut. When Watts doubled over, Mick hit him with an uppercut, slamming him back against the wall. Watts growled and charged Mick, grabbing him around the waist and smashing him into the opposite wall. Mick's head bounced off the wall and he barely saw Watts drawing back to punch him in the face. He jerked to the left and instead of Watts' fist slamming him directly in the middle of his face, he hit Mick's cheek, the pain sharp. When Watts drew back for another, Mick blocked his arm, bringing his fist up and punching Watts in his side. Watts groaned and shifted back, enough for Mick to land a few more blows until Watts charged again, slamming Mick back against the wall, his shoulder hitting the air compressor pipe running down the wall. Mick winced in pain as he pushed forward, now grappling with Watts in the middle of the room.

Mick could vaguely hear Laurel in the background, but he was more concerned with putting Watts down, hurting him so he couldn't hurt Laurel again. He brought his knee up and slammed it into Watts' thigh. Watts released Mick and stumbled back and Mick rained blow after blow on him, ignoring the pain in his shoulder as he swung, until Watts dropped to one knee, his arms crossed above his head. Even though he knew he should stop, he kept going. He couldn't save Sarah from Austin, but maybe he could save Laurel from Watts. It all combined into one blinding rage and he kept punching, hitting Watts on his arms, shoulders, head, cheeks. He kept going until someone dragged him back, flinging him against the wall. He almost groaned when he saw two of Watts' friends, one holding him against the wall and the other standing over Watts.

"Get that fucker," he heard Watts mutter.

The one holding him, a guy about his height, with long greasy hair, swung his fist into Mick's midsection. He doubled over, only to be brought upright by a punch to his jaw from the other guy, a skinny runt of a man with bad teeth. He heard Laurel scream as they took turns, hitting his gut, his ribs, then his face. He managed one punch to the skinny guy, happy to see a tooth fly along with a mouthful of blood. At least he did some damage.

From his rapidly swelling eyes, he saw Watts stand slowly, blood dripping down his face from his nose, his mouth and a cut near his eye. "You fucked with the wrong person," he rasped as he unclipped the knife from his belt and advanced on Mick.

Another Marine flew in. He was a big man, as tall as Mick but more solidly built. His skin was dark, his eyes were darker. "What's going on here?" He asked, pushing Watts away and moving between Watts and Mick. Watts' friends stepped away from Mick and he sagged briefly on the wall, but pulled himself up before anyone noticed.

"He attacked me," Watts said, spitting blood on the floor.

"And the rest of you assholes?"

"They were just defending me," Watts said. "He fights dirty."

"I think three on one is pretty dirty, Watts." He turned to Mick. "Did you attack him?"

Despite the beating he had just received, Mick wasn't done. He wanted to obliterate Watts and his friends. "Yeah, after I came in and saw him smacking Laurel."

"Laurel?"

She wrapped her arms around herself as she looked at the newcomer. Watts' handprint was still visible on her cheek. "He hit me," she said softly.

"Bullshit!" Watts exclaimed. "She likes it!"

Mick growled and tried to get to Watts again, but the big Marine put a hand into his chest and held him in place easily. "No, you don't move." He turned back to Watts. "You have to come in, Watts, you know that."

"Fuck that." Watts spit blood on the floor again.

Mick then noticed the "MP" on the Marine's arm. "I'm taking him to the Major, but all three of you better be there in five minutes, or I'll come for you and you won't like it."

"Fuck you, Jones," Watts spat.

"Yeah, fuck me, but if you aren't there, you're fucked, Watts." He looked over at Laurel. "You need to come, too, Laurel, and tell the Major what happened."

She shook her head. "I can't. I can't get involved."

"If you don't, then this guy here is fucked. Is that what you want?"

Laurel's eyes found Mick's. "Do what you need to do, Laurel. Don't worry about me," Mick said.

Jones looked at Mick. "Aren't you the gentleman?"

"More so than most of the assholes here."

Jones grunted. Watts and his companions bristled. Jones pulled his hand from Mick's chest and in one quick motion, had Mick spun around and pressed to the wall. Mick felt his arms being pulled behind his back. It had been years since he had been handcuffed and he didn't like it then; it was worse now. When Jones pulled his arms behind his back, his shoulder screamed in pain. The click of the cuffs on his wrists caused a touch of panic, but he fought it down. "Let's go, buddy."

"My name is Mick."

"I really don't care." He took Mick's arm to lead him out. "Remember what I said, Watts."

"Yeah, yeah."

"Don't touch her again, Watts," Mick said as Jones led him away. "Next time I'll kill you."

CHAPTER TWELVE

Jones led Mick through the camp, holding him by his arm. While no one stopped to stare, he felt the gazes on him. He knew he looked a mess. His face was smeared with blood, his clothes were dirty and disheveled, and the cuffs were around his wrists. "Just another night, another bar," he muttered to himself.

"What did you say?"

"Nothing. Where are you taking me?"

"The Major. You tell him what happened, maybe he'll go easy on you."

Mick laughed. "That'll work."

"What's the problem? The Major likes Laurel." Jones steered him around a puddle on the street.

"Yeah, maybe a little too much."

"What are you talking about?"

"Nothing. Let's just get this shit done."

Jones shook his head. "This isn't a game. Civilians can't fight Marines. The Major is not going to be happy about this. If you're lucky, he'll just throw you into the brig for a while."

"And if I'm unlucky?"

"Banishment. Execution. Who knows?"

"Execution?" Mick stopped. "What the fuck? For punching an asshole?"

Jones grabbed his arm and pulled him along. "Assault on a Marine during wartime."

"We're not at war."

They were at the building that housed the Major. "We're under martial law. Same difference."

Mick stopped again. "Can you let Campbell know what happened? Tell him I won't be back for my shift?"

"That's what you're worried about?"

"It's my job to protect this place, civilian and Marine alike." Mick pulled away from Jones. "No matter what kind of assholes they are." He walked to the door and waited for Jones to open it.

Jones opened the door and pushed Mick inside. Once the door closed behind them, Jones looked around to make sure no one else was in the vicinity. "Look, I know Watts is an asshole. He was a civilian a few months ago and now he thinks he's a big man because he wears the uniform. But you can't go around beating the shit out of every asshole here."

"If that asshole is hurting someone else, and has been told previously about their asshole behavior, then yeah, I beat the shit out of that asshole." Mick nodded towards the stairs. "Let's get this over with."

They walked up the stairs, Mick exuding a bravado that he really didn't feel. He had no idea what the Major would do. Would he banish him from camp? Not a problem, he was done with their asinine camp, anyway. But execution? For what amounted to a bar fight? That couldn't happen. He couldn't die miles away from his daughter, never seeing Sarah's smile on her little face again. He took a deep breath, wincing at a pain in his ribs.

Jones steered him to the office he had visited before. He opened the door and nudged Mick through. A different Marine was at the desk. "Is the Major in?" Jones asked.

"Yes, sir. He's getting ready to leave, though." The man peered at Mick. Mick flashed him an insincere smile.

"Thanks." Jones stepped around the desk and knocked on the door. He didn't wait for an answer before he opened it, pulling Mick in with him.

"Whatever it is, I'm leaving. I don't have time, Lieutenant." The Major was standing behind his desk. He returned Jones's salute.

"Sir, there was a brawl at the garage," Jones said. "I brought one combatant with me; the others are to follow."

The Major looked at Mick. "A civilian? Were the others Marines?"

"Yes, sir, but there were mitigating circumstances."

The Major shook his head. "Civilians don't attack Marines under any circumstances." He looked closer at Mick. "Is that the guy that came in with McGuire and Sullivan? Cooke?"

Jones looked at Mick, who nodded. "Yes, sir, it is." Jones turned back to the Major.

"Same guy who fell over the wall and killed a bunch of those monsters?"

"Yes, sir," Mick said, avoiding the middleman.

"Why were you fighting my Marines?"

"One was abusing a woman, sir. I don't believe a man should abuse a woman."

"Neither do I. Who was it?"

Sure you don't, Mick thought, unless it's you.

"It was Laurel, sir," Jones said.

"No, who were the men?"

"Watts, sir, and two of his cronies."

The Major arched an eyebrow. "He took on three Marines?"

Mick shook his head. "No, sir. Just Watts. His friends came in to assist."

The Major sat back in his chair and tented his fingers. After a few minutes, he said, "Civilians cannot attack Marines. That is a hard and fast rule." He put his hands on the desk. "I could execute you for that."

Mick fought off a tremor. "Yes, sir."

"But mitigating circumstances. Hurting a woman. Laurel, you say?"

"Yes, sir," Jones answered.

"So I could just banish you, and confiscate of all of your possessions." He searched Mick's face for some sign of distress. He saw nothing. Mick kept his face completely impassive. "But I'm feeling generous today. Plus, you're a good hard worker. A month in the brig."

"What about Watts, sir?" Jones asked.

"Give him a week."

"A week?" Mick said. Jones squeezed his arm, trying to get him to shut up. But Mick would have his say. "He was trying to rape her! He slapped her in the face!"

"Two months for you, civilian." The Major stood and narrowed his eyes. "One more word and you won't like the next punishment."

Mick clenched his jaw. He gave a slight nod.

The Major motioned to the door. "Get him out of here. See if Bradley can look at him." He casually returned Jones's salute.

Jones pulled Mick from the room, past the guard and down the hall. "Why did you have to open your mouth?" Jones said. "You could have done a month easy. Two months is going to be hard."

"Because it's bullshit. A week for slapping a woman and trying to rape her?" Mick shook his head. "This place is a fucking cesspool."

Jones didn't respond. He held tight to Mick's arm as he led him down the stairs and back outside. They walked a few blocks before stopping in front of the military police station. "I'll do the best I can for you, but it's not going to be easy," Jones said.

Mick looked over at him. "Why do you care?"

"No man should ever hit a woman, but especially not a Marine." He shook his head. "I can't even call that shitstain a Marine. Look, just try to keep your head down. Do what you're told. I'll see if I can get the Major to release you early. He seems to like you."

"Who the fuck cares?" Mick nodded towards the door. "Just get me inside so I can do my time and get the fuck out of this shithole." Jones opened his mouth and Mick interrupted "And don't tell me I can't leave. I'm tired of hearing that shit."

Jones opened the door and ushered Mick inside. A desk sat just inside the door. A thin black Marine sat, relaxed with his feet up, leafing through an old magazine. "What do you have there, Jones?" He asked when the door closed.

"Major sentenced him to 2 months in the brig."

"Sentenced?" Mick repeated with a snort.

Jones squeezed his arm. "Can you go get the doc? Major wants him looked over."

"Sure thing." He swung his feet down off the desk and stood up. He was surprisingly tall, at least 6 and a half feet. "Need help with him?"

"I got him, Richards." He pulled Mick past the desk and through the room. He came to a second desk. He pushed Mick into the visitor chair while he slid behind the desk and dropped onto the worn chair. He opened a drawer and pulled out a sheet of paper. "Name?" He asked.

"Oh, so we're treating this like it's legal now?" Mick said. He was slumped in his chair, too proud to ask Jones to help him sit up.

"It is legal. Name?"

"Michael Cooke."

"Date of birth?"

"What the fuck do you need all this for? I'm guilty, throw me in a cell and forget about me."

Jones tapped the pen on the paper and looked at Mick. "You can make this easy or make it hard. Work with me, here. Don't be an asshole."

"I've been told that's my best asset."

"I'm starting to agree with whoever said that," Jones muttered.

Mick laughed despite himself. He decided to just get it over with. He answered the questions with a minimum of bullshit, but he still didn't tell the whole truth. Who knew what they would do with their paperwork?

"I need your knife and your belt." Jones put the form he had just filled out into another drawer.

"Little hard for me to give them to you now." Mick leaned forward and wagged his cuffed hands.

Jones barked out a chuckle. "Yeah, that's true. Can I trust you'll give them to me when we get to your cell?"

"Yes."

Jones helped him to his feet and led him past the desk to another door, which he unlocked with a key from his pocket. He swung the door open and pushed Mick through to a hallway lined with metal doors. There was a small window at the top of each door and what looked like a small rectangular door about midway down. Jones pulled a ring of keys from a hook near the entrance and walked down the hall, pulling Mick along. He stopped in front of the second door on the left and unlocked it.

The room was small, maybe 7 by 7 feet. There was a sink and a toilet and a bed bolted to the wall holding two blankets and a thin pillow. "In you go," Jones said. He pushed Mick through the door and closed it. "Turn around, put your hands against the door." Mick did as he said. He heard the small door open, then his hands were grabbed and he was pulled backwards. He winced, but then sighed with relief when the cuffs came off. The small door slammed shut.

"Knife and belt, please."

"Not my bootlaces?" Mick asked as he unsnapped his sheath from his belt and threw it on the bed. He began to unbuckle his belt.

"No, if you can hang yourself with those, then you are a determined motherfucker and I will salute you before I cut your body down and let you drop on this nasty floor."

He passed the items throw the slot, then, rubbing his wrists, looked out the small window at Jones. "Now what?" He asked.

"Now you wait for the doc."

"Will you let Campbell know what happened? He needs to get someone else on the wall." Jones nodded. "Thanks." Mick sat on the hard bed and sighed.

Dr. Bradley showed up about an hour later. With very little conversation, he checked Mick over, pronouncing his shoulder strained and his ribs bruised. He threw a tube of Neosporin and a clean rag at him and left the cell. Mick wet the rag in the sink and wiped the blood and grime from his face, wincing when he hit a cut. His knuckles were cut and bruised as well. He scrubbed up as best he could, then sat back on the bed with the Neosporin.

"Cooke, you have a visitor."

Mick tossed the tube of medication on the bed and stood in front of the door. Campbell's face appeared. "What the fuck did you do?"

"Beat the fuck out of Watts."

"Looks like you took a pretty good beating yourself."

"His buddies."

Campbell shook his head. "Why?"

"I don't like his attitude." Campbell cocked his head and stared at Mick. Mick sighed. "He was beating on Laurel. He was trying to rape her."

Campbell shook his head. "I've told them about him, but no one fucking listens."

"Because they do it themselves," Mick spat.

"What are you talking about?"

Mick shook his head. "Nothing. Never mind."

"Would you just spit it the fuck out? You've been alluding to shit for weeks and I'm fucking sick of it."

Mick smirked. "You told me not to trust you. Just following orders, sergeant."

Campbell faked a laugh. "You're a funny fuck, aren't you?" Mick shrugged. "Just tell me, Mick."

Campbell had never used his given name. Mick leaned his head against the window. "The Major assaults her, too."

"Fuck!" Campbell swore. "Who else?"

"I don't know. I just know about Watts and the Major. She said there were others. Tom kept most of them away when he was working with her."

"I'll see if I can get Tom there again. Might not stop the Major, but it'll stop the others."

"Then what the fuck is the point, Campbell? If even one guy forces her, it's wrong."

"Mick, sometimes you have to take what you can get." Campbell scratched at his beard. "I'll see what I can do."

"Thanks."

"How long are you in for?"

"Two months." Campbell winced. Mick shrugged. "It's not so bad. I can catch up on my reading."

"No, you can't. You get nothing while you're in here." Campbell shook his head. "Two months alone with your thoughts is going to be pretty bad. Two weeks almost drove me nuts."

"You got two weeks when you went AWOL?" At Campbell's nod, Mick swore. "Watts got a week for attempted rape and slapping Laurel." He looked up at Campbell. "This isn't right, man."

Campbell sighed. "I know, man. I'm sorry. I wish there was more we could do." He turned his head as the door to the cells opened. Jones was framed in the doorway.

"Time's up, Campbell."

"Alright, Jones, don't get your panties in a wad." Campbell turned back to Mick. "Just hang on. I'll see you in a couple months."

"You're not coming back?"

Campbell shrugged. "If I can, but you're supposed to do two months solitary confinement. Depends on who's on duty." He slapped a hand on the door. "I'll keep an eye on Laurel."

"Thank you." Campbell nodded and walked away. Jones closed the door behind him.

Mick sat back on his bed and leaned his head against the wall. He found the tube of Neosporin and opened it, smearing the salve on the worst of the cuts on his face. He figured the knuckles could heal without. He capped the tube and threw it back on the bed.

A while later, he heard a commotion beyond his door. He stood back up and looked out the small window. Jones was leading Watts down the hall.

"I don't know why I'm even here," Watts said. Mick was happy to see that his eye was blackened and he was limping.

"Because you beat on a woman and tried to rape her," Jones said.

"No, I didn't! I don't know why that fucking civilian is lying."

"Watts, I saw the bruise on her face myself. And even if I didn't, I'd believe a civilian I met an hour ago over a piece of shit like you."

"Fuck you, man."

Mick couldn't see them anymore, but he guessed Jones was putting him in his cell. "Turn around, asshole, and put your hands at the door."

A moment later, he heard Watts cry out. "Shit, man, that hurt."

"Like a slap to the face?"

"Fuck you."

"You need to work on your retorts, Watts. They're getting repetitive."

"Get me a magazine or something. C'mon, man."

"You know the rules, you've been here before."

"You can't leave me here without something. I'll go nuts."

"Please, do us all a favor."

Mick saw Jones walk by his cell again. He turned and looked at Mick, who stared impassively back. Jones disappeared out the door and Mick heard the lock click. He stepped back into the tiny cell and sat back on the bed.

Rather than letting his mind take over, Mick amused himself by bouncing the tube of medication off the wall and catching it, trying to see how many he could do in a row. He was up to 272 when the lights abruptly cut out. The cell went completely dark with the barest hint of light coming through the small window in his door. He stood slowly, carefully, so as not to smack into the few things bolted to the floor of the unfamiliar room and walked to the door. He looked out of the window, seeing the hallway lit with emergency lighting. He stood at the door for five minutes, then gave up, making his way back to the bed. He set the Neosporin on the sink and proceeded to make his bed in the dark, laying one blanket on the thin dirty mattress and setting the other at the foot of the bed. He sat, wincing as his ribs pulled, and toed off his boots. He swung onto the bed fully clothed and pulled the thin blanket over him. He put his hands behind his head and waited for morning.

The lights came back on sometime later. Mick had already been awake for over an hour. He sat up, pushing the blanket to the end of the bed, and scraped his hands over his eyes. He used the toilet, then washed his hands and face. He folded his blanket and sat back on the bed, waiting.

After another hour, he heard the outside door open. He got up and stood at his door, watching out the small window as a cart holding three trays with covered plates was pushed through the door. The cart stopped across the hall at the first door. He watched as the Marine that pushed the cart grabbed a tray from the top and pushed it through the slot. "Come on, Chester, get up and get your breakfast," the Marine said. "You got thirty seconds or I'm dropping it on the floor." Chester must have made it to the door because Mick didn't hear the sound of anything hitting the ground.

The Marine grabbed another tray and walked across the hall to Mick. "Breakfast," he said as he thrust it through the slot. Mick took the tray and murmured his thanks. The Marine grunted and walked away.

He sat back on his bed with the tray on his lap. It held a covered plate, a plastic cup full of a light brown liquid and a spoon. He lifted the cup to his nose and sniffed. Smelled like herbal tea. He took a small sip. Yup, herbal tea. He set the cup back on the tray and took the plastic cover from the plate. He saw his breakfast, his first meal since lunch before his shift the day before. A small scoop of scrambled eggs and a bowl of canned peaches. Even as he devoured the food, he thought of how hungry he would still be once he finished. When nothing was left but a few smears of grease, he contemplated licking the plate. With a sigh of disgust, he pushed the tray to the end of the bed and sat with his back to the wall.

About a half hour later, he heard the door open again. "Bring your trays out."

Mick picked up his tray and waited at the door. As soon as the Marine came to the door, Mick slid his tray through the slot. "When do we get fed again?" he asked.

"At lunch time." The Marine took the tray, then pushed it back in the slot. "Keep your cup, in case you want water. Give it back at lunch."

Mick hated himself for asking. "Is there any way I can get more food? I missed dinner yesterday." He took the cup from the tray and the Marine pulled it back out.

"Lunch time."

"What time is it?"

He looked at Mick for the first time. "Does it matter?" He pushed away from the door.

After he tired of playing catch with the Neosporin tube, Mick tried to nap. It was a rousing failure. He barely slept at night, why did he think he would be able to nap during the day? He sat back up on the bed and rubbed his eyes. Sarah would think this was funny, he thought, just before she broke me out of here. He shook his head. He didn't want to think about her. Not here. Not now. Not with the hours of time he had ahead of him.

He turned his mind to the Laurel problem. As soon as he was released, he was getting out of here with her, if he had to fight his way out. It would be mid-August, if he counted right, prime zombie season, but they should be able to make their way back without issue. They could scavenge along the way, plus there was the garage stocked with food. Might take more than a few days, but it was doable. Getting out would be the hard part.

Sarah would have a plan, he thought. She would figure… "Shit!" he whispered. He took a deep breath and picked up the tube of medicine again.

♦

"Cooke! Back to the door, hands out the slot." He didn't even hear the outer door open. He dropped the tube on the bed – 743 this time – and stood as instructed. He felt his hands being cuffed, then a gentle nudge forward. He turned as the door opened.

It was the Marine from the day before, who had been sitting at the desk. He could see "Todd" written across his breast. "Come on out."

Mick stepped out of his cell. "What's going on?"

"Exercise." He took Mick's arm and pulled him along the hall, past the cell where Watts was housed. He unlocked the door at the far end and they were in a small fenced area about 10 x 10.

Mick took a deep breath of the air. Even though he got a faint whiff of exhaust and burning corpses, it was still better than the stale air in the cellblock. "How long do I have?"

"Hour." He undid Mick's cuffs and turned to go back inside.

"Wait!" Mick reached out, but thought better of touching him. "Aren't you staying?"

"Rules say you get an hour of exercise a day, they don't say you get company." Todd walked back through the door. Mick heard it lock behind him.

Mick turned from the door. The enclosure was surrounded on three sides by cyclone fence, the fourth by the building. There was another fence, presumably the barrier around the camp, about 6 feet from the end of the enclosure. Mick walked to the fence and curled his fingers around the wire. He looked down as far as he could see on both sides. There were a few zombies far off to his right, about half a dozen down to his left. He pushed his head against the fence to try and see a bit further. It looked like the wall he had been working on was to the right. Maybe. It was hard to tell.

He pushed back off the fence, hearing the metal clang as it bounced back. He paced the area, thinking about the zombies he had seen, thinking about life beyond this fence, the outer fence. The door opened and he whipped his head around to see Jones heading out. "That was a quick hour," he said.

"Hour's not up yet." Jones walked over to where Mick stood. "We're not all assholes, you know. Some of us do care about what happens here." He reached in his pocket and pulled out two granola bars. He handed them to Mick.

"Thank you," Mick managed before he ripped the wrapper off the first one and ate it in two bites.

"Laurel's not safe," Mick said after he swallowed. "She needs to get out of here."

"We can protect her."

Mick shook his head. "No, you can't. She needs to get out of here. I'm planning to take her when I go, but can she hold out two more months?"

"I said we'll protect her."

Mick smiled sadly. He didn't trust Jones enough with the truth. "I hope you can." He tore open the second granola bar. "Thank you for this." He motioned with it before he took another bite.

"Lunch is about two and a half hours. That should hold you over." Jones nodded his head at him before he unlocked the door and went back into the building.

After his brief sojourn outside, in which Mick did some sit-ups and push-ups, since he had nothing better to do, Todd came back out with the handcuffs. Mick turned so he could put the cuffs on. "So, is Todd your first name or last name?"

Todd rolled his eyes. "Like I haven't heard that before."

"Sorry. You'd think with all this free time with nothing to do, I'd come up with better jokes." He was surprised to see a brief smile on Todd's face.

"Maybe you'll get better." He opened the door to the building and gestured Mick through. "But I doubt it." When Mick headed back towards his cell, Todd took his arm and led him through another door near the end of the cell block. Mick raised his brows, but Todd was quiet. They walked down a short hall and stopped in front of another door. Todd opened it and nudged Mick through.

It was a bathroom, complete with shower stall. Todd undid his cuffs and said, "You have fifteen minutes. Your bag is on the sink."

"Thank you." Todd nodded and left the room.

He rubbed his wrists as he walked to the sink. A sealed plastic bag sat on the counter. He tore open the plastic and pulled out the contents: a towel, a washcloth, a toothbrush and small tube of toothpaste, a small square of soap, two pairs of brown pants and two brown long-sleeved shirts, two tan tees, three pairs each of boxers and socks. He grabbed the toothbrush and toothpaste and immediately brushed his teeth. He was paranoid about his teeth since the ZA began. No dentists. Or rather, no painkillers if something happened to his teeth. He brushed for about five minutes, until he was actually getting nauseated from the taste of the toothpaste. But his teeth were clean.

He shed his clothes as he walked to the shower, carrying the square of soap and washcloth. He turned the water on, not even waiting until it warmed before he stepped under the spray, rinsing days of sweat and grime from his skin. He soaped up quickly, not knowing how much time he had left. Months of showering at Thornville had honed his skill. He was clean and rinsed in seven minutes, stepping out of the shower with the small towel wrapped around his waist. He quickly dried and pulled on the clean clothes. The pants were about two inches too short, the shirt not even coming to his wrists. He shrugged, then looked in the plastic bag, hoping he had missed the razor and shaving cream in the bag. He had not.

Todd walked in. "Let's go."

"I need to shave," Mick said.

"Why?"

"Because I need to shave." He rubbed a hand over his bristly cheek. "I hate beards." He winced when he thought of the last time he had had a beard.

"Time's up."

"Come on, Todd. You can even shave me if you're worried I'll use the razor on you."

Todd arched an eyebrow. "Yeah, like that could happen." He sighed heavily. "Wait here." He was back in about five minutes with a small can of shaving cream and a disposable razor. "You better be able to shave quick."

Mick smiled. "Bless you, Todd." He took the items from Todd's outstretched hand and turned to the mirror. He shaved quickly, grooming his goatee into the proper shape. He finished in less than three minutes.

"Why don't you just keep the beard?" Todd asked. "It's quicker and easier. Major doesn't care, one of the few rules he actually suspended."

"I don't like them. This is how I've looked for years; this is how she – uh, I see myself."

Todd cocked his head and looked at Mick. "Yeah, didn't help." He held out his hand.

Mick laughed as he handed him the razor and shaving cream. "Think I could do that every day?"

"You shower once a week."

"What about during exercise? I'd be willing to forgo time outside."

"I'll think about it. Now let's go. Leave your civvies on the sink and get your shit together. You're already over your allotted time."

Mick threw his stuff in the plastic bag. He folded his civilian clothes and set them on the sink. Todd handed him back the shaving cream. He nodded his thanks as he threw it on top of everything else. He turned, holding the bag between his arm and his side, and held his hands out to Todd.

The Marine looked at Mick and nodded. He snapped the cuffs over his wrists and led him out of the bathroom and back to his cell. Mick stepped in and moved his arm, releasing his bag to drop to his bed. He turned his back to the door and moved his hands to the slot. He felt Todd unlock the handcuffs and turned immediately. "Thank you," he said to the Marine. Todd nodded and walked away.

Mick felt a hundred times better now that he had showered and shaved. He sat back on his bed, folded his hands beneath his head and leaned against the wall.

♦

Lunch was a bowl of watery stew and more peaches. Mick wolfed it down, this time actually licking the remains from the bowl. Who cared anymore? He laid back on his bunk after he finished, wondering how he was going to occupy so many hours of time. His fingers started drumming on the mattress. When he realized he was actually thumping out the tune of one of his songs, he sat up. Smiling slightly, he positioned his hands as if he was holding his guitar. He closed his eyes and began to play.

That was how Campbell found him hours later. "What the fuck are you doing, Cooke?"

Mick's head whipped up to see Campbell at the window. "Trying not to go crazy." Perversely, he finished the song before he stood up.

"Air guitar? Really?"

Mick shrugged. "Used to play. Good way to occupy my time." He moved closer to the door. "How'd you manage to get in?"

"I still have friends." He looked left and right then back at Mick. "Here." The slot in the door pushed open and Mick saw two MREs on the shelf. He hurriedly grabbed them and shoved them under his blanket.

"Thanks, Campbell."

"Tom is working with Laurel full time now. Keeps most of the assholes away."

"But not the biggest."

"No, not him. But I'm doing the best I can."

"I know, Campbell. And I thank you."

Campbell leaned back from the door. "You should. Now I'm short two people on the wall. I have to go up there myself."

Mick laughed. "Earn those stripes."

"Yeah, fuck you, Cooke." He slapped a hand on the door. "Take it easy."

"Only way I can."

♦

Days slowly dragged into weeks. Each day was maddeningly the same. He woke after a fitful sleep, ate a meager breakfast, then practiced air guitar. At some point after breakfast, he got his exercise hour. Each hour, he studied the zombies, then did his push-ups and sit-ups. If Todd was in charge, he got to shape his goatee. He and Todd had become friends of a sort. He didn't even cuff him anymore when he left his cell. Once a week, he got a shower.

Occasionally, Campbell or Jones stopped by, usually with extra food. A miserable lunch, then hours until the mediocre dinner. He filled his time with air guitar, silently playing every song he had ever learned. When he ran out of those, he tried to teach himself new ones. Anything to avoid thinking. To avoid remembering.

He watched when Watts left. Watts looked towards his cell and Mick eye-fucked him through the small window. He saw another guy brought in for a week-end stay. He never saw the guy who was in the cell across from him. If he was in for longer than Mick, then God help him.

Just under a month into his sentence, Sully showed up. "What the fuck did you do, Mick?"

"What I told you I would." Mick stood up from his bunk where he was remembering the chords to the last song he had written. "Watts was beating on Laurel, was probably going to rape her. I told you I wouldn't put up with that shit."

"You're lucky the Major seems to like you."

Mick snorted. "If this is his way of showing he likes me, I'd hate to see what happens if he loves me."

Sully laughed. It sounded rusty, like he hadn't laughed in a while. "You need to behave yourself, Mick."

"I do what I can." He moved closer to the door. "How are you doing?"

Sully shrugged. "I'm doing what I can. We all lose people." He looked up at Mick. "You know that better than I do."

Mick nodded. It almost broke him. "What are you doing now?"

"I'm here for a couple days, then back out. I may drop by Thornville if I have a chance. Any messages?"

"Just that I'm still here. And I'll be back soon." His chest hurt when he thought of Josey. "Give Josey a hug for me."

Sully smiled sadly. "I will. And you stay out of trouble."

Mick spread his arms wide. "Can't get into much trouble here."

"If anyone could find a way, it would be you."

♦

He had been in for nearly six weeks. He had run through all the songs he had learned and was getting frustrated trying to learn new ones without an actual instrument. He threw himself on his bed and rubbed his hands over his face. Exercise time and lunch had come and gone; dinner was still hours away. How the fuck was he going to pass the time? He still had more than two weeks to go.

Without warning, Sarah appeared in his head. She was smiling at him, her gorgeous smile turning her plain face into something approaching perfection. He shook his head, not wanting her in the cell with him. But there she was. And she wasn't leaving.

The day he met her, going after her with a machete, thinking she was undead, until she spoke. She never let him forget that. The first time she saved his ass. The look on her face the day Ryan hurt her so badly. How she cried in his arms the day she had to shoot Gail. The day they finally kissed, after rescuing April and the rest from the zombies. The first time they made love. How scared she was when she told him she was pregnant. How angry she was when she found out Ryan had been kidnapped.

The pain in her eyes and the bruises on her face when she returned after rescuing Ryan, having miscarried their child in the process. The horror she felt when she had to kill Becca after she had been bitten. Her laughter when they bathed in the cold, cold river at Thornville. The pain and fury when Ryan was murdered. The fierceness when she left his killer to die, zombies circling him. The first time she told him she loved him. The joy mixed with sadness when she told him she was pregnant again, over the body of his murdered brother.

How she blossomed during her pregnancy, never stopping her normal routine, yet loving his pampering at the end of the day. The look of awe on her face when she held Josey for the first time. How happy she was – they were – as a family. How strong she was as she led their community. The determination not to let George win, even though they were backed into a corner. Sarah, covered in her blood and George's, touching Josey's cheek for the last time. How calm she looked in death. The hopelessness he felt as he put a knife through her temple.

He didn't realize he was crying. He didn't realize he was sobbing for all that he had lost.

CHAPTER THIRTEEN

Todd came with dinner. "Cooke, dinner." Mick didn't move from the bed. "Hey, Cooke, come get your dinner." Mick still didn't move. Todd banged on the door. "C'mon, Cooke, I don't have all day."

Mick slowly pulled himself from the bed. He walked to the door and accepted the tray Todd had slid through the slot. Without a word, he set the tray on the sink and went back to his bed.

"You okay, man?"

"Go away, Todd." Mick slung an arm over his face.

Todd looked through the window at him for another minute, then set off to deliver his last tray.

When Todd came back a half hour later, the tray was untouched on the sink and Mick was still on his bed. "Dude, what's up?"

"Go away, Todd."

"You need to eat. Get up and eat. Or give me the damn tray."

Mick stood, taking the tray and thrusting it through the slot. "Here's the tray. Now go."

Todd barely caught the tray before it fell to the floor. He put it on his cart and with a last look at Mick, pushed the cart to the opposite side of the hall to the next prisoner.

Todd came back ten minutes later, Mick's tray in hand. "What's up, Mick?"

"Just go away, Todd. Leave me alone."

"What the fuck, dude? You giving up? You're almost out."

"Go the fuck away, Todd."

"Mick, come on, man. You're almost done. You need to get up, eat, get outside of your head."

Mick turned on the too-small bed, facing the wall. He didn't respond.

Todd watched him for a few minutes, then trudged back out of the cell block.

Jones was next. "Cooke, Todd told me you aren't eating. What's going on?" Mick didn't respond, just stared at the wall. Jones had gotten to know Mick over the last 6 weeks. He was a good guy, trying to do the right thing and got punished for it. After a moment of debate, he unlocked the cell door and stepped inside. "Cooke, you have to eat. You've only got a few more weeks to go."

Mick ignored him. He just wanted to be left alone. Alone with his pain and misery and knowledge of what he would never have again.

"Cooke, you have a kid. Don't you want to get out of here and see her?" He noticed Mick tense up. He had struck a nerve. "If you don't eat, you won't be able to get back to her. Just ignore what's in your head and eat." He waited in vain for Mick to respond. Sighing, he opened the cell and stepped back into the hall. He re-locked the door and turned to Todd. "Go find Campbell."

Todd nodded and headed out. Jones leaned against Mick's door, watching him.

Campbell showed up about ten minutes later. "What's going on?" he asked Jones.

"Cooke isn't eating or talking. I think the time finally caught up with him."

"Let me talk to him. Open it up." Campbell waited for Jones to unlock the cell door.

"You sure you want to go in there? You didn't fare so well last time."

Campbell rolled his eyes. "Just open it up." Jones unlocked the door and Campbell stepped in. He leaned against the sink. "Cooke, what the fuck are you doing?" No response from Mick. "Get your ass up and eat something. You only have a couple weeks left. You made it this far, the rest is a cakewalk."

"Get out of here, Campbell." Mick's voice was thick from the tears he had shed.

"When you get your ass up, I'll leave." He looked back at Jones. Jones shrugged. "Mick," Campbell said, his voice a register lower than his usual. "You need to get up. If you want to get out of here, if you want to get Laurel somewhere safe, you need to get up."

"Get out, Campbell. I'm done. I don't fucking care anymore."

"You have a daughter; don't you want to get home to her?"

"She's better off without me."

"Fuck if she is, you're her father. You're all she has left." Campbell reached out and smacked Mick's leg. "Get your lazy ass up, Cooke."

"Get the fuck out of my cell, Campbell! Your goddamn Marine bullshit isn't going to work on me."

"What will? Knowing that your daughter is going to grow up without either of her parents? Knowing that every minute you fuck around feeling sorry for yourself, Laurel is getting hurt? Or do you just not give a shit about anyone but yourself?"

Campbell waited for him to speak, but Mick remained silent. Finally, he pushed open the cell door and stepped outside into the hall. "I'll be back, Mick. I'll keep coming back until you man up."

For two days, Mick refused to eat. He refused his exercise hour. He just laid in his bed, his arm over his face. Campbell came every day, cajoling Mick, teasing him, anything to get him up and out of bed. Tom was there as well, to no avail. Mick wasn't moving. He was done.

Why should he live without Sarah? What was the purpose? Annie and the rest would take care of Josey. Laurel was resigned to her fate, let her have it. No one else seemed to care, anyway. Why should he bust his balls to help?

He closed his eyes and tried to sleep. Instead, he remembered. He and Sarah on the floor of an abandoned house, in front of a warm fire. "You know we have to help everyone we can," she had said. He took a deep breath and swallowed hard. Another memory: Sarah talking to Lyn, who was being terrorized by Chad. "It's my job to keep everyone safe." He blew out another breath even as he felt the tears gather in the corners of his eyes. That was who she was. Who he needed to be.

The next morning, Mick was standing at the door when Todd came with breakfast. "Cooke! Glad to see you up and about." Todd pushed the tray through the slot.

"Thanks." Mick picked a pear from the bowl on his tray with his fingers and popped it in his mouth. "Think I can get a shave today?"

"Sure thing." Todd smiled.

"Thanks, Todd. For everything." Todd nodded as he left to deliver the rest of the trays.

Mick ate every scrap of his breakfast. When Todd returned to take the tray, he slipped Mick a power bar, which he devoured. He needed to get his strength back. He only had a few more weeks, then he was out. Of the brig and out of the camp. He needed to get home and see his daughter.

Jones came to take him to his exercise hour. "Glad you decided to join us again," he said as he unlocked the cell.

"Thanks for sticking around, Jones," Mick said as he stepped into the hall.

"Shit, guy dies on my watch, there's too much paperwork." He slapped Mick on the back as he led him to the exercise yard.

Once they were outside, Jones asked, "You OK?"

Mick hooked his fingers in the fence and looked out. He couldn't meet Jones' eyes. "Yes, I'm fine now. It just got to me, is all."

"It gets to the best of them, Cooke. And you've been in longer than most."

"Are there more zombies over there?" Mick asked, pointing to the left.

Jones walked to the fence and looked out. "Maybe. I can't tell."

"I've been watching them every time I'm out here. Looks like a lot more over there than the last time."

"I'll let someone know. I'm sure it's nothing." He nodded at Mick. "I'm glad you're okay." He left before Mick could respond.

Mick did his push-ups and sit-ups, getting winded way too quick. He'd have to build his numbers up again. When his hour was up, Todd collected him and led him to the bathroom. Mick splashed water on his face before accepting the razor and shaving cream. He quickly removed three days' worth of stubble, shaping his goatee, looking like the man she knew he could be, the man he needed to be.

"Much better," Todd said when Mick finished.

"I know." Mick grinned as he handed the razor back.

"You're good now?"

"I'm good." He followed Todd from the bathroom. "Just hungry."

"Damn, dude, you're always hungry!"

♦

The next week passed uneventfully. Mick was still bothered by the number of zombies against the fence, but Jones said it was being handled. Mick trusted his word. Campbell came to visit, giving him shit as usual. Mick was surprised to find that Campbell had become a true friend. He could only hope he could talk the Marine into coming with him when he left. He'd make a good addition to Thornville.

"Good news, Cooke," Todd said as he unlocked the cell on Mick's shower day, his last shower in the brig.

"Finally get some hot water in the shower?"

"Nope, you're out of here."

Mick stopped gathering his toiletries and stared at Todd. "Seriously?"

"Seriously. The Major figures you learned your lesson."

"I sure as fuck have. As long as I don't see that asshole Watts again."

Todd shook his head. "No, you have learned your lesson. Period. Don't attack him – or any other Marine – again. Next time won't be so easy."

Mick laughed. "You think this was easy?"

"Easier than being dead. Come on, get your shit. One last shower before you go out."

Mick's civilian clothes were sitting on the sink, along with his knife, belt and a disposable razor. He grinned as he undressed for his last shower in the brig. He made it last, not knowing when his next one would be. He only got out when he realized he still needed to shave. He dried and dressed quickly, happy to be wearing clothes that fit, albeit a little looser. He slathered his face with shaving cream. He was just finishing up when Todd came back in.

"Let's go, Cooke."

"Sure thing, Todd." He splashed water on his face, removing the last traces of shaving cream. "What do I do with the prison clothes?"

"Throw them in that bin over there, they'll get washed for the next guy."

Mick gathered the clothes and towel and dumped them in the bin. "I'm ready to get the hell out of here."

"Just make sure you don't come back."

Mick laughed. "I shall do my best."

Todd led Mick to the outer room, where Jones sat at his desk. "You're to report to Campbell on the wall. He doesn't know you've been released."

"So I can tell him I overpowered you and broke out of jail?"

Jones laughed. "Yeah, like that could happen." He stood up and put out his hand. "Stay out of trouble, Cooke."

"Thanks for everything, Jones." Mick shook his hand. "I'll be seeing you."

"I hope not."

Mick stepped out onto the street and took a deep breath. While he had been outside in the past seven weeks, it was his first breath out of incarceration. It still smelled like exhaust with a faint whiff of burning flesh, but it was freedom. He knew he was supposed to report to Campbell on the wall, but a stop before was necessary. He walked down the street towards Laurel's garage.

He was surprised to hear laughter when he entered the outer door. He stepped past the truck on the lift – was it the same one? – and headed towards the back room, where Laurel did her welding. He opened the door and saw Laurel and Tom and a Marine he hadn't met chuckling about something. "Hey," he said.

"Mick!" Laurel exclaimed. She ran over to him as if to hug him, but stopped short and held out her hand. Mick smiled and shook her hand. "When did you get out?"

"This morning." He shook Tom's outstretched hand. "How's things going?"

"Good," Tom said. "Working here has been really good."

"I'm glad, Tom."

"This is Danny Williams," Tom said. "He's been working on the wall."

Mick shook his hand. "Nice to meet you."

"So you're the famous Mick," Williams said.

"Famous or infamous?" Mick asked with a smile.

"Both?" Williams said.

Mick laughed. "Yeah, that's about right."

"Campbell can't stop talking about how you jumped over that wall and just started killing them, like a machine."

"Campbell talks too much." He looked over at Tom. "Got a minute?"

"Sure."

As Mick started to walk away, Laurel walked up to him and placed a hand on his arm. "Thank you for everything, Mick. I'm really sorry you had to –"

"You're welcome, Laurel," he interrupted. "I'm just glad things are working out for you."

Laurel smiled. "Me, too."

Mick nodded at Williams and left the shop, Tom trailing behind him. "How are things here?" Mick asked as soon as they were on the street.

"Good, real good. Guys were coming around at first, but with me here, we haven't seen anyone for a while. Except the Major, of course."

Mick shook his head. "What about Williams?"

"He's just sweet on her, which is understandable, she's a great kid. Reminds me a lot of my daughter."

"I'm working on getting us out of here, along with her, maybe a few others," Mick said, as he looked down the street towards the building where he spent the last two months. "I'll let you know when I have a plan."

Tom looked a bit uneasy. "Sure thing."

"I'm going to head to the wall. I was supposed to go there first thing but I wanted to check on you and Laurel."

"I've got this, Mick. At least, as best as I can."

"Thanks, Tom." He clapped the older man on his back. "I'll see you later." Mick put his hands in the pockets of his jeans and walked down the street towards the wall.

Mick walked by the civilian settlement on his way to the wall. Conditions still looked grim. If anything, they seemed to have worsened. The tents seemed even more crowded together and the people he could see looked worn and beaten down. Except for one man, a young blond man, average height and heavily bearded. He defiantly watched Mick as he moved down the street. Mick lifted a hand in greeting and the man nodded, then turned away.

As he approached the wall, he noticed some commotion on top. He jogged the remaining distance to the ladder and climbed up. "Need a hand?"

Campbell looked surprised to see him. "What are you doing out? You still have another week."

"Good behavior." He looked over the wall and saw about a dozen zombies with more coming. "What's going on?"

"Wagner tripped and fell partially over the wall. Fucking new guys." He thrust his spear at Mick. "Here, get to work."

Mick smiled as he took the spear. "Good to see you, too, Campbell." He turned and started spearing ghouls.

After two hours of zombie killing, Mick realized how out of shape he was. Despite all the push-ups and sit-ups during his exercise hours, sitting stagnant for 23 hours a day made him weak. When Campbell called a break, he dropped to his ass on the wall and breathed heavily. Campbell walked up to him and smirked. "You're such a pussy."

"Fuck you, Campbell," Mick laughed. "I'm out of shape."

Campbell held out an arm. Mick reached for it and Campbell pulled him up. "You'll get it back. Go down and get some water."

Mick climbed slowly down the ladder and walked to the shack, where bottles of water sat in the shade. He plopped down, leaning against the wall of the shack and drained most of a bottle of water. "What I wouldn't give for some ice," he said when he finished.

"I'll make a request," Campbell said as he sat next to Mick, a bottle of his own in his hand. "How are you doing?"

"I'm better." Mick reached for another bottle of water. "Just lost my head a bit."

"I'm surprised it took that long." Campbell took a drink of his water. "I think I lost mine in 3 days."

"Not much to lose."

"Oh, you're a funny one."

Mick shrugged. He drank some more water. He was getting his breath back. "Campbell, when I leave, would you want to come with me?"

"You're not leaving."

Mick sighed heavily. "Yes, I am. Soon. I'd like you to come with me. We could use you at Thornville."

Campbell didn't think Mick was going anywhere. "Sure, I'll go with you." It wouldn't hurt to humor him. "I've had enough of this place."

"You aren't the only one."

♦

After his shift, Mick collapsed into bed. He didn't even stop to wash up. Every muscle ached. He fell immediately to sleep and to his surprise, he slept for a solid seven hours before waking up. He hadn't slept like that since Sarah was alive.

After a quick breakfast with Tom, he headed to the gate. Sgt. Bender was on duty. "How do I get my weapons back?" Mick asked after he shook his hand.

"Major has to approve," Bender said. "Why?"

"I'll need them when I leave. Do you keep them here or somewhere else?"

Bender pointed to a locked cabinet. "Right here."

"Thanks." Now he needed to meet with the Major.

He still had time before his shift, so he headed to the brig. Jones was behind the desk. "You miss us that much?"

Mick laughed. "Hell, no. I was wondering if you could get me in to see the Major."

"Why?"

"I want to thank him for my early release. And ask for my weapons back."

"He won't give you your weapons," Jones said with a shake of his head. "No civilians are to be armed in camp."

"I'm leaving. I'll need them."

"Cooke, he's not going to let you leave."

"He can't keep me here. I've volunteered my time. I haven't even seen another civilian volunteer since I came in. I'm ready to get back home and see my daughter."

"Haven't you realized he's a dictator here? He does what he wants, when he wants and he doesn't give a fuck about 'legalities.'"

"I know that," Mick spat. "I know what he does and who he does it to. I don't give a shit if he thinks he's fucking God, he's not keeping me here."

"What are you talking about?"

"He rapes Laurel. Oh, sure, he makes sure she gets pleasure out of it, but when the woman doesn't want it, it's rape."

"What?"

"You heard me."

Jones sat forward. "How do you know this?"

"Laurel told me." He snorted. "She was pretty much fair game for lots of guys, not just the Major and Watts. That's why Tom's working with her now, he keeps the assholes away."

"Why didn't you say something?"

"Like you all would believe a civilian."

"I would," Jones said softly.

Mick sank into the chair next to Jones' desk. "I'm sorry, I know you would." He sighed heavily. "I just can't stay here anymore, Jones. I realized while I was in that cell that I was just running away from my problems. I need to do something, to be the man my wife wanted me to be. Even if it's just to go home and raise our daughter."

"I understand." He blew out a breath. "I can get you a meet with him, but I think you're wasting your time. I think you're here for the duration."

"Thanks, Jones." Mick held out his hand and Jones shook it. "Let me know when you can arrange it."

"You have time now? May as well get it done."

Mick nodded. "I'm not on the wall for a few more hours."

"Then let's go."

The Major had five minutes to spare. Mick told himself on the way over to show the utmost respect. It might make a difference. As long as he didn't forget.

"What can I do for you?" The Major asked from behind his desk.

"I wanted to thank you, sir, for the early release from my sentence," Mick said. He mimicked Jones' stance, with his hands clasped behind his back.

"You're welcome. Like I said before, there were extenuating circumstances behind your crime. I thought you had served enough time."

Mick nodded. "I'd also like to request the return of my weapons. I'm planning to go back to Thornville. I had a lot of time to think when I was locked up and I'd like to go home and take care of my daughter."

The Major leaned back in his chair. "I'm sorry, I can't spare you. You're too good at your job and we don't have any replacements."

"Sir, I volunteered to come here. I was told it wouldn't be permanent." He struggled to hold onto his temper.

"We're not getting any more volunteers and I have a limited supply of men for the wall. I can't let you go."

"Why aren't you recruiting volunteers, then?" He couldn't reveal what Tony and Sully told him in confidence. "There are more people in settlements out there that would be eager to come to your camp."

"Recruiting is off limits now. If someone comes to camp and volunteers, that's one thing. Like you did." He smiled thinly. "I can detain you as long as necessary. And it is necessary."

Mick took a deep breath before speaking. "Thank you, sir. I'm sorry I wasted your time." He nodded once at the man, then turned on his heel and left the office. After snapping off a salute, Jones was right behind him.

Once they were in the hall, Jones said, "I'm sorry, Cooke, but I knew he would be like that. He doesn't like to lose."

"He's losing me. One way or another, I'm leaving if I have to break out to do it."

CHAPTER FOURTEEN

Mick left Jones at the Major's office and headed towards the wall. He needed an outlet for his anger. He was passing by the civilian's camp when he noticed the same man from the day before staring at him. "Can I help you with something?" He asked, a touch of irritation in his voice. Maybe this guy would do.

"Why do you get so much freedom?" The guy asked, walking up to Mick. "Why aren't you stuck in a tent in the middle of this shithole?"

"I kill zombies on the wall."

"How'd you get that gig?"

"I volunteered."

The guy scratched his beard. "So if I volunteer for something, I can get freedom? Better food?" He nodded at Mick. "You don't look like you're starving."

"If you mean freedom from tent city, then yeah." He grimaced. "You're not getting any other kind of freedom."

"Who do I talk to?"

Mick sighed. "Come with me, I'll see if Campbell can help you." He started walking and the man fell in beside him.

"We've been here about three months, me and my friend, Dalton. I'm Evan, by the way," he said. "Evan Wright." He had to quicken his steps to keep up with Mick.

"Mick Cooke."

"I used to see you a lot, moving around, then you disappeared for a while. What happened? Where were you?"

"Jail."

"Jail? They have a jail here?" When Mick answered with a look, he moved on. "How'd you end up in jail?"

"Assault."

"Really? I didn't think they went in for much law and order around here. There's all kinds of stealing and fighting in the civilian camp." He stumbled on the curb, but righted himself quickly. "I'm from a small settlement about thirty miles away. We ran out of food, so we set off to find some more and found this place instead. Where are you from?"

"Thornville."

"You're a man of few words, huh?" Evan asked with a smile.

"Yup." Mick picked up his pace. Evan's innocent questions were just fueling his anger. They were at the wall just a minute later.

"What are you doing here?" Campbell asked when he saw them. "Your shift doesn't start for an hour."

"I need to work out some anger. What better way to do it?"

Campbell was pretty sure he knew why Mick was angry. He gave Mick a slight nod. "Who's this?" He indicated Evan.

"Evan Wright. Wants to help. Talk to him and give me your spear." Mick held out his hand. Campbell put his bloodied spear in Mick's hand. Without another word, Mick walked to the ladder and climbed up on the wall.

He nodded at the Marine on the wall, then walked past him to an empty spot on the wall. Without a pause, he started on the zombies, taking each one out with a single shot to the head. Within an hour, he had killed every creature within a twenty-foot radius.

"Jesus, Cooke, you're a machine," Campbell said, stepping up beside him.

Mick whipped around, nearly hitting him with the spear. The anger was still there. "Don't sneak up on me."

Campbell held his hands up. "Sorry, man. Are you okay?"

"No," Mick spat. "That fuck told me I was too 'necessary' for him to allow me to leave." Mick looked at Campbell, the anger still raging in his eyes. "Fuck him, I'm getting out of here one way or another."

"Mick, just take it easy."

"No, Campbell, I can't take it easy. I don't want to be here anymore, I want to be back home, with my daughter."

"I told you he wouldn't let you leave," Campbell said softly.

"I should have believed you." Mick leaned the spear against his leg. "I just didn't think he'd be able to hold a civilian."

"He can do whatever he wants until he's replaced."

"And when will that be?"

Campbell's shrug said it all.

The anger barely subsided over the next few days. He knew he could leave if he wanted to, just jump over the wall and be done with it. But that would mean leaving Sarah's things behind, along with anyone else who wanted to come with him, like Laurel. Even though things were better for her, they still weren't as good as they could be. One abuser was just as bad as multiple abusers. So he maintained his daily routine, wondering if eventually the Major would relent. If he would allow him to go back home.

Somehow, Campbell got approval from the Major to allow Evan to work on the wall. Mick was assigned the job of training him. The kid wasn't bad, just way more talkative than Mick had the patience for.

"What did you do before all this shit? I just graduated college, was getting ready to start working at a non-profit. All my loans would have been forgiven if I worked there ten years." Evan laughed. "Guess they're all forgiven now."

"Yup," Mick said as he speared another zombie.

"Wonder what I'd be doing now if the zombies hadn't shown up?" Mick bit back his answer. "Probably something stupid." Evan thrust down at a zombie and missed. "You make this look so easy."

"Practice."

"Are you killing them all or are there less of them?"

Mick finally looked at Evan. "What?"

"Does it seem like there's less of them?"

Mick looked out over the area beyond the wall. Evan was right. There were substantially fewer zombies than there had been. "Huh," Mick grunted. "Wonder what's going on."

"Maybe they're dying out."

"We're only about twenty miles from the state capital," Mick said. "There should still be tons of them around. Especially since just about everyone can become one now."

"Maybe you're just that good at killing them."

Mick laughed and hefted his spear. "Let's just get rid of what's here."

♦

The next day, there were even less zombies. "Maybe the kid is right," Campbell said when Mick remarked on it. "Maybe they are dying off."

"I don't think so. There's something going on. Maybe they're all herding somewhere else, but you'd think they'd be drawn here, to the noise." Mick shrugged. "There's no sense trying to figure those fuckers out."

"I don't know why you're bitching about it. Less work for you."

"And you, too, you lazy fuck," Mick said with a laugh. Campbell flipped him the bird, then headed back down the ladder. He reminded Mick a lot of his brother. The same sophomoric sense of humor, the same struggle when doing the right thing just wasn't possible. Ryan would have made a good Marine, he thought. He slammed his spear down into a zombie's skull, then waited for the next one.

A scream ripped through the air. He turned his head towards the sound, which came from the camp. He took a step forward, then heard another, followed by a gunshot. Gripping his spear tightly, he climbed quickly down the ladder. "We have a breach," he said to Campbell as he ran past him. Campbell was right on his heels.

They rounded the corner and saw pandemonium. People, civilian and Marine alike, were running, screaming. Other Marines were heading towards the back of the tent city, where it looked like streams of zombies were breaking through. Campbell pulled his Glock 19 from his holster and began firing. "Be careful not to hit the civilians," Mick yelled. "I'm heading to Laurel's to get more weapons."

He ran quickly, passing Marines heading towards the fighting. Tom and Laurel were already in the doorway when he arrived. "There's a breach," Mick said. "We need weapons."

"I don't – I don't have any here," Laurel said, her eyes filled with fear.

"Pipes, crowbars, lengths of metal, anything you have that we can use to bash their heads in," Mick said.

"I'll gather some." Tom went back in the garage.

Mick watched the area, his spear ready just in case. The invasion seemed to be concentrated by the fences. The wrought iron and chain link fences that he figured to be a problem when he first arrived.

"What's – what's going to happen?" Laurel asked softly. He had forgotten she was there.

"We'll get them, don't worry."

A scream rose over the gunshots and she flinched. "Are you sure?"

He looked down at her, the naked fear on her face. "Stay here, lock yourself in. Don't open unless it's me, Tom, Campbell or Jones, OK?" She nodded. "Go on in."

Tom came out as she was heading in, makeshift weapons cradled in his arms. "This is what I could find," he said.

"Good enough." Mick pulled a crowbar from the pile and hooked it to his belt. "Let's go."

They jogged to the civilian tent camp and saw chaos. People running and screaming, zombies rampaging, Marines firing, taking down zombies with nearly every shot. "Hey!" Mick yelled as they stopped in the center of the camp. "Grab a weapon." Most people ran past without stopping. Mick grabbed the next woman, a thin woman with long dark hair. "Hey! Quit running and start fighting!"

"I – I can't," She sobbed.

"Either that or die, now fight!" He thrust her towards Tom with his armful of weapons.

Her hand shaking, she grabbed a length of pipe. "What – what do I do?"

"Hit them in the head as hard as you can. Hit them till they drop."

"O-OK." She walked away, gripping the pipe tight.

Mick turned to his companion. "Tom, stop anyone you can and give them a weapon. Keep one for yourself then start killing."

"Alright. You be careful."

"You, too, man." He slapped Tom on the back then headed towards the fight.

He killed three before the spear broke. He left the broken end embedded in the zombie's skull and pulled the pry bar from his belt. He forced his way through a clot of civilians, huddling together. "Get out of here!" He yelled. "Go find a weapon and help!" He swung on another creature, a short fat one. Its head nearly exploded, black ooze spraying in all directions. He leapt over a body, hopefully a ghoul and not a person.

He ran deeper into the camp, swinging as he went. Gunshots cracked through the air, screams overlaying the sounds. He prayed the Marines were good enough. He made it to the edge of the civilian camp, having dispatched half a dozen ghouls on the way. He spotted Marines and civilians, working together to save the camp. He swung on a close one, nearly decapitating it, before he moved to another spot. He kept moving, swinging, killing and stepping to another spot to kill another one.

Gunfire shattered the air right next to him. He heard a grunt that sounded human. He looked to his left and saw the Major firing into the crowd. Every other bullet missed a zombie, and instead, hit a civilian. "Hey!" Mick screamed. "You're killing civilians!"

The Major ignored him, firing again and again. Mick raced towards him, hoping to stop the carnage. The Major turned and saw him coming. "What happened?"

Mick ignored his question. "You're killing civilians," he said. "Watch your aim."

"I can't tell them apart!"

"The ones running away are civilians, asshole." Mick pushed past him and headed back into the fray.

The damn things kept coming. His arms were tired, but he couldn't stop. He swung, stomped and moved on until it was all he could think about. Civilians and Marines were doing the same, taking down every creature that moved. Some were too slow, getting bit before the creature was dispatched. Mick saw the gruesome sight of a Marine out of ammunition who was swarmed by four zombies and wrestled to the ground. He watched as another Marine fired into the crowd, giving the doomed Marine a mercy killing. He whispered a prayer to a God he didn't believe in as he kept on killing.

Mick made his way to the chain-link fence, which was laying on the ground, covered in blood and gore. He could see the wrought iron fence twisted out of shape, presumably from the press of thousands of bodies. Fewer zombies were getting through, but the hole needed to be closed. "Hey!" He yelled to a nearby Marine. "Is there some way to block this back up?"

"What?" The Marine's eyes were wide and full of shock in his young face.

"Go get a truck or tank or something!! Block this fence up!!"

The Marine swiped a hand over his gore-streaked face before running down the street. Mick positioned himself in front of the downed fence and took down another half a dozen zombies before the young Marine came back driving some sort of green truck that reminded him of a Humvee. It had big wheels, which would allow zombies to crawl underneath, but it would be better than nothing. Mick moved away from the fence and pointed to where he had stood, hoping the Marine got the idea. He pulled the truck up to the gap in the fence, parking it directly between the uprights. He hopped out and ran to where Mick was standing. "Thanks," he said as he pulled his sidearm.

"For what?"

"You woke me up." He took aim and dropped a zombie.

"You're welcome." Mick swung on a tall black zombie that reminded him of Jones. He hoped Jones was okay.

Mick and the young Marine stood in front of the truck and worked their way forward. Mick heard fewer screams, but the gunshots were still constant. Finally, as his shoulders were aching and his arms starting to quiver, the gunshots slowed, then petered out, with only an occasional pop. Mick dropped his arm to his side, the blood and gore thick and heavy on his pry bar. His breathing was heavy and he wanted nothing more than to drop to the ground.

"Nice work," the Marine said, holding out his hand.

Mick wiped his blood-spattered hand on his jeans and shook the Marine's hand. "Same to you."

"Luke Davis."

"Mick Cooke."

"What now?' Davis asked, staring at the bodies littering the ground.

"Now we clean it up, see who needs help."

His prybar gathered another layer of gore as he slammed it through the skull of every body that didn't have a head wound, zombie, civilian or Marine. He didn't know if the people who died had the virus or not, but he was taking no chances. He did stop to check each of the Marine bodies, hoping he didn't see someone he knew. Until he did.

Watts had been bitten in the neck from behind and bled out. Was it wrong that he felt satisfaction slamming the pry bar through his eye socket and into his brain? He didn't think so.

"Mick!"

He looked up from Watts' corpse to see Campbell running towards him.

"Good to see you," Mick said, holding out his hand, then taking it back when he realized how grimy his gloves were.

"Fuck, I thought maybe they got you. You weren't by the wall."

"No, I worked my way to the fence where they got in." Mick nodded in that direction. "Something still needs to be done. Some guy named Davis just moved a truck in front of it, but they can still get through."

Campbell nodded. "Major's dead."

"What?"

"Shot. Not sure if it was intentional or not."

"I'd like to say something sad about that, but I'm not that much of a hypocrite." He wiped the sweat from his brow with the back of his glove. "Who's in charge now?"

"I think Jones is ranking, but I'm not sure."

"So he's OK, then?"

Campbell nodded. He looked down at the corpse at Mick's feet. "Watts, huh?" He looked up at Mick, a grin on his face. "So was he already dead when you put the pry bar through his skull?"

Mick laughed. "Fuck you, Campbell."

It took over an hour to make sure all of the corpses were really corpses. One unfortunate that had been bitten turned on the field. Mick got it with his prybar just before it could bite another Marine. There were a handful of people bitten, but not turned. Jones directed them to one of the unused office buildings where they could be kept comfortable until the end. A couple people had gunshot wounds from stray rounds. They were ushered to the infirmary. All that was left was the cleanup of the bodies.

Mick had just dropped on the sidewalk at the edge of the civilian camp. He leaned up against a building. He was spent. Every muscle ached, but he knew that he wasn't done. He needed a few minutes. "Hi," he heard a soft female voice.

He looked up and saw the dark-haired woman from earlier. She was covered in blood and gore, the pipe gripped in her right hand streaked with red and black. For a split second, he saw Sarah. "I'm glad to see you're okay," he said.

"I am, thanks to you."

"No, you did it yourself. I just gave you the weapon."

"Nevertheless, thank you." Mick nodded. She gave him a slight smile and walked away, dragging the pipe on the ground.

Mick leaned back against the wall and closed his eyes. He just needed a few more minutes before getting back up.

"Cooke!" He snapped his eyes open to see Jones heading towards him.

"Hey, Jones." He patted the concrete next to him. "Pull up a seat."

With a brief smile, Jones squatted down next to him. "Thanks for your help today. I don't think we would have gotten a handle on it so soon without you."

"You're welcome. But you would have taken care of it, you're Marines."

"Regardless, thanks." Jones cleared his throat. "The Major is dead."

"So I heard." Mick looked at his friend. "I also heard that puts you in charge."

"Temporarily, I guess. They'll send someone else."

"Hopefully someone better."

"Yeah, that's my hope, too." He looked out over the camp, at the death and destruction. "You're free to go. You and any of the civilians. If any of the Marines want to go, as long as they've finished their tour, they can go, too."

"Thanks, Jones, I really appreciate it."

"But I'd like you to stay. Just a little bit. Help us get this cleaned up, get back on our feet."

"Are there going to be changes? With the civilians?"

Jones nodded. "We have room in the buildings. I'm going to put them to work, but it'll be worth it for them."

"And I can leave whenever I want?"

"Even if you don't help, you can leave whenever you want, Mick."

As much as he wanted to go home, he owed Jones. "I'll stay and help."

"Thanks," Jones held out his hand. Mick shook it. "Get some rest, you'll need it."

♦

It took two days to clear the carnage. Twenty-seven civilians and eight Marines had been killed. Ten people had been hurt with what Dr. Bradley called "survivable injuries." Nearly half of all deaths and injuries had been from gunfire. They collected the dog tags from the Marines and any identification from the civilians so they could keep a log of those that had died and those that were remaining in the camp. Jones was going to run the camp more like Thornville rather than a military base. The civilians had been assigned housing in the buildings. He even appointed a civilian council to act as a liaison with the military. He planned to do better than his predecessor.

At the end of the second day, after consulting with Jones on his council, Mick had enough. He was ready to go. As he and Jones were heading away from the now full school building, he said to Jones, "I'm leaving tomorrow."

Jones nodded. "OK, I guess I can't ask for anything else."

"I'm sorry, Jones, but I'm really missing my daughter. I need to get home to her."

"I understand, Mick. I told you that you could leave whenever you wanted." He looked over at Mick. "Are you going alone?"

Mick shook his head. "Campbell wants to come with me. Plus Tom and Laurel. I think that's it."

Jones nodded again. "I like Campbell, but damn, he can be a pain in the ass. Now he's your pain in the ass."

Mick laughed. "He'll do fine." Mick coughed as the stench of the former civilian outhouses wafted towards him. "I'll need my weapons."

"You can pick them up on your way out of camp. I'll leave word at the gate."

"Thanks, Jones." Mick held out his hand.

"Thank you, Mick." Jones shook his hand, clapped him on the back with the other one.

Mick sought out Campbell, who was back to overseeing the wall. "I'm leaving tomorrow," he said as soon as he saw the Marine. "Are you still coming with me?"

Campbell looked out over the wall, at the few zombies that approached. "Yeah, I think I've had it with this place. I gotta tell Jones I'm leaving."

"He knows," Mick said. "I told him earlier."

Campbell nodded. He looked down at the ground and asked, "Are you sure it'll be okay for me to come back with you?"

Mick laughed, then stopped when he saw the look on Campbell's face. "It'll be fine. I want to leave in the morning, so be ready."

"I'm a Marine, I'm always ready." The concern was gone, the cocky Marine back in place.

"Sure, Campbell."

Mick's next stop was Laurel's garage. He walked through the garage, to the work area at the back of the shop. Tom and Laurel were laughing as they shared an MRE. "Hey, guys," Mick said as he stepped into the room.

"Mick!" Laurel put her MRE down and slid off the bench she was sitting on. She crossed the room. This time, she engulfed him in a big hug.

Mick awkwardly patted her on the back. "Hi, Laurel." He looked over her shoulder at Tom, who was smirking. He gently disengaged himself and took a step back. "We're leaving tomorrow, so get together whatever you want to take."

Laurel looked at Tom. He dropped his head, then looked back up at Mick. "We're not going."

"What?"

"We're staying here. With the Major gone and Jones in charge, Laurel doesn't have to worry anymore. And if someone starts shit, I'll be here to stop it." Tom set his meal on the bench next to him. "And here…Here people don't treat me like a pariah. I have friends."

He knew he had to let him live his life. He still felt bad about how Tom had been treated in Thornville. But it was hard to let a friend go. He nodded. "If you change your mind, our doors are always open for you. Both of you."

"Thanks for understanding." Tom took a step towards Mick and held out his hand.

"Of course, Tom," Mick said as he shook the older man's hand. "Thanks for coming with me and keeping me out of trouble."

Tom laughed. "Didn't do such a good job, did I?"

Mick grinned. "Yeah, well, you did your best." He nodded at Laurel. "See ya."

Hands in his pockets, Mick left Laurel's shop. At least he wasn't going back alone. He'd have Campbell. That should be a fun and interesting journey.

"Hey, Mick!" He lifted his head to see Evan running towards him.

"What's up, Evan?"

Evan fell in step beside him. "Campbell said you're leaving tomorrow?"

Mick nodded. "It's time for me to get home. I miss my daughter."

"You have a daughter? Wow, that's weird. I never would have thought you had a kid. How old is she? What's her name? Why did you leave her? I don't know if I'd leave my kid, if I had one, that had to be pretty hard. How come you –"

"Something I can help you with, Evan?" Mick interrupted.

"Oh. Yeah. Can I go with you?"

Mick stopped walking. "You want to go with me to Thornville? Why?"

Evan shifted his feet. "I just – I don't – my friend, Dalton, died. I don't have anyone else here but you and Campbell and both of you are leaving. Can I please go with you? I can pull my weight, I swear. I just don't want to be left behind here." He stopped suddenly, looking anywhere but at Mick.

Mick sighed. It was going to be a long trip home. "Sure, you can come. We're leaving at first light, so be ready."

"I will! Thanks so much, Mick!! I won't let you down. I –"

"I know, Evan," Mick interrupted again. "Just go get your shit together, OK?"

"Sure thing, Mick! Thanks again!" He bounded away and Mick shook his head, smiling. Well, this trip just got longer, he thought as he resumed walking.

He headed back to the wall, for his last shift. Campbell was instructing two civilians on the best way to kill the zombies from the top of the wall. Mick waited until he was finished before he approached. "Fresh meat?"

Campbell laughed. "Yeah, we'll see how long they'll last. Actually, we won't. It's Freeman's problem now."

"Where's my spear?"

"You're done here, Cooke. Go get your shit ready, get some rest. We're leaving at first light."

Mick smiled. "Evan's coming, too."

"Jesus fuck, really? I'm going to have to listen to him for the rest of my life?"

Mick laughed. "He's not so bad, you just have to tune him out, nod a few times so he thinks you're still listening."

"I'm starting to rethink this journey."

"Fuck you, Campbell, I'm not walking for two days with just Evan."

CHAPTER FIFTEEN

The sun was barely over the horizon when Mick and Campbell left their room. Both had backpacks filled with MREs and water, just in case they couldn't find anything along the way. Campbell's was twice the size of Mick's. Campbell had his Glock 19 on his hip and his M16A2 rifle slung over his shoulder. Mick would pick up his weapons at the gate.

Where Jones was waiting. "Had to see you off," he said, shaking Mick's hand.

"It's a bit early, don't you think?"

Jones shrugged. "I'm not planning on much sleep any time soon." He moved to the metal footlocker stacked onto two saw horses and flipped open the lid. "Come here and get your weapons."

Mick walked over and peered inside. On the right was Sarah's 9mm and the shotgun with the string threaded through the trigger guard. "Those two," he pointed before he reached inside.

"What the hell is that string for?" Campbell asked.

Mick smiled as he took the shotgun from the locker. He slid the string over his head and put his arm through. The shotgun hung by his side within easy reach if need be. "Now do you understand?"

After a moment, Campbell started laughing. "Holy shit! That makes you 'the ugly!'"

Jones joined in. Mick laughed, too. "Sarah said I was better looking than Tuco." For the first time, it didn't hurt when he thought of her. A small ache, yes, but the deep pain was gone.

"She didn't wear glasses, did she?" Campbell asked, still laughing.

"Fuck you, Campbell." Mick reached into the locker and pulled out the 9mm and holster. He slid the weapon from the holster and popped the magazine, checked to see that it was still full, then pushed it back into place. He snapped the holster on his belt.

"Am I late?" Evan came running up to them. "I'm so sorry. I couldn't find my spare pair of boots, so I just left without them." He had a small pack on his back. "Are we leaving? How far is it, anyway?"

"Couple days' walk," Mick said. "You ready?"

"Oh, yeah, I'm ready. I've been ready. I can't wait to get out of here." Evan looked at Jones. "No offense, sir."

"None taken." He turned back to Mick. "You're welcome back anytime."

"Thanks, Jones. Same goes for Thornville."

Jones nodded. "You better get on your way."

Mick held out his hand to Jones. They shook again. "Thank you for everything, Jones."

"Thank you for what you did, and what you tried to do."

"I'll see you again."

"I hope so," the Marine said.

Mick stepped towards the gate as Campbell and Jones said their goodbyes. Now that the day was here, he was eager to go. But he was apprehensive, too. How much had things changed in Thornville? How much had Josey changed? Would she remember him?

Campbell and Evan moved up beside him. Campbell looked over at Mick, sensing his conflict. "Let's go, Cooke. Your daughter awaits." Mick favored him with a small smile. The gates slowly opened, just enough for them to step through. Mick didn't look back as they closed behind them.

The morning was just this side of cool, but Mick knew the temperature would climb through the day. He hoped they could get a lot of walking in before they had to stop. He adjusted his pace to Campbell's and Evan's as they walked down the road.

"So what's Thornville like?" Evan asked. "Is it big? What will I do there?"

"It's not so big," Mick said when Evan stopped for a breath. "About 50 people when I left. We all stay in 3 buildings because they have generators. One building has full solar power, Bobby was working on outfitting the rest when I left."

"Pretty small, then?" Campbell remarked.

"Nothing like the camp we left, no. But it's good enough."

"What else is there? Do you have women there?"

Mick turned to Evan. "Yes, there are women there. But no one does anything they don't want to. That means no chasing after women who don't want you, understand?"

"Well, yeah, who would do that?"

"Who, indeed?" Mick looked at Campbell, who shook his head.

They walked in silence for a few minutes before Evan started talking again. "What do you eat there? Do you have enough food?"

"We scavenge and we send out hunting parties. They bring back all kinds of game, once even a wild pig."

"Shit, you have real bacon?" Campbell asked.

Mick shook his head, smiling. "Of course you'd care about the bacon. We didn't know how to butcher it properly, so we screwed it up. We have a book for next time so we can get some bacon out of it. If we get another one."

"I used to hunt back home," Evan said. "I could be on a hunting party."

Mick nodded. "When we get back, you can talk to Troy, tell him what you can do. He'll find a spot for you."

"Who's Troy?" Evan asked.

Mick spent the next hour explaining who everyone was in the camp. Whenever he'd mention a name, Evan would ask about them. Mick regretted not knowing more about the people who came in from Kittington and the few stragglers thereafter. Once Sarah was killed, he lost interest in the day-to-day running of the settlement. All he cared about was Josey and where his next drink was coming from. At least that part of his life was over.

The conversation petered out and they walked in silence. Evan, not used to walking so long at such a pace, decided to save his breath and quit asking questions. Mick enjoyed the quiet.

Other than quick bathroom breaks, they walked without stopping for nearly five hours. They had just entered the small town of Bardley when Campbell called a halt. "We should eat," he said. "Let's stop in that park over there."

The park was small and overgrown, the grass over a foot tall. Two picnic tables were still visible among the weeds. They made their way over the cracked and weed-infested asphalt to the tables.

Evan collapsed on a bench with a heavy sigh. "Whew!" he blew out. "Didn't expect this much walking. My feet are killing me." He bent to untie his boots.

"Don't do that," Mick said as he shrugged out of his backpack. "You won't get them back on."

"Oh." Evan sat upright. "So what do I do?"

"Embrace the suck," Campbell said as he swung his backpack off his shoulders.

Mick laughed. He was almost afraid to sit down, fearing he wouldn't want to get back up. He still wasn't in the best of shape after his incarceration and the morning's walk had worn on him. In the end, he sat on the bench and opened his pack.

They each had an MRE, washed down with water. Campbell allowed an additional fifteen minutes of rest after they had eaten, then he got them on the move again. With a heavy sigh, Mick shouldered his pack and started walking. Evan was only a few steps behind.

As Mick predicted, the day turned warm and muggy. All three of them were down to tee shirts before another hour had passed. They spoke little, saving their energy for the walk. They were three hours into the second leg of their walk when Campbell spoke up. "I don't like the look of those clouds."

Mick looked up at the sky. There was a line of black clouds drifting towards them. "Maybe they'll pass over."

"Not with our luck. We should move faster, see if we can find somewhere to hole up if it starts pouring."

"I think the garage we sheltered in on the way here isn't far," Mick said.

"I hope so. That shit's going to be nasty when it comes down."

The wind picked up as they walked. They started moving faster, but the rain caught them, big fat drops that heralded the coming storm. Lightning flashed, then barely a second later, the thunder boomed. Without a word, they started jogging, hoping to find the garage before the rain completely engulfed them.

They were soaked by the time Mick spotted the building. "Come on!" He yelled over the roar of the storm. He could barely hear his own voice, so he didn't know if they heard him, but they were following. Mick hit the man door and opened it quickly, without checking for anyone inside. Campbell and Evan followed and Mick slammed the door shut behind them, his hand going to the knife on his belt just in case.

"Little wet out there?" Sully was sitting by the fire ring, a small fire burning, a pot on top of the grate. His gear was spread out around him. They heard the soft nicker of his horse, stabled in the corner of the garage.

"Sully! What are you doing here?" Mick asked.

“I think that’s a better question for you three.” Mick watched as he slid his hand away from his Glock 19 and reached inside his pack.

"I'm going home," Mick said.

"And you, Campbell? Does the Major know you're out?"

"Major's dead," Campbell said to Sully. "Jones is in charge."

"What?" Sully put aside the socks he had pulled out of his pack. "What happened?"

"Can we talk about it while we build up that fire?" Mick asked. "We need to dry out." He was shivering in the cold of the garage.

"Sure, sure." Sully stood up and walked to where the wood was stacked. Mick joined him. Both carried logs to the fire and shoved them under the grate, sending sparks flying. Sully headed to the shelves built into the wall.

Campbell and Evan walked to the fire and sat on the bench surrounding it. They leaned forward, feeling the heat, steam rising from their clothes. Mick plopped down on the bench next to them. Once the heat hit him, he stopped shivering.

"So what happened?" Sully asked. He walked back to the fire with another pot, which he set next to the first one on the grate.

"There was a breach," Campbell said. "About forty people were killed. The Major was one of them."

"No great loss," Mick muttered.

"And now Jones is in charge?"

“Temporarily," Campbell answered Sully. "He's the ranking officer."

"Huh." Sully was silent a moment. "And he just let you go?"

"Anyone who finished their tour could leave. I had enough of that place, and Mick's lost without me now, so here I am."

"Fuck you, Campbell," Mick said absently.

Sully chuckled. "And you?" He nodded at Evan. "Who are you?"

"I'm Evan. Evan Wright. I didn't like it there anymore so I decided to tag along." He looked over at the horse. "Is that your horse? Why do you have a horse inside? What do you feed it?"

Mick closed his eyes and smiled, glad that someone else was dealing with Evan's unending questions. He let the conversation flow around him as the fire dried his wet clothes, the sounds of the storm in the background.

"Food’s ready,” he heard Sully say. He opened his eyes to see Sully walking back from the shelves with four plates in his hand.

"Campbell, why don't you grab a couple bottles of water?" Sully asked as he dished out the meal from the pots.

"I have something better," Evan said as he unzipped his pack. He reached inside and slowly pulled out a mason jar filled with clear liquid.

"What's that?" Campbell asked, standing in front of the shelves.

"Moonshine. They were making it at the camp. I traded my spare knife and some socks for it."

"Hell, yeah, that's better than water!" He grabbed four cups from the shelf.

"None for me, thanks," Mick said. "Can you just grab me some water?"

"C'mon, Mick, live a little," Campbell said.

Mick shook his head. "I don't drink." He caught Sully's gaze. Sully favored him with a slight smile.

"Really?" Campbell shook his head as he put the cup back on the shelf and took a bottle of water. "Loser."

"How many times do I have to say it? Fuck you, Campbell," Mick said with a laugh.

Campbell came back to the fire. He handed the water to Mick and set the cups next to him. "Pass over the hooch."

Evan handed the jar to Campbell and he unscrewed the lid, the strong scent of alcohol filling the room.

"Damn, don't spill that near the fire, this whole place will go up." Sully sat back, away from the fire.

"I'm a professional, I don't spill." Campbell poured a measure into the three cups, then recapped the jar. He handed it back to Evan – near half full – then passed around the cups of liquor.

Sully gave everyone a plate of the corned beef hash that he had heated on the fire. They ate without talking, the only sound the storm raging outside. Lightning flashes filled the garage with light, thunder directly on its heels, rattling the windows. "Wow, sounds bad out there," Evan said.

"It's a big one," Sully replied. "I skirted the edges of it for a couple hours. I barely made it here in time." He forked up the hash. "I got here about twenty minutes before you guys."

"Hope it lets up soon," Mick said. "I want to get home."

"Sorry, I didn't make it there this trip," Sully said. "But I guess it doesn't matter, since you're heading back."

"Can't wait," Mick said as he finished the last of his hash.

"You – uh – you think I could join you?" Sully asked. "Not right now, I have to take the horse back, but since Jones is letting us go, would I be welcome?"

"Why wouldn't you be?" Mick set his plate aside and reached for his water. "I'd be honored to have a real Marine at Thornville."

Campbell laughed. "You're such an asshole." He picked up his cup. "A toast to Thornville." They all lifted their cups, Mick, his water bottle. "May it be all Mick claims it to be." They drank.

"Jesus Christ!" Sully sputtered after he had swallowed. "Where the hell did you find this shit?"

Campbell and Evan both choked after their drinks, then Campbell shouted, "All right! Now that's a drink!"

"You can have the rest," Evan whispered. "I don't think I can feel my tongue anymore."

Mick laughed. He was enjoying himself, for the first time in months. He didn't think she would mind.

The storm showed no signs of abating. It seemed to grow in strength, the rain whipping the windows, the thunder and lightning sounding like it was right on top of them. "I think we're better off staying here until it stops," Campbell said, peering out a grimy window. "It looks like the road's flooded anyway."

Mick agreed. "I don't relish walking in the rain," he said. "I had to walk in the snow to get there."

"Hey," Sully said. "It didn't start snowing until we were almost there."

Mick shrugged. "Still snow."

Sully laughed. "Payback for you holding me at gunpoint."

"What?" Evan asked, his eyes wide.

"He did not," Campbell retorted.

"Yeah, he did. He and –" Sully looked over at Mick. Mick nodded, a slight smile on his lips. "– He and Sarah, when we first got to Thornville."

"I have got to hear this." Campbell leaned forward and took a swig of his moonshine. He barely suppressed a shudder.

Sully looked at Mick again before he related the tale. Mick didn't mind. It was good not to feel the stabbing pain every time he heard her name. The pain was still there – it would always be there – but it was hurting less and less.

"Damn, Cooke," Campbell said when Sully had finished. "How'd you get a badass chick like that?"

"Just lucky, I guess." He smiled a little.

"Oh, jeez, none of this feelings shit," Campbell said, finishing off his moonshine.

"Hey, Campbell?" Mick said.

Both Sully and Evan yelled "Fuck you!" Mick laughed. Friends were good.

They stayed the night in the garage. The rain had let up just after dark, but no one wanted to walk the muddy roads in the dark. Mick and Evan laid out the bedrolls while Campbell cleaned up and Sully tended to his horse. They bedded down early, hoping to get an early start in the morning.

Mick volunteered for first watch. Campbell stopped before he went to his bedroll. "I'm sorry I never got to meet your wife," he said softly. "She sounds like she was awesome."

Mick nodded. "She would have liked you. You both have the same juvenile sense of humor."

"Hey!"

Mick laughed. "Get some sleep. I'll wake you in a few hours."

♦

Dawn was barely lighting the sky when Mick woke up. He had managed five straight hours of sleep without nightmares. He rubbed his eyes as he watched Sully fill a percolator with coffee. "'Morning," Mick said, sitting up. "Coffee?"

"Yeah, we replenished it last time we were by," Sully situated the pot on the grate over the coals. He poked at the fire with a metal rod.

"How are you doing?"

Sully shrugged. "I'm a Marine, we embrace the suck."

"If you need to talk…"

Sully laughed. "Like you did? Nah, thanks, but I'll work through it."

"I don't suggest my method. You know, solitary confinement for months."

They ate a quick breakfast, then cleaned up the garage. They were all ready to go less than an hour after Mick awoke. "Be careful out there," Sully said. "There was a small herd when I came through that way a month ago."

"Probably long gone," Mick said. "You be careful. We'll see you soon?"

"Yeah, I'm going to turn in the horse and tender my resignation from the USMC."

"Look forward to having you, Sully."

"Likewise." They shook hands.

"Hey, Campbell, stay away from Donna," Sully said as he shook the big Marine's hand.

"Who's Donna?"

"Don't worry about it, just stay away from her."

Mick laughed. Guess he wasn't as immune to her charms as we thought, he thought.

"Evan, nice to meet you. Guess I'll see you soon." Sully shook Evan's hand.

"Same here, sir."

"Don't 'sir' me. I'm Sully."

Evan nodded rapidly. "Sully."

"See you guys soon." Sully mounted the horse and led him down the still wet road.

"Alright, let's get. We should get there today barring another storm." Mick adjusted his pack on his back and set out in the opposite direction. Campbell and Evan were right beside him.

CHAPTER SIXTEEN

"Were all the zombies at the base or what?" Evan asked. They had been walking three hours and hadn't seen one creature.

"Don't jinx us, kid" Campbell said. "I like not having to kill the fuckers for a change."

"How many have you killed?" Evan asked. "Have you killed people?"

"A lot and yes." Campbell's tone didn't invite questions.

"What about you, Mick? Have you ever killed a person?"

"You can't go around asking people that, Evan," Mick said.

"Why not? Old rules, sure, but this is a new world. I gotta know who I'm dealing with, if they could hurt me."

"Everyone can hurt you, you fucking wimp," Campbell muttered.

Mick fought off a smile. "You ask the wrong person that question, they just might kill you. So how 'bout you don't ask it anymore."

Evan sighed heavily. "Fine." He walked a few more steps. "So what can I ask? What can we talk about?"

"How 'bout we enjoy the quiet," Campbell said. "I know I am."

Mick smiled at Evan's heavy sigh. Silence was best.

The silence only lasted another ten minutes before Evan was bursting with questions and comments. Both Mick and Campbell just let him go on, occasionally answering or acknowledging his comments. Evan didn't seem to mind. He just liked to talk.

They had walked for about four hours before they came to a familiar looking town. "There was a settlement here when we went through before," Mick said, pointing at the small bank. "I think it was five people. I sent them to Thornville."

"Do you think they made it?" Campbell asked.

Mick shrugged. "I hope so." He wiped the sweat from his brow. "We're only about four or five hours away. Let's get a move on."

They walked a few more hours, the heat starting to wear on them. They were rounding a curve when they saw a group of zombies milling about the road. Mick put out an arm to stop Campbell and Evan. "There's only a handful," he whispered so low they barely heard him. "We can take them out, but we need to do it quietly in case there are more in the trees."

Campbell nodded. He withdrew his knife from his belt. Evan reached around and pulled out the bat that was protruding from his backpack. Mick unclipped the poker from his pack. They advanced on the crowd.

Mick took out the first one, a short fat one wearing overalls. Campbell put his knife thru the brain of what was once a woman. Evan swung on a third, knocking its head nearly off its shoulders. There were only four left, then the path was clear. Evan tripped and fell, his bat clattering to the road. A chorus of groans came from the trees.

"Shit," Mick said. "Let's move before they see us."

Evan pulled himself up, scooping his bat from the road and swinging on the next one in his path. Campbell put down two more, turning for the next one, but it was already on the ground, Mick moving away from the corpse, his poker clenched in his hand. He looked into the trees, saw a mass of zombies. "Let's go!"

They ran for a half hour, finally slowing to a jog, then a full out stop. Evan dropped onto the asphalt, gulping air. Mick was breathing heavy, but Campbell was fine. "A little winded?" he asked with a smirk.

"Fuck you, Campbell," Evan wheezed out.

Mick laughed. "Quick break to catch our breath, then we'll go on." Mick could have made it – he really didn't want to stop – but he needed to give Evan a chance to recover.

They resumed walking after a fifteen-minute break. Mick had to pace himself. He knew he was about an hour away from his daughter and every step seemed a lifetime.

"Hey, Mick," Evan said.

"What, Evan?" Mick prepared himself for endless questions and comments.

"Will they – will they like me there?"

Mick looked over at his companion. "What do you mean? Of course they'll like you."

"I just – I never had a lot of friends. I can be annoying, I know, but I want to be a part of something. I don't know if I'll fit in."

"You are annoying." Mick tempered his words with a smile. "But you'll be fine. There are a lot of people there with similar quirks and everyone accepts them." His thoughts flew to Tom, how he was never accepted by Thornville. He shook his head. "Besides, you said you have hunting skills and the person who brings the food is always welcome."

Evan laughed. "I guess that's true."

"What about me, Dad?" Campbell said. "Will I fit in?"

"Fuck you, Campbell." Mick clapped him on his back. "Come on, I want to see my daughter."

"Who is Donna, anyway?"

"Stay away from her, Campbell. There are plenty other women there."

They walked another hour, then Campbell remarked. "Is that a river over there?"

"Yes, we're right along a river." Mick smiled. "Sarah and I took a bath in that river when we first got here. It was so cold I thought my balls were going to jump off my body to find shelter." The guys laughed. "It was worth it, though. To get clean, to see her so happy…" He shook his head. "It was a good time, even though I was frozen when we finished."

They walked just a little further and Mick caught sight of the wall. He stopped.

"Is that it?" Campbell asked.

"Yeah." Mick stared at the wall, the bus and truck nose to nose, the metal welded on to make it more secure. His eyes drifted up to the roof of the restaurant to see a figure staring back at them. He saw Sarah, her braid hanging over her shoulder, the grey Henley she loved paired with worn jeans, the guns strapped to her waist, those old boots she was so fond of.

She smiled at him, that smile that made her plain face absolutely breathtaking. He watched as she beckoned to him with her head, telling him to come home.

"How do we get in?" Evan asked and she disappeared.

Mick cleared his throat and swiped a hand over his eyes. "I'll show you."

He started walking again, Campbell and Evan right behind him. When they were within ten feet of the barrier, he stopped, looking up at the sentry. "Did you grow another couple inches while I was gone? I swear, you're taller than me now," Mick called up.

"Mick?" The sentry leaned over, a grin on his face. "Is that you?"

Mick smiled. "It's me, Jack. I've come home."

Made in the USA
Monee, IL
31 December 2020

56017347R00114